AVALANCHE

Peril in the Park Series

Book one: Avalanche

Avalanche

Book One of Peril in the Park

By
Gayla K. Hiss

Avalanche
Published by Mountain Brook Ink
White Salmon, WA U.S.A.

The website addresses recommended throughout this book are offered as a resource. These websites are not intended in any way to be or imply an endorsement on the part of Mountain Brook Ink, nor do we vouch for their content.

This story is a work of fiction. All characters and events are the product of the author's imagination. References to real locations, places, or organizations are used in a fictional context. Any resemblance to any person, living or dead, is coincidental.

Scripture quotations are taken from the *Holy Bible*, *New International Version®,* NIV® Copyright ©1973, 1978, 1984, 2011 by Biblica, Inc.® Used by permission. All rights reserved worldwide.

Words to *Amazing Grace* are by John Newton, published in 1779. Public Domain.

ISBN 978-1-943959-17-4

The Team: Miralee Ferrell, Nikki Wright, Cindy Jackson
Cover Design: Indie Cover Design, Lynnette Bonner Designer

Mountain Brook Ink is an inspirational publisher offering fiction you can believe in.

Printed in the U.S.A. 2016

For my husband, Jeff,
who has blessed me with many exciting adventures.

Acknowledgements

Special thanks to Kevin Bacher, National Park Service, Mount Rainier National Park, for sharing his vast knowledge about the beautiful Cascade Mountains. To Eric and Don, Ed Pavone, and Christina McConnell, who helped with the technical research for this book. To my critique partners, Dawn Lilly and Harry Wegley, for their constructive feedback, encouragement and support of my writing, and for persevering with me through all the critique sessions and remaining such great friends. To those who read my manuscript and provided valuable feedback: Lynda Dodson, David Akers, Christina Portillo, Ed Pavone, and Jeanne Hiss. And to all those who supported, encouraged and prayed for me as I wrote this book.

Many thanks also to Miralee Ferrell for her encouragement and enthusiasm for this story, and for fulfilling my dream of seeing it published.

In His hand are the depths of the earth,
and the mountain peaks belong to Him.

Psalm 95:4

CHAPTER ONE

Fireworks exploded across the dark sky, but Jenny Snowfeather hardly noticed. The news about the cabin break-in had cast a shadow over her brother's Fourth of July barbecue. She'd suspected a bear at first, until she learned two hunting rifles and ammo had been stolen, along with food and blankets.

A bright flash startled her.

"Watch out!" a man cried as the stray spark zoomed toward her like a small meteor.

She spun around to escape, slamming right into the man and his plate of barbecued chicken.

He grabbed her, stumbled, and pulled her with him to the ground.

A second later, the blazing miniature rocket whizzed over their heads and crashed into the lawn only a few feet away.

She squeezed her eyes shut at the near miss. When she opened them, Jenny found herself face-to-face with the handsome stranger.

His large, brown eyes stared back in surprise.

Her gaze traveled to his arm, sheltering her body.

Quickly, he withdrew it and rolled over, raising himself to his elbows. "That was a close one. Are you okay?"

She sat up and lightly brushed the grass from her blue sweater and faded jeans. "Other than a few grass stains, I'm fine." Glancing back at him, she noticed the food plastered to his chest and smiled. "But you're not."

When she leaned over to flick the remnant of baked beans from his white cotton shirt, her eyes zeroed in on the holstered Glock beneath his jacket.

She drew back. "Look, I don't know who you are or why you're here, but nobody comes to my brother's Fourth of July party packing a gun."

He glanced at the exposed weapon on his belt and pulled his jacket over it. "I can explain."

She scrambled to her feet. "Save it for Deputy Patterson. I'll go get him."

As she turned away, he jumped up. "Wait, Jenny, let me explain." His voice was low and insistent.

How does he know my name?

"Are you okay, Jenny?" Billy Norton stood nearby with his grunge-style stringy hair, Nirvana T-Shirt and baggy jeans. Concern shrouded his freckled face.

The tall stranger wrapped his arm around her before she could respond. "She's fine. Aren't you, Jen?" He smiled at her as if they were sharing a private joke.

His bold move stunned her. And what was up with the familiar way he addressed her? No one called her Jen except her father and brother.

His disarming smile diffused her temper long enough to notice he was not much older than she, probably in his late twenties. Black, wavy hair framed his tanned, chiseled face. Like dark mirrors, his eyes flashed, pleading for her not to give him away.

She paused, then shifted her gaze to her old friend. "It's okay, Billy."

The crimson stain on the man's shirt captured Billy's attention. "What happened to you?"

The stranger glanced at his chest and returned a wry grin. "A head-on collision with a plate of barbecued chicken."

Billy looked at Jenny. "Are you sure you're okay with this guy?"

The man met her scrutinizing stare with an affectionate squeeze and a wink. She flinched, but the boyish gleam in his eye and his playful smile sparked her curiosity and overruled her better judgment. "Yes, I'm fine, Billy. Go on back to the party now. Don't worry about me."

As soon as Billy left, she turned and confronted the mystery man. "Okay. The show's over. Now get your hands off me or you'll wish you were packing more than that Glock."

He complied, removing his arm from her shoulder. "Sorry, I guess I got a little carried away." Despite his tough masculinity, he looked like a boy caught stealing a piece of candy.

She put her hands on her hips. "All right. Out with it. Who are you, and why did you bring a gun to my brother's barbecue?"

"I'm Chase Matthews, a friend of your brother, Joel." He extended his hand, which she ignored.

"Funny, I didn't know my brother had any friends. Did you come here to shoot him?" She narrowed her eyes. "And how do you know who I am?"

"Joel has pictures of you around the house. I recognized your face."

She glared at him, unconvinced.

He smiled. "Ah. You're still wondering about the gun. Let's start over. I'm Deputy U.S. Marshal Chase Matthews." He took out his ID and handed it to her.

The encircled, five-point star emblem appeared authentic enough. She scrutinized his face, comparing it with the one in the photo. A perfect match. Satisfied, she returned his badge to him. "Why all the secrecy?"

"I'm trying to keep a low profile."

"How come? Is something going on here in Eagle Valley?"

He looked away. "I can't discuss it."

"Oh." Her gaze drifted to the stain. "Well, you won't keep much of a low profile wearing that. I'm afraid I've ruined your shirt."

He shrugged it off. "It's okay. I'm staying here at the house. I'll go in and change."

Jenny paused. "You're staying where?"

"Right here. Joel invited me to stay with him."

The ear-splitting blast of the next round of fireworks caused Jenny to jump. Ears still ringing, she peered at the marshal.

The look on his face frightened her more than the noise. Horror and shock contorted his features as he stared at the red stain bleeding through his shirt as if the explosion had triggered a war, and he was its victim.

"Chase?"

No response.

She touched his arm. "Chase!"

He blinked a couple of times and put his hand to his head as he recovered from whatever nightmare he'd been living. "I . . . I'm sorry. What did you say?"

"Are you all right?"

He managed a crooked smile and pointed to his ear. "It's the noise. I think I'm deaf now, thanks to your brother."

"It is loud."

He stared at her for a moment as if he wanted to say more. "I better go in."

Jenny watched him walk away. A tug at her pant leg caused her to glance down.

Her three-year-old nephew, Adam, peered up at her. "I liked the blue one the bestest."

She hoisted him in her arms. "That was my favorite too."

Carrying the boy, she strolled across her brother's back lawn where friends and family had gathered in clusters for the fireworks show. The tempting aroma of burgers grilling on the open barbecue pit and the fresh scent of flowers and cut grass proclaimed that summer had finally arrived in the Pacific Northwest. After the unusually long, harsh winter, Jenny welcomed the change in seasons.

Another firecracker blasted her eardrums.

Adam leapt in her arms and covered his ears, nuzzling against her. "I don't like that kind."

"Neither do I." She suspected Chase would agree with them.

After the noise stopped, an impish grin appeared on Adam's face, and his brown eyes shone with mischief. "I've got a secret."

She tried to keep from laughing as she played along with his game. "What kind of secret?"

"It's about you."

"Me? Well, if it's about me, I'm not interested. I already know all my secrets."

He giggled. "Not this one. Daddy told his friend he wants him to meet you."

Before Jenny could respond, her brother Joel appeared.

He reached to take his son from her. "I wondered where he ran off to."

Like her own, Joel and Adam's features were dark and striking, a poignant reminder of their late father and his Native American roots.

She eyed her brother with a shrewd look. "Adam was letting me in on a little secret."

The boy smiled, very pleased with himself. Joel looked him in the eye. "Won't you even tell your own dad?"

Adam shook his head.

Jenny studied her brother, wondering what he was up to now. "I met your house guest tonight."

A curious expression crossed Joel's face. "Chase?"

"Since when do you have strangers staying at your house, and why didn't you tell me?"

Joel shifted Adam to his right arm and faced Jenny. "First of all, Chase isn't a stranger. He's an old Army buddy. Second, I didn't know myself until he called yesterday and said he was in the area and could he come by for a visit? I invited him to stay with us. But since you're so interested in him, why don't you go hiking with us tomorrow?"

Jenny arched a brow. So Adam was right. Joel did want to fix her up with Chase. "I have to work."

"You could take the day off."

She rolled her eyes and crossed her arms.

"Then come over for dinner Saturday night." Joel didn't give up easily.

"Would you give it a rest? He's not even my type."

"How do you know? And what is your type anyway, someone with fur or feathers?"

She glared back at him. "Tell Lori goodnight for me." She kissed Adam goodbye and tussled his hair. "'Bye, buddy."

Joel followed her with Adam. "Come on, Jen, don't leave yet."

She stopped when he caught up to her.

He took a more conciliatory tone. "Look, I'm sorry for what I said back there, but I don't think you should be alone right now."

She shook her head and sighed. "Joel, what's it going to take to convince you that I'm fine?"

"If you were, that would be enough, but I know you're not. Since Dad passed away, you've changed. You've withdrawn from us."

"That's not true. I came to your barbecue today, didn't I?"

"I practically had to beg you to come, and you haven't been to church in weeks. With both our parents gone now, we need to stick together."

She saw the concern on his face. He looked so much like their father her heart ached. She clutched the small silver cross dangling from the chain around her neck, the cross her father had given her when she turned sixteen. "Don't worry about me, Joel. I'll be okay. Just give me some time and space."

"Okay, but promise me you won't shut us out."

"Goodnight, Joel."

Jenny arrived at the rangers' station in the North Cascades National Park half an hour late on Monday morning. She groaned when her supervisor, Clint Newman, met her at the door.

Impeccably dressed in his crisp ranger shirt and shorts, Clint had always been fastidious about his uniform. Unfortunately, his nerdy-looking white, hairy legs did nothing for his professional image.

The balding man in his early 60s moved to let her pass. "So you made it to work after all. I was beginning to get worried. What happened to you anyway? You look like something the marmot dug up."

She tucked in her shirt and pulled her ranger ball cap over her head and ponytail, tucking a stray lock of her straight, black hair under it. "I was at Joel's Fourth of July party last night."

Clint followed her to the front desk. "Must have been quite a party."

"I left early, but the fireworks at Joel's place kept going well past midnight, so I didn't get much sleep." She moved behind the desk and turned her attention to the bulletin board on the back wall. "Any news on that cabin break-in near the park?"

"Nope. I spoke to Deputy Patterson about it this morning, but he doesn't have any leads yet. Whoever it was came in through a broken window. Probably kids up to no good." Clint paused and scratched his ear. "I hope it's not a new trend."

Gus Patterson, the deputy sheriff, was a good friend of Clint's. "I'm sure Gus will get to the bottom of it. Has he notified the owner?" Jenny asked.

"Yeah, he spoke to Frank Baker about it yesterday. Slim Baker, Frank's cousin, has been keeping an eye on the place since Frank's father died and left it to him. Slim's the one who reported the break-in." Clint released a heavy sigh. "He's got heart trouble . . ."

"Who, Frank?"

"No, Slim. Says he's moving to Bellingham to live with his daughter and her family."

Jenny faced Clint. "That's too bad. What's Frank going to do with the cabin?"

"He told Gus he wants to rent it out as-is. Says he can't get away from Seattle long enough to come here and clean the place out himself. You don't know anyone who'd be interested, do you?"

"I might be, if I can afford it."

Clint chuckled. "Tired of living next door to Joel, huh?"

She grinned. "I need more space."

"More space? You already live on an acre of land, half a mile down the road from him."

"Sometimes I think I could live in Africa, and it still wouldn't be far enough away from that brother of mine."

She pointed to the weather report posted on the board. "The forecast looks good today." Her cell rang. She glanced at the caller ID and saw Joel's number.

Clint grimaced at the noise when it rang for the second time. "Well, either answer it or turn that noisemaker off."

"Okay, okay. You know, Clint, one of these days you're going to have to accept the fact that you live in the twenty-first century."

He grunted. "First it was the computer, now it's the smart phone. Next thing you know I'll be working for a robot."

She went outside and answered the call. "What's up, Joel?"

"Something's wrong with Chase. I think he was stung by something. I need your help." She listened carefully as he gave her directions.

After the call, she rushed back in the office to grab the emergency first aid backpack. "I've got to run, Clint. Got a bee sting emergency near Cascade Pass."

Sprinting up the trail, Jenny met Joel halfway to the top. He quickly helped her shed her pack. "He's over there."

Her gaze traveled to Chase who was sitting on the ground with his back against a rock and his legs outstretched in front of him.

"We meet again," he said with a labored breath.

She strode to him and gently touched his shoulder. "No fireworks this time."

A faint spark lit his eyes. "Who says?"

She glanced over her shoulder at Joel. "He's delusional."

"I heard that," Chase replied.

She knelt beside him and pressed her finger to his neck. His weak pulse sent hers racing. "Chase, listen to me. You're having an allergic reaction. I need to give you a shot of adrenaline."

He frowned like a petulant child. "No shots. I hate shots."

"Hmm. Let me see if I have any pills." She turned away from him and searched through her first aid supplies until she found an EpiPen. She glanced up at her brother who stood beside her. After she jerked her head a couple of times in Chase's direction, Joel caught her hint to distract him somehow.

"Wow, look at that!" Joel pointed his finger away from Jenny.

When Chase turned his head to see, she spun around and jabbed the epinephrine needle deep into his thigh.

He howled in pain and shot Jenny a piercing glare. "What's the matter with you? I said no shots. Are you trying to kill me?"

Shifting to Joel, Chase's eyes narrowed. "And *you*. I thought you were my friend."

Jenny downplayed his drama. "Don't be such a baby. It was going to hurt one way or the other. I thought it might be easier if Joel distracted you. That's what we do with Adam when he gets stung."

Chase stared back at her. "I'm glad you're not my dentist."

She gave him a cheerful pat on the head, tempted to tousle his hair the way she did her nephew's. "Did you see what stung you?"

"A wasp or bee with yellow stripes."

"A yellow jacket. Have you ever been stung by one before?"

"When I was little. I think I was five. My whole arm swelled up, but nothing this bad."

"You should see a doctor and start carrying an EpiPen with you all the time."

Chase stared at his trembling hands. "What was in that shot anyway? My heart's racing like I've had twenty cups of coffee."

"It's okay. It's the adrenaline taking effect."

While they waited for Chase to recover, Joel motioned to her. "Can I talk to you for a minute?"

She followed him a short distance away from Chase. The earnest expression on Joel's face surprised her. "What's going on?"

"Thanks for coming when I called."

She shrugged. "It's my job, but you know how to treat bee stings as well as I do, Joel."

"I didn't have an EpiPen on me."

"That's not like you. Are you sure you didn't plant that wasp on Chase to get me out here today?"

He snorted back. "Don't flatter yourself. I wouldn't do that to an old Army buddy."

"You know," Chase said, silencing them, "where I come from, it's rude to talk about someone behind their back."

Jenny blushed and exchanged a guilty look with Joel.

Joel strode back to Chase. "Jenny was telling me that she's coming over for dinner Saturday night."

Her mouth fell open, and she stormed up behind her brother, ready to set him straight.

"As long as she knows I've got dibs on Lori's apple pie," Chase said with a brilliant smile that stopped Jenny in her tracks.

When Chase moved to get up, she forgot about her tiff with Joel and rushed to his side. "Wait. Not so fast." She turned to her brother. "Give me a hand."

Joel moved to Chase's opposite side.

Jenny stooped down. "Chase, put your arm around my shoulder."

"I thought you'd never ask."

She rolled her eyes and peered past him to Joel. "I think your friend is having a relapse. I should give him another injection."

Chase raised his hand in surrender. "Okay, okay. I'll be

good."

She sent him a stern look. "Promise?"

"You like this power you have over me, don't you?"

She tossed him a smug grin. "Yes, I do, actually."

Joel interrupted them. "Whenever you two are finished, I'd like to get on with this."

"I'm the one who should be complaining," Jenny replied, "I need to get back to work." Pressing her shoulders against Chase's powerful body, she strained to push up. Her knees nearly buckled from the unexpected mass.

Joel hefted Chase from the other side. "You okay, Jen?"

She shrugged it off. "Yeah. Guess I wasn't prepared for Mr. Iron-Marshal here."

Chase sighed impatiently. "This is ridiculous. I can stand on my own. Give me a few minutes, and I'll beat you both down the mountain."

Jenny ignored his protest. "Joel, I've got him now. Let's try again."

After she and her brother helped Chase to his feet, they paused to give him a moment to regain his balance.

Chase stared at her with a strange, mystified expression. "You saved my life."

Jenny found herself gazing into his eyes as the scent of his sweat and aftershave hung in the air. She looked away and stiffened under his weight. "It's my job. Don't get all choked up over it."

She caught her brother's attention. "You got him, Joel?"

"Yeah."

"He's all yours." She carefully slipped out from under Chase's arm.

Chase straightened. "Wait a minute. Don't I get a vote?"

"You look well enough to me. Joel will help you down the mountain if you need it." She waited while her brother released Chase to stand on his own.

Chase's gaze settled on her park ranger uniform. "Nice

outfit." His eyes shifted from her shorts to the SIG Sauer 9mm semi-automatic handgun holstered on her belt. His brow arched. "And SIG. I didn't realize park rangers carried guns."

"It's for protection."

"Protection from what, wild animals?"

"People, mostly."

Chase shot Joel a doubtful look. "Tell me she's not serious."

Joel grinned back at him. "You don't know my sister. Don't mess with her—Jenny was the state skeet shooting champion a few years back."

Chase noticed the special badge on her uniform. "You're a law enforcement ranger."

She stepped up to him and planted her hands on her hips. "That's right. So unless you're a criminal, you don't have anything to worry about." She scanned his belt. "Speaking of guns, where's yours?"

Joel eyed her with the big-brother look he used whenever he thought she was wrong and needed to be corrected. "Chase is on vacation, Jen. He's not carrying a gun."

"Really."

Like sharp arrows, her eyes darted back to Chase. He glanced away, confirming her suspicions.

He was still keeping secrets.

Jenny spent the afternoon checking camping permits, chatting and sharing information with the campers, and assessing bear activity in the campgrounds. As she descended the forested trail to the road where her ranger car was parked, the rustling of bushes from behind drew her attention.

She turned around, expecting to see a hiker or animal, but no one was there.

Resuming her hike to the road, footsteps echoed hers.

When she peered over her shoulder, the sound stopped. She paused, looked around, and confirmed no one else was on the trail. Her ranger instincts kicked in, and she reached for her gun. Cautiously, she turned and backtracked the trail. "Who's there?"

Silence.

"Come out so I can see you."

Nothing but the whisper of leaves.

Then rustling came from her left.

A chill crept up her spine, but she shook it off as her training kicked in. She followed the noise and headed off-trail through a salmonberry thicket.

Movement in the overgrown brush caught her eye. She glimpsed something white. Was that a T-shirt? Whatever it was, something big crashed through the dense canopy of leaves beyond her vision.

"Stop!" She hesitated for a moment, not wanting to corner a bear, but the memory of what might have been a T-shirt spurred her forward. She bushwhacked through the thorny berry branches but couldn't keep up. Whatever it was, it didn't want to be discovered. At least, not by her.

After waiting a few minutes and hearing no suspicious sounds, Jenny pivoted. Holstering her weapon, she glanced down and noticed something in the mud on the forest floor. Footprints of a man's athletic shoes. And it looked like he'd been standing—waiting—for a long time.

CHAPTER TWO

IT WAS LATE MORNING WHEN CHASE and Joel returned to Joel's ranch. At Jenny's insistence, Joel stopped by the medical clinic on the way home, but the office was closed for the entire Fourth of July week. Concerned about his health, Joel and Lori invited Chase to join them at her parents' that afternoon to celebrate her mother's birthday, but Chase declined.

The truth was, he wanted to be alone. He still wasn't feeling a hundred percent, but mostly he needed time to come to grips with what had happened.

Death had come close a few times in his life, but he never thought a bee sting could do him in. If not for Jenny, he might be meeting his Maker right now. It wasn't a pleasant thought. There was too much he'd have to explain and try to excuse.

After removing his pistol from his backpack, he unloaded it and hid it on the top shelf of his guest-room closet, well out of Adam's reach. The suspicious look on Jenny's face when Joel insisted Chase wasn't carrying a gun concerned him. He couldn't let her beauty blind him to her shrewdness.

Now that she knows I'm keeping Joel in the dark about why I'm here, she'll be watching me like a hawk. He frowned as he finished unloading his pack. Maybe he shouldn't have confided in her, but at least she hadn't given him away—yet.

A twinge of guilt needled him for not telling Joel the truth. He pushed it aside. The fewer people who knew why he was really there, the better. But how long would Jenny keep it from her brother? Of course, what did she really know? Only that he might be here on a case he couldn't discuss—nothing more.

A short while later, Chase leaned against a post on Joel's back porch, sipping on a soda, while he surveyed the picturesque landscape. The large porch spanned the entire back side of the house and provided an incredible view of the valley meadows. He watched Joel's sheep grazing peacefully, surrounded by the majestic Cascade Mountains, and found himself envying his friend's idyllic life.

The ring of his cell shattered his serenity. He pulled it from his pocket and pressed it to his ear. "Matthews."

"Chase, where in the world are you? I've been calling and leaving you messages for three days now!" His friend and fellow deputy marshal, Kate Phillips, was not happy.

"What's up, Kate?"

"*What's up*? I've been worried sick about you. That's what's up. Why aren't you returning my calls?"

"I'm on vacation, remember?"

"You really went somewhere to get away? That's what this is all about?"

Chase gazed at the mountains. "Would I lie to you?"

Silence.

"Okay, don't answer that. The truth is I'm visiting an old Army buddy in Washington State."

"For your sake, I hope you're telling the truth. A vacation is exactly what you need right now. Mack was just saying . . ."

At the mention of their supervisor, Chase pushed off the post he had been leaning against. "What did Mack say about me?"

A couple of seconds ticked by before she responded. "He said that after everything you've been through, a vacation would be good for you."

"He wants me out of the way. He thinks it was my fault, you know."

"Why do you say that?"

"Kate, he pretty much ordered me to take this vacation."

"If that's true, it's because you've been under so much pressure. Anyone who's been through what you have needs time off."

A bald eagle came into Chase's view and circled in the air. "Have they caught him yet?"

"No . . . not yet. But you need to forget about it and get some rest. Boss's orders, remember? You need to take it easy and enjoy the break from this crazy place."

Chase growled through his teeth. "How can I take it easy while that killer is still at large?"

"Look, I've gotta go. I'll talk to you soon. Take care of yourself, and try putting everything else behind you."

After Kate hung up, Chase's thoughts drifted back to his partner, Jim. A lump lodged in his throat and made him choke.

He gazed at the soaring eagle. Today he almost died, but now he had another chance. Jim deserved a second chance at life more than he did. Regardless, he wasn't ready to die today. There was still too much left for him to do.

He called out to heaven. "Jim, buddy, tell God thanks for giving me another chance today."

Like a distant echo, Chase could almost hear his friend shouting back to him. *Why don't you thank Him yourself?*

Tuesday morning, Jenny reported to work extra early. The first one in, she came to the computer at the front desk and checked the local weather and trail conditions.

Clint arrived and removed his broad-rimmed Stetson. "What's this? You're in before me?"

"I'm turning over a new leaf."

"I thought maybe you were bucking for a promotion."

She smiled. "That too."

He joined her behind the counter. "What's the forecast? Is this sunshine going to last?"

"It doesn't look like it. Rain is moving in tomorrow with a major cold front. There's even a chance of snow in the higher elevations." She swiveled the computer screen on the desk to show him the latest park weather report.

Studying the forecast, Clint frowned. "Snow in July? Then again, it has been known to happen, but it's pretty rare. So much for summer. After that record-breaking cold, snowy winter, I was really looking forward to a little sunshine."

"You know how crazy the weather can be here in July. If you want sun, today is the day to get it." She grabbed her ranger ball cap from under the counter and headed toward the door. "I'm going to check on the Hidden Lake trail today."

Clint glanced up from the computer. "By the way, you have a visitor."

She gave him a surprised look. "I do? Who is it?"

The twinkle in his eye belied his serious expression. "She's waiting outside."

"Now you tell me." Jenny went to the door and when she opened it, she smiled. "Wendy!"

The young woman ran to her and gave Jenny a big hug. "I told Clint I wanted to surprise you."

Jenny studied her for a moment. The messy divorce between Deputy Patterson and his wife last year had devastated their daughter. It was good to see her looking so well now. "I thought when you went away to college, you'd forget all about us back here. How long will you be home?"

Wendy's blue eyes sparkled. "The rest of the summer."

Clint leaned over the front desk. "Here to keep an eye on your old man, huh?"

Wendy laughed. "Yeah. Dad can't get along without me, you know."

Jenny touched a lock of Wendy's thick, brown tresses. "You've grown out your hair. The last time I saw you it was a lot shorter."

"You like it?"

"Yes. It's a whole new you." Jenny turned to Clint. "She could be a model, couldn't she?"

"Pretty enough to be the cover girl on the National Parks calendar," Clint replied.

Wendy giggled, obviously delighted with the compliments.

Jenny couldn't help smiling at her friend's youthful exuberance. "How long have you been here?"

"Since yesterday. I flew into Seattle and Dad picked me up."

"And how are things with your mother in California?"

Clint left them to go into his office.

Wendy shrugged, her radiance fading. "Okay, I guess. She's getting remarried this fall."

"You don't sound too happy about it."

"He's not Dad, you know?"

Jenny gave an understanding nod, thinking of her own father. "Yeah, I know."

"With Mom living in California and Dad here, it feels like my life has been split in two. When I'm with one of them, I feel guilty for not being with the other. It's been such a relief to go away to college in L.A. and get out from under all of their problems."

"Well, I'm sure your father is thrilled to have you home again, and so am I."

Wendy returned a wistful smile. "I've missed you, Jenny."

Jenny put her arm around her young friend's shoulder, giving her an affectionate hug. "Now that you're back, we've got a lot of catching up to do."

"What's been happening in Eagle Valley while I was away?"

"Come with me on my rounds, and I'll fill you in."

Chase had always prided himself on being fit, at least until he hiked the mountain with Joel earlier that morning. His friend made the steep climb look easy, but Chase had to work at staying with him. Then again, Joel had been hiking these mountains all his life.

Since Chase's bee sting ended their hike yesterday, Joel had chosen this strenuous trail because of its breathtaking views, and they were definitely worth the effort.

As the men descended the mountain, they encountered Jenny

coming up the trail.

Sporting a pair of stylish sunglasses, she wore her hair pulled back in a ponytail under her ball cap, looking surprisingly chic in her ranger uniform. Her striking appearance eclipsed the pretty, younger woman with her.

Jenny raised her sunglasses and rested them on the bill of her cap. Her exotic, almond-shaped eyes were underscored by high cheekbones that framed her oval face. Chase couldn't help studying her like a captivating mystery he wanted to unravel.

Resting a hand on her hip, she eyed them both. "What's this, Army survival training?"

Joel grinned at her remark. "Only a quick refresher."

She gestured toward Wendy. "Joel, you remember Wendy. She's home from college for the summer."

Her brother shifted his attention to the girl. "How's college treating you?"

"I survived my freshman year. Does that count for survival training?"

He swapped a humorous look with Chase. "I'd say that deserves a medal. Or maybe that should go to your father for paying your tuition."

"Shh," she kidded with him. "Don't tell him that. He wants me to transfer closer to home, but I like going to USC."

"Better you than me. Too many people and cars in L.A. for my taste." Joel turned to Chase. "Now my friend here lives in a big city, so he's probably used to all the hustle and bustle."

Wendy eyed Chase with interest. "Hi. We haven't met before." She extended her hand to him. "I knew everyone in Eagle Valley before I left for college, and I would definitely remember your face."

Chase shook her hand and smiled politely. "Nice to meet you."

"Where are you from?"

"Nashville, Tennessee."

"Oh, my mother loves Elvis."

Chase gave her a brotherly smile, not wanting to encourage her flirting "You're thinking of Memphis, not Nashville."

Wendy returned a carefree shrug. "Whatever."

Joel turned to Jenny. "Why don't you bring Wendy with you when you come over for dinner Saturday?"

"I have a date, but thanks for the offer," Wendy said.

"You are still coming, aren't you, Jen?" His question sounded more like an expectation.

She stubbornly shook her head. "I don't think so . . ."

Chase understood Jenny's reluctance and gave her a perceptive smile. "You know your brother. You'll never get any peace until you say yes. If it makes it any easier, I promise I won't bite. Personally, you'd be doing me a big favor."

Jenny's features softened as she pivoted in his direction. Tilting her head slightly, her eyes flickered with interest. "Why is that?"

Chase leaned closer and covered his mouth as if to share a secret. "I wouldn't have to listen to Joel's sheep-shearing stories for a change."

Joel cast Chase a mock glare. "I heard that."

Laughter escaped Jenny's pouty lips, temporarily easing the tension between her and her brother. "Okay, I'll go, but you'll have to share Lori's apple pie with me."

"No worries. I'll ask Lori to bake two of them. One for you, and one for me."

"Better make that three pies," Joel said with a wry grin. "I'm glad that's finally settled. I was afraid Chase was going to offer you the ranch next. Speaking of Lori, Chase and I better get back, or we'll be late for lunch."

Despite the joking, Jenny's espresso-brown eyes, astute and intense, regarded Chase with concern. "I'm surprised to see you hiking again so soon after yesterday."

Joel intervened. "We decided to give it another shot today—excuse the pun—since yesterday's hike was cut short."

She ignored her brother. "Did you bring an EpiPen with you

this time, Chase?"

"Yep," Joel answered for him. "I got one of Adam's from home." He glanced at Chase and explained. "He's allergic to bee stings too."

Chase glared at him. "Good thing you didn't tell me you were carrying that thing or I wouldn't have come with you."

A loud rumble shook the earth. Chase looked around. "What was that?"

They all moved to the ledge a few feet from the trail, and peered across the valley. Jenny pointed to a plume of snow barreling down a mountain on the other side. "An avalanche."

Surprised, Chase turned in her direction. "I thought avalanches only happen in winter."

"They are more common then, but with the record-breaking snowfall we experienced last winter and the cooler-than-normal summer so far, the threat of avalanches persists in the upper elevations throughout July." She glanced at the sunny sky. "You picked a good day for your hike. A major cold front is moving in tomorrow and conditions will deteriorate. The avalanche risk will increase too."

"Why is that?"

"When it's unusually cold and wet, the top layers of the snow become unstable, and the looser wet snow can slide over the more stable snowpack layers. Also, if it's unusually hot, the top layers of snow can become mushy and unstable, which increases the risk of avalanches too."

With an adventurous gleam in his eye, Chase rubbed his hands together. "Hey, Joel, what do you say we go mountain climbing tomorrow and check it out?"

Jenny was incredulous. "What? The bee sting wasn't enough? Now you want to try avalanches?"

Chase turned to Joel, relishing the sparks flying from Jenny's lovely eyes. "What do you say, buddy?"

Joel frowned. "Not in these conditions. I've had enough experience with search and rescues from avalanches to know better than to go looking for one."

At his friend's response, Chase cleared his throat. "What other exciting things are there to do around here?"

Wendy laughed. "If it's excitement you're after, you've come to the wrong place."

Chase's gaze traveled back to Jenny. "Oh, I don't know. I think there are still a few possibilities."

A thunderous boom reverberated from across the valley.

Chase and the others immediately turned and looked.

A giant wall of snow collapsed and hurtled down the huge mountain, sweeping away everything in its path.

Chase stared at the devastated landscape, stunned.

"As I was saying," Joel responded, "avalanches are no joke."

CHAPTER THREE

Saturday evening, Chase shook his head with disgust after inspecting his face in the mirror. He hadn't nicked himself this bad since he was in junior high.

It seemed like ages since he'd shared dinner with an attractive, single woman. Now he knew why. It wasn't worth the hassle. Not only was his face raw, but he'd spent thirty minutes ironing the only decent shirt he had left after the barbecue incident ruined his best one.

He heard Lori's voice through the door. "Dinner's almost ready, Chase."

When he emerged from the bathroom, she was no longer there. He entered the large den that adjoined the dining room and noticed the candlelit table with four plates and a fire glowing in the fireplace.

He met Lori and Joel in the kitchen. "Did the power go out or something?"

Lori checked on the vegetables roasting in the oven. "No, why?"

"I thought with the candles and the fireplace going in July there must have been a catastrophic power outage."

Lori and Joel exchanged amused expressions, then she glanced at Chase with a slight shrug. "It's not often we have a babysitter for Adam and we can entertain. With the rain and chilly weather, I thought it would be cozier with candles and a warm fire." Her gaze met Joel's again, and he winked at her.

Chase cleared his throat. "I hope I'm not encroaching on an anniversary or something. You'll let me know if I'm wearing out my welcome, won't you?"

Joel patted Chase on the back. "Relax, buddy. When we want to be alone, I'll let you know. Now go make yourself useful and finish setting the table."

When Jenny arrived at the kitchen door, Lori let her in and greeted her with a warm hug. "I was afraid you were going to back out at the last minute."

Jenny took off her rain jacket and sniffed the air. "Is something burning in the den?"

Lori laughed as she took her jacket and hung it on the hook by the door. "Yes, there is, but don't worry. It's under control."

Lori's dark brown hair was swept neatly off her neck, revealing the pearl necklace and matching earrings Joel had given her for their sixth wedding anniversary last year.

Noticing her sister-in-law's skirt and blouse, Jenny glanced at her own jeans and light green sweater. "I must have missed the memo on what to wear tonight. Did I forget someone's birthday or anniversary?"

Joel had returned to the kitchen. "Why can't we all have a nice dinner together without it becoming a federal case? Now let's take this food out to the table. I'm starving."

Jenny grabbed the basket of rolls and followed them through the swinging door of the kitchen into the dining room. She found Chase setting the silverware around the plates. Dressed in a blue cotton shirt and navy slacks, he was definitely easy on the eyes, even if he didn't know how to set the table.

She placed the basket across from him. "The fork goes on the left and the knife and spoon on the right."

He glanced down and swapped the order of the utensils around a plate. "I knew something wasn't right." He picked up the remaining silverware and offered it to her. "Maybe you'd like to finish the job. You're obviously more domestically-inclined than I am."

Joel and Lori erupted in laughter. "Jenny knows more about

rock climbing than she does about cooking," Joel remarked.

Jenny crossed her arms. "I may not know much about cooking, but I do know how to start a fire."

Chase's face beamed. "That I believe."

Lori took the silverware from him. "Here, I'll finish up." She glanced at Joel. "Is the salmon ready, dear?"

"Should be. I'll bring it in from the grill." Joel disappeared through the door and quickly returned with a platter of thick, pinkish fish fillets. "Okay, let's eat." He gestured toward the chair at the opposite end of the table from him. "Chase, why don't you sit there? Jenny, you sit across from Lori."

On his way to his seat, Chase moved behind Jenny's chair and held it out for her. She glanced over her shoulder at him, surprised by the unexpected display of chivalry.

He whispered in her ear. "Relax. I promised not to bite, remember?"

The fresh scent of his aftershave aroused her curiosity. Had he shaved and dressed up for her?

She studied him until he took his seat and caught her staring. His subtle smile set her face on fire, and she glanced down at her plate.

"Is something wrong, Jenny?" Lori asked.

Jenny lifted her dish. "Is this your wedding china?"

Lori's eyes twinkled. "You know it is. We use it all the time."

"Really? It looks different in candlelight."

When they were all seated and Joel had said the blessing, they passed the food around and took turns serving themselves until their plates were full.

Joel took a bite of Lori's roasted carrots and zucchini. "The veggies are great, hon."

Chase raised his glass of ice tea. "I second that. And I have a toast to make. To Lori and Joel, for being such great hosts." Then he turned to Jenny. "And to Jenny . . . for saving my life this week."

When she looked his way, he gave her a humble nod.

Joel raised his glass. "To Jenny."

The sound of clinking glasses filled the room as they toasted her.

A strange fever seared Jenny's flesh. She didn't know if it was due to the candles, the blazing fireplace, or her brother's mysterious friend.

"Jenny?" Lori's distant voice brought Jenny's focus back to the conversation.

"Sorry, Lori, what did you say?"

"I said it's a good thing you were there when Joel called."

Jenny shrugged. "Any of the rangers would have come. You'd be surprised how many insect bites we treat each year."

Her focus shifted to Chase. "Did you ever see the doctor?"

He cleared his throat uncomfortably. "No. The office was closed all week . . . It was a fluke anyway. What are the odds I'll ever get stung by a wasp again?"

Annoyed by his cavalier attitude, she couldn't let it go. "The odds are nearly 100% that you'll have another serious attack if you do, perhaps even a fatal one."

"Why don't you tell us about Nashville, Chase?" Joel asked.

Jenny shook her head at her brother's interruption. He obviously thought she was out of line.

Lori passed the rolls around for the second time. "Yes, being a marshal must be very exciting."

"It's all right, but sometimes it's not all it's cracked up to be." A hint of ruefulness darkened his expression. He turned to Jenny. "I'm sure being a park ranger is much more interesting."

Jenny took a roll and set the basket down. "It has its moments. The best part is being outdoors most of the time and in the mountains." She turned to her sister-in-law. "That reminds me. Guess who is back in town, Lori."

"Who?"

"Wendy Patterson."

"Really? For how long?"

"The rest of the summer. She stopped by the rangers' office

today."

Joel wiped his mouth with his napkin. "I forgot to tell you, hon, Chase and I ran into her on our hike today. I hardly recognized her she looks so grown-up now."

Lori turned to Jenny, her eyes bright with interest. "And how is she doing?"

Jenny shrugged. "She seems okay, all things considered."

"It was such a shame," Lori explained to Chase. "Wendy's parents had a nasty divorce last year. The whole church was praying for them, but it didn't work out the way we hoped. Jenny was there for Wendy through the whole thing."

"She was Wendy's youth leader at church," Joel added.

"Really." Chase turned to Jenny. "Do you still lead the youth?"

"No. I quit after Dad passed away . . ." At the mention of her father, tears welled up in her eyes. Embarrassed, she quickly dabbed her face with her napkin and tried to compose herself.

Joel mercifully broke the awkward silence. "I should take you on a backpacking trip in the mountains, Chase."

"I'd like that. I haven't been camping in years."

"Let's plan on Friday. I need to finish a few projects around here first."

Chase washed down the last bite of his salmon with some tea. "Anything I can help with?"

"Are you good with a hammer?"

"I worked in construction while I was in college before I became a marshal."

"You're hired. Too bad we're past sheep shearing season. We could have used an extra hand last spring." Joel's eyes shifted to his sister. "Jenny's an expert sheep shearer, by the way."

"All it takes is a little patience and gentleness, Joel." She sent her brother a significant glance.

"You should check out her zoo sometime," he said to Chase, ignoring her dig.

Chase looked at Jenny, his eyes wide with interest. "You have a zoo?"

"Joel is exaggerating again," she said. "I simply rehabilitate a few injured animals we find in the park. What we really need is a good vet."

"Why isn't there one in Eagle Valley?"

"Doc Lincoln died, and we haven't been able to find someone to take over his practice. It's not like we don't have enough business."

Joel snorted. "That's for sure. Jenny, alone, could keep a vet busy for years with her injured critters."

A loud commotion erupted outside.

"What on earth is that?" Joel shot up from his chair and headed for the back porch.

Jenny followed him. She groaned when she saw her two Husky-mix dogs, Fred and Ginger, roaming Joel's yard, barking and growling.

"Hush up!" Joel yelled at the dogs. Then he glared at Jenny. "You better stop those two wolves of yours before they harm one of my sheep."

"Fred, Ginger, come!" At the sound of Jenny's command, the agitated canines whined and scampered toward her. Like small children who knew they'd been bad, they skulked up and stopped a few feet in front of her. But instead of obediently receiving their due, they turned away, pacing and growling again.

The dogs' strange behavior baffled Jenny. "I've never seen them like this. There's something out there, Joel."

"That's what my sheepdogs are for."

Jenny noticed his dogs were nowhere in sight. "So where are they?"

He looked around. "Good question." He raised his hand to his mouth to call. "Shep! Fleece!" They didn't come. "Come to think of it, I haven't seen them since this afternoon."

The disturbed look on her brother's face matched Jenny's thoughts. His dogs weren't the type to run away.

Fred and Ginger erupted again. Joel shook an accusatory finger at them. "Maybe those wolves chased them off. This is the third time they've escaped from their pen."

"They're not wolves, Joel."

"But they have wolf-blood in them. That's close enough for me. I warned you about raising them as pets. Now that they're grown, they've become unpredictable."

She watched her mixed-breed canines bark and growl with fangs bared. What on earth was wrong with them?

She shifted to her brother and made an effort to be more contrite. "They need a larger pen now that they're almost grown."

"You better do something quick, Jen. They are getting out of control." Joel turned and walked way.

With her hands on her hips, she looked at her furry partners in crime and shook her head. "What am I going to do with you two?"

The dogs whimpered and trotted toward her. The frenzied wolves had morphed back to her loveable Huskies.

She couldn't bring herself to punish them. Instead, she stooped to give them a vigorous rub down. Soon their long, furry tails were wagging again. "I believe you guys," she said in a low voice, "but how do I convince that big, stubborn brother of mine that you really were barking at something?"

Jenny came to the porch where Joel waited for her with Lori and Chase. The couple's sympathetic looks helped to lessen the brunt of Joel's previous scolding.

Fred and Ginger heeled at her side like furry, four-footed angels and stopped at the base of steps.

After studying her dogs, Jenny turned to Joel. "Whatever was out there, it's gone now. It must have been a coyote. You should do a headcount of your sheep in the morning."

His mouth twitched. "I'm sorry, but you're going to have to keep Fred and Ginger locked up from now on. They've become a nuisance, and I'm afraid it won't be long before they start killing sheep for sport. It's one thing to keep a few animals in cages temporarily, but I won't stand for those wolf-dogs running loose on my property any more, especially with Adam around."

As much as she hated to admit it, Joel had a point. He was right to be concerned for Adam and his sheep, and if locking up Fred and Ginger gave him the peace of mind he needed, she couldn't refuse him. "Okay. I'll keep them in my trailer until I can get a bigger fence installed."

Joel seemed satisfied for the moment.

Jenny ascended the steps to the porch. "What about Shep and Fleece? Where did they go?"

He frowned. "I wish I knew. Sometimes they wander off, but they're always home before dinner."

"Let's hope they return by morning."

His expression changed as he shifted back to his role as host. "Now that the excitement is over, let's go in and finish dinner. Remember to save room for dessert. Lori baked a delicious mountain-size apple pie."

Lori laughed. "It was easier than baking a pie for each one of you."

As the group headed inside, Jenny stopped at the door. "Thanks, Lori, but I think I should take my dogs home."

Lori and Joel turned around with surprised stares. Her brother switched to his persuasive tone. "You can't leave yet. It's still early."

"Maybe Fleece and Shep will return if Fred and Ginger aren't here."

"We could put them in the barn."

Jenny sighed. "No, it's getting late anyway." She turned to Lori and gave her a peck on the cheek. "It was a wonderful dinner. Thank you for having me over."

Lori raised her hand. "Wait. Don't forget your jacket. It's chilly tonight."

While Lori ducked inside, Jenny turned to Chase. "I'm sorry my dogs spoiled dinner."

The corner of his mouth lifted. "They didn't. It was the most exciting thing that's happened around here since I arrived. Except, of course, the fireworks and the plate of barbecued chicken."

She smiled at his levity in the awkward situation. "Don't forget the bee sting and the avalanche." Then she warned him. "You can't ignore that allergy, Chase."

"At least let me walk you to your car."

"Thanks, but I didn't drive."

He eyed her with an incredulous expression. "You're not planning to walk all the way home in the dark, are you?"

She pointed at the sky. "There's a break in the rain and the moon is out."

"Still, I'd feel better if I went with you."

Lori returned and handed Jenny her jacket and a small plastic container. "It's your dessert."

Chase appealed to Lori and Joel. "Would you mind keeping my piece of pie warm while I walk Jenny home?"

Joel deferred to Lori. She shrugged and smiled. "Looks like it's you and me and a candlelit dessert for two."

Jenny couldn't think of a good enough reason to refuse Chase's offer to escort her home, especially since she wanted to be with him. That should have been reason enough. Besides, it would give her a chance to get to know him better. And find out what exactly he was *really* doing in Eagle Valley.

CHAPTER FOUR

CHASE ADMIRED JENNY'S EBONY MANE AS he strolled beside her. The bright moon illuminated the vast countryside, and her long hair shimmered like strands of black silk.

He gestured toward her dogs trotting alongside them. "Where did you get the names Fred and Ginger?"

She gave him a sidelong glance. "Where do you think?"

"You actually named your dogs after Fred Astaire and Ginger Rogers?"

Grinning, she shrugged. "What can I say? I'm a fan of old movies and television shows."

"You mean reruns."

She raised her nose in the air. "I prefer to call them classics."

"I like old war movies and westerns myself. Anything with John Wayne in it."

"Hmm."

"What? Those are classics too, you know."

"I was thinking that you can tell a lot about a person by the movies they watch."

He caught the subtle meaning in her tone. "I suppose you think I crave violence because I like war movies and westerns."

"Actually, I was thinking that Joel likes those same kinds of movies. So did my father . . ."

Chase smiled. "Well, at least I'm in good company. I've never been much for music or dancing." The sweet smell of her hair combined with the fresh scent of rain-soaked wildflowers created an intoxicating fragrance that clung to the damp, night air.

Fred's collar jingled, and Chase reached down to give him a

friendly pat as they strolled along. "You'd never know these dogs were capable of terrorizing Joel's sheep to look at them now."

"They only get aggressive when a predator is close." She sighed. "But I am a little concerned that their wilder instincts could take over now that they're almost grown. I've never seen them act the way they did tonight. They usually obey me."

"Are they really part wolf?"

She nodded. "The result of breeding dogs with wolves for profit. They're mostly Husky though."

"Did you buy them from a breeder?"

"No. They were abandoned as pups in the park. They would have starved to death or turned feral, so I brought them home and raised them."

As Chase thought about the abandoned dogs, he frowned. "I don't understand. Why breed dogs with wolves in the first place?"

She shrugged. "Human nature, I guess. We're fascinated with the wild, but we also want to tame it."

Chase chuckled.

She tilted her head. "What's so funny?"

"I never realized how much people and animals have in common."

She turned in his direction. "I'm not following you."

"I've chased down plenty of dogs with some wolf in them. We lock them up, hoping they'll act more like dogs when they get out, but most of the time they revert to their wolf instincts, reaping havoc on innocent sheep. I guess the moral of the story is once a wolf, always a wolf."

"But you're not talking about animals. People have souls and a free will to choose against their natural instincts, and we have a God who gives us the power to resist evil."

Chase scoffed. "Now you sound like my father."

Jenny stopped, her eyes wide with interest. "You don't share your father's faith?"

He paused and shook his head. "I've been the proverbial thorn in his side for years."

"Why?"

"Oh, I don't go for all that talk about forgiveness and turning the other cheek. I've seen enough evil in my life to know there's only one way to stop it. You've got to snuff it out like a brush fire, before it has a chance to burn someone else."

Her eyes searched his face. "Who burned you, Chase?"

The question threw him off guard. He never confided in anyone. Emotions were a dangerous thing. Totally illogical and counter-productive. They left you vulnerable to anyone who knew you had them. He'd seen enough people let their hearts overrule their heads, sometimes paying for it with their lives.

"Everybody's got a hard luck story. I won't bore you with mine, especially on a beautiful night like tonight." He gazed up. "Wow, look at those stars." The vast array of distant lights was more profound and beautiful than any fireworks show.

He sensed Jenny watching him.

"You're very good, you know, acting like you're so in control, yet keeping yourself at a safe distance from everyone. That's part of your game, isn't it? Never let anyone too close to you."

He laughed. "Are we talking about me, or *you*? If being distant were a game, you'd be the master of it."

She flinched.

He realized his words had hurt her, which was the last thing he'd wanted to do.

Jenny stooped to pet her dogs. As she stroked them softly, she glanced up at him. "You're right, Chase. I do shut myself off from people, especially people I don't know."

"You mean *men* you don't know."

A stubborn glare flickered in her eyes. "I haven't exactly come through this life unscathed either, but the fire that's burned me hasn't consumed me."

He regarded her for the first time as a fighter and survivor, traits he admired more than her beauty. "What's going on with you and Joel? Why do you two fight all the time?"

She stood and stuffed her hands in the pockets of her jacket. "Well, for one thing, he's a controlling big brother, who thinks it's his duty to protect me. I'm twenty-eight, but he still treats me like I'm a kid. He's gotten even worse since Dad passed away."

Regret chided Chase for sounding so callous earlier. "Sorry about your father."

She glanced down. "It's been hard on both of us, especially since it was so unexpected." After a moment, she lifted her gaze toward him. "Anyway, Joel needs to learn to mind his own business and let me live my own life."

"I know he can be overbearing, but he does care about you."

Determination sparked in her eyes. "Maybe, but I don't need his protection. I got over Russ a long time ago."

Chase eyed Jenny, intrigued. "Russ?"

"Russ Webb. He's the mistake I made when I was sixteen that Joel won't let me forget. I was a bit of a rebel back then . . ."

Chase paused and arched his brow. "What? You?"

She shrugged. "I was also young and naïve. Russ sort of swept me off my feet. Thank heavens, we never tied the knot."

"What happened?"

Jenny released a long sigh. "Russ talked me into running off with him. He said we'd get married and he'd take care of me. Joel got wind of it and caught us before we crossed into Canada." She looked down and shoved her hands deeper in her pockets. "I was so angry . . ."

"I don't blame you. That Russ-character sounds like a thug."

"He was, but at the time, I was more furious at Joel."

"But he rescued you."

She nodded. "I know, and I thank God that he did, but back then, I was young and confused. I refused to believe the truth."

"And what truth was that?"

She snorted self-derisively. "Russ never intended to marry me. He didn't even love me. He only wanted to use me. You see, I worked at a bank as a teller, and Russ would come there sometimes. That's how we met. Now I know he was really scoping out the place. Before we left town together, he wanted to stop at the bank and get some money. He asked me to stay in the car. I thought he was making a withdrawal or cashing a check. Little did I know he was robbing the bank—with me outside waiting for him like a complete idiot. Turns out, I was nothing more to him than an alibi and accomplice."

"What happened to Russ?"

She removed her hands from her pockets and rubbed her arms. "When Joel found us, Russ got away. All Joel wanted was to bring me home. Like me, he didn't learn about the robbery until later. When I returned, not only did I have to face my father, which was bad enough, but also the police. Meanwhile, Russ disappeared and got off scot-free, never to be heard from again."

Chase shook his head, anger boiling inside him. "It's good you got away from him. Guys like that are nothing but trouble."

"At least I was still a minor and didn't have to serve time. Anyway, it's ancient history now." She paused, staring in his direction. "Why are you so upset?"

He looked away, clenching his fists in the dark. "Comes with the territory, I guess."

"What's that?"

"Being a marshal. I don't like it when someone breaks the law and gets away with it." He peered at her from the corner of his eye.

She relaxed her arms by her side and resumed walking. "Since we're being so honest, why are you really here? And don't tell me it's to see Joel."

He kept pace with her. "But I *am* visiting your brother."

"You mean you're using my brother and his family as a cover for your secret operation." She shot him an adamant look. "And if you're putting them in danger, you'll have to answer to me for it."

Chase halted. "It's not like that."

Jenny stopped and faced him. "Then what is it like?"

He paused, frustration setting in. "You have to trust me. I know what I'm doing."

"You don't trust me enough to tell me the truth, but I'm supposed to trust you?"

He shook his head. "You don't let up, do you?"

"Not when it comes to my family."

He rubbed his mouth, realizing he was running out of excuses. After all, she had a point. Why should she trust him when he wasn't being honest with her own brother?

He sucked in a deep breath and exhaled. "My partner, Jim, and I were guarding a key witness for a high-profile case against the leaders of a powerful drug cartel. This witness also happened to be a convicted felon, whose sentence was reduced to parole in exchange for testifying in court. We'd been guarding this guy for two weeks when . . ." His throat constricted from the painful memory. It was the first time he'd talked about what had happened.

Jenny softly touched his arm, somehow empowering him to continue.

"That morning I got a call that another witness involved in the case had been murdered. I rushed downstairs to get the car so we could quickly transport our witness to another location." He paused, recalling the tragic details of that day.

"And?" Jenny quietly asked.

He looked down. "As I was climbing the stairs I heard a gunshot. By the time I got there, Jim was on the floor, bleeding out. He'd been shot in the leg with his own gun, and the witness had escaped down the backstairs."

Everything turned to red as the memory again lurched him into his recurring nightmare. He frantically pressed his blood-soaked hands against Jim's thigh, desperate to stop the bleeding...

"Chase?"

Jenny's voice returned him to the present. He shut his eyes to purge the haunting image from his mind. "I couldn't save him, Jen. The bullet hit his artery. There was too much blood. I tried, but it was too late. *I* was too late."

Jenny gently touched his face. "Listen to me, Chase."

He opened his eyes and gazed at her.

"It wasn't your fault."

"It doesn't matter. I won't rest until I find that miserable scumbag and . . ."

"Snuff him out?"

Her remark surprised him. He waited, expecting her to criticize him or lecture him on forgiveness.

Instead, only compassion shone in her eyes.

"You're the first person I've shared this with. I can't talk about it with the people at work. They already think I'm on the ragged edge. I can't tell my parents. They'd tell me to forgive and forget."

He couldn't believe he was spilling his guts like this, but he was grateful to her for caring enough to listen. For the first time, he could breathe easier, like a huge mountain had been lifted off his chest.

She gave him an earnest look. "Why do you think this man who shot your partner would show up here?"

"It's a theory, based on experience. When someone's on the run they often go back to their roots. Being back home makes them feel safe."

"Is this witness is from Eagle Valley?"

Chase hesitated, mulling over how much he should tell her. But then again, maybe she could help. "Not exactly. He's a drifter. He's never lived anywhere for very long, but he did live near here once. The mountains are a good place for a man to hide out. I know it's a long shot, but you'll tell me if you hear anything suspicious?"

"Okay . . . but I wouldn't hold my breath if I were you. This place isn't exactly known as a safe haven for fugitives."

He caught her teasing look. The moonlight danced in her

eyes, captivating him. "I'm glad you're so amused, even if it is at my expense."

She laughed at first, then gazed at him with tenderness. "Maybe you should take a few days off and enjoy your vacation with Joel. You've been through a lot, you know."

"Maybe I should. I have to admit I'm having a much better time than I expected."

They walked the remaining distance together in contented silence. The bright light outside Jenny's trailer shone ahead as their northern star. The occasional jingle of Fred and Ginger's collar tags and the night sounds of crickets and frogs in the distance filled the calm night air with a simple beauty and sweetness Chase was unaccustomed to.

He wished their walk didn't have to end yet. He'd never felt so at ease with anyone before. Certainly not with a beautiful and intriguing woman like Jenny.

She stopped when they reached her trailer. "Well, this is it. My castle. Thanks again for escorting me home."

"I'm the one who should be thanking you. For saving my life and listening to my problems."

"That's what friends are for, right?"

"Friends?" He repeated the word with an ironic smile. "Is that what we are? I wasn't sure what to call it."

Her eyes smiled back at him. "Would you like to meet my other friends?"

He hesitated, wondering if other people lived with her. "Sure, I guess."

"Come with me."

Chase followed her around the side of her trailer to the back.

She illuminated the cages with her flashlight.

Two pairs of orbs glowed in the darkness.

When Chase joined her near one of the cages, he smiled, realizing she had been referring to the animals, not people. "This is your zoo, huh?"

"Not much of one at the moment. I only have two residents

right now. This is Sage." The large owl peered back at them with strange, luminous eyes.

Jenny touched the cage. "We found her in the park with a broken wing. She's healed now but will never be able to fly again."

She shifted to the cage housing a small fox. "And this is Lucy. I call her that because of her red hair."

He noticed the creature had only three legs. "What happened to her?"

Jenny gave a sad sigh. "Someone found her in a trap. She practically chewed her leg off to free herself, so it had to be amputated. She's almost recovered now. Soon I'll set her free."

"Can she survive like that?"

"Sure. Animals, like people, are amazingly resilient."

"Now I see why you became a park ranger, so you can protect the wildlife."

She turned the flashlight off, and Lucy and Sage's eyes glowed in the darkness. "If I hadn't become a ranger, I probably would have been a vet. When my mother died, I was very young, so Dad had to raise Joel and me alone while he managed a ranch. I used to help him with the animals and livestock."

As Chase's eyes adjusted to the dark, he noticed how the moonlight highlighted Jenny's pretty face. "You must have the healing touch."

She shrugged modestly. "My ancestors on my father's side were Snohomish, and my great grandmother was said to have the gift of healing. She was also fiercely independent. I'm told I take after her." A hint of pride flickered in her eyes.

"Stubborn, you mean." His teasing provoked a reluctant grin from her lips. "So where did the name Snowfeather come from?"

"Nobody knows exactly. There's an old legend, but I won't bore you with it."

He smiled. "I happen to like old legends."

She glanced away from him.

He didn't budge. "I'm waiting."

"Oh, all right." She cleared her throat. "They say long ago, when my people were moving from the mountains to the winter camp in the valley, a boy got separated from his family. A big snowstorm came, and the boy miraculously survived. When they found him, he was playing with a feather in the snow."

Jenny looked at Chase with a demure expression. "It's probably a myth, but I used to love hearing my father tell it to me."

"Actually, I'm jealous."

She gave him a doubtful look. "Of what?"

"I wish I knew more about my ancestors."

"Can't you ask your parents about them?"

He shook his head. "My biological parents died when I was young. I know my grandfather was full-blooded Cherokee, but not much else. After they died, I was in foster homes for years before I was finally adopted."

She tilted her head. "Your adoptive parents are Christians?"

"Right." He smiled and rubbed his chin. "You would get along great with them. I think they've been praying I would meet someone like you for a long time." He meant it to be charming, but it came out sounding pathetic.

Since coming to Eagle Valley, a growing awareness of the emptiness and isolation of his life was becoming impossible to ignore. Jenny was as committed to her work as he was, but she possessed something he lacked. A sense of peace.

At night he rarely slept. Minutes turned to hours as his mind raced with questions he couldn't answer, problems he couldn't solve, and people he couldn't save. How many more innocent lives would be destroyed at the hands of criminals? How many more would suffer as he had suffered?

The maimed fox's retinas reflected an eerie glow in the darkness as she stared at him with a palpable mixture of fear, distrust, and a desperation to be free. Chase watched the caged animal with unexpected empathy.

Jenny called Chase's name, drawing him from his dark

thoughts. Her smile faded when he allowed her to see the wounded animal inside him. Like staring into the sun, the hidden, vulnerable side of him was exposed. He might very well get burned, but to feel the warmth of her compassion and understanding was a risk worth taking.

"Chase," she said softly, her eyes shining with sincerity. "I'd like to help you."

Looking down, he softly touched her hand. "You already have." He sighed. "I should be going. It's getting late and it would be rude not to eat a piece of Lori's pie after she made it for me."

"Think you can find your way back?"

"I'll manage."

He paused as he turned to leave. "I know you think the odds of a fugitive turning up here in Eagle Valley are pretty slim, but still, be on your guard."

After Chase left, Jenny brought her dogs inside with her. As soon as she entered her trailer, she felt a chill. She looked around her living area and kitchen, but the windows were all shut. As she strode down the hall to her bedroom, she detected a distinct draft.

Seeing the window by her bed open, she halted. Surely, she'd closed it before going to Joel's for dinner that night.

Her dogs followed her into the room and immediately began barking.

When Billy Norton appeared outside her window, Jenny gasped. "Billy!"

"Hey, Jenny," he said with a carefree wave.

"What are you doing out there?"

He shrugged and smiled. "Sorry to scare you. I was going to knock, but then I saw you at your window."

"You didn't scare me. You surprised me. What's up?"

"Can we talk?"

"Only if you come to the front door like a normal person."

Moments later, Jenny met him at the door and held it open for him. "What's with the long face, huh?"

He frowned as he walked in. "I lost my job today."

"Uh-oh." She gestured to her kitchen table, then moved to open a cabinet. "Have a seat while I get us a snack and drink."

"That's all right. I'm not hungry or thirsty."

Billy refusing food? This was serious. She put the glasses away and joined him at the table, sitting across from him. After propping her arm on the table, she rested her chin in her palm, ready to listen. "What happened?"

"My boss told me I was too careless. That I had to follow all their stinkin' rules."

"Well, it is a sawmill. That's a pretty dangerous place to work. They have to have strict regulations."

He shrugged and sighed. "My mother is threatening to kick me out if I don't get a job and help her with expenses."

"Oh. There will be other jobs," she replied in a more cheerful tone.

"I'm running out of options in Eagle Valley. I may have to move out of town."

"There must be something around here you could do."

His face brightened a little. "You don't have any ranger openings at the park, do you?"

She shook her head. "Not at the moment."

He slumped in his chair, then squinted at her. "Hey, who was that man leaving your place when I walked up? He looked like the guy from your brother's barbecue."

"Chase."

"Yeah. What's he still doing here?"

"He's visiting my brother. They're old Army buddies."

"Oh . . . So when's he leaving?"

"I don't know. Why?"

"You're not dating him or anything, are you?"

"I told you, he's a friend of my brother's."

"Then go fishing with me next week."

Jenny sighed. "Things are really busy with work right now, Billy. Besides, you need to look for a job."

He eyed her with a crooked grin. "I'd rather be fishing."

Jenny couldn't fall asleep after Billy left. The mystery of her open window kept her awake. Either she was mistaken and hadn't closed the window before she went to Joel's for dinner, which was hard to believe, or someone else had opened it.

While her dogs slept on the floor, Jenny grabbed a flashlight and took it with her outside. She illuminated her bedroom window and examined it. She distinctly remembered closing the window but couldn't recall locking it. Though she usually locked things up before she left, she'd never worried if she happened to leave a window or a door unlocked. After all, this was Eagle Valley. It bothered her that her oversight may have left a calling card for an intruder, especially after the cabin break-in.

She made one more sweep with her flashlight and froze. The wet ground was illuminated, revealing fresh prints. But there was not one, but two distinct sets. As she studied the shoe patterns more closely, she noticed one set was longer and narrower than the other. In fact, it looked identical to the prints she'd discovered off the trail earlier that week.

She rushed back into the trailer, closing and locking the door behind her.

Fred and Ginger were awake now, anxious and whining. They followed her into her bedroom.

Jenny searched her closet and drawers, doing a quick inventory. So far, everything appeared to be accounted for. When she came to her bed, she sat on the floor to remove a square wooden board under her mattress, uncovering her hidden gun safe. She quickly unlocked and opened it. Finding her service weapon still there, she breathed a big sigh of relief.

Only one other place to check. She came to her nightstand and slowly opened the drawer to look inside. She bent down and reached all the way to the back, searching for the small, carved box her father had made, where she kept extra cash, pocket change, and ten fool's gold coins he had given her as a child. She pulled the drawer completely out and dumped its contents on her bed, confirming her suspicion. The box was gone.

CHAPTER FIVE

Early the next morning while Jenny fed her animals, the sound of a car engine caught her attention. She came around her trailer to her driveway. Chase stepped out of a shiny, new Jeep Grand Cherokee. It made quite a contrast to her green, 1990 Ford pickup parked next to it.

He joined her in her front yard while she checked out his SUV.

"Nice wheels," she said. "If I'd known you were driving that, I would have asked you to drive me home last night. We would have made better time too."

He grinned. "Yeah, but it wouldn't have been near as much fun." His pleasant expression turned more serious. "Sorry to bother you so early, but one of Joel's sheep was killed last night, and your brother wants you to take a look at it."

She glanced at her dogs, who had followed her to the front yard, hoping one of them hadn't done it. "Wait while I put Fred and Ginger inside."

Like fussy children being told to go to bed, the dogs barked and whined in protest when she locked them in her trailer. She hurried to the Grand Cherokee and hopped in beside Chase.

He quickly backed out of the drive and headed to Joel's. "Things sure look different in daylight, don't they?" He pointed toward the Cascades. "Last night, I couldn't even see those mountains."

She silently brooded over the break-in that tainted the pleasant memory of her evening with Chase.

"Is something wrong?" he asked.

Should she tell him about the theft? He'd want to report it to the sheriff. She'd have to tell them about Billy showing up last night too. If he got mixed up with all this, it could hurt his chances of finding a job. "You didn't get lost on the way back, did you?"

"Of course not. I made it in record time."

She sent him a teasing grin as he drove into Joel's driveway. "That's not saying much, since our walk last night wasn't exactly a speed run."

He parked the car and killed the engine. "There you go, spoiling my victory. And I was going to ask you out to dinner."

Jenny arched her brow. "You were?" She caught the hint of a smile on his face.

"Yeah. I was thinking of going to that nice restaurant at the lodge, but now . . ."

She cast him a sidelong glance. "I suppose there's no harm in one dinner. We do have to eat, after all."

Joel approached Chase's side of the SUV and leaned against it. "Are you two going to sit in there all day?"

Jenny rolled her eyes and got out. "I hear one of your sheep was killed."

"Yeah. I don't know what killed it, but it probably happened last night around the time your dogs went ballistic."

At least he hadn't accused her dogs of doing it. "Did Shep and Fleece come home yet?"

"No." His tone was gruff. "Come on. I put a tarp over the sheep's remains to keep the vultures away."

Jenny and Chase followed Joel to the field behind his house. They traipsed through the meadow toward the woods. Joel pointed to the mound under a blue vinyl tarp. "There it is."

After he removed the covering, Jenny knelt down to inspect the carnage. She examined it for teeth and claw marks then glanced up at Joel. "This wasn't done by a dog, if that's what you're thinking."

She searched the ground on her hands and knees and pointed to a print in the dirt. "See. Those tracks and the bite at the throat of the sheep are consistent with a cougar. My dogs must have scared it away last night, or it would have dragged the carcass deeper into the woods."

Joel wiped his face with the back of his hand. "A cougar. That's all I need. Now that it's found my herd, it'll come back."

Chase looked from Joel to Jenny. "Isn't there something we can do to prevent it from happening again?"

Joel shook his head in frustration. "It'll take forever to raise a fence high enough to keep it out, let alone the cost involved."

"What about running an electrical current through the barbed wire?"

Joel rubbed the stubble on his chin. "If that cat can scale a barbed wire fence, an electric shock won't keep him out, not unless it's powerful enough to knock him unconscious. Even then, there's no guarantee he won't jump over it. No, the only thing to do is to trap it and kill it."

Jenny rose. "You don't have to kill it. We can catch it and set it free somewhere else."

Joel rolled his eyes. "I know how opposed you are to killing wildlife, but this cat is encroaching on my property. If you set it loose again, chances are it will come right back and start all over again, or it will kill another rancher's sheep."

"It's only doing what it was created to do. It has a right to eat and provide for its young."

"We're talking about an animal, not a human being, and I have a right to protect my sheep and my family —"

"Look." Chase took a step closer. "I don't know anything about cougars, but why don't you two quit bickering and try to work out a compromise?"

Joel and Jenny stopped arguing and stared at him as if he was crazy.

Chase shook his head. "That's the problem with you two."

Joel's face twisted. "What are you talking about?"

"You preach one thing and do another."

"Come again?"

"Why are you always arguing? Whatever happened to blessed are the peacemakers, huh?"

The truth behind Chase's remark pierced Jenny to the core.

She and Joel exchanged chagrinned looks.

Her brother crossed his arms and spoke first. "Okay, Jen, I'm willing to hear your ideas, if you'll also consider mine."

Surprised, she glanced at Chase.

He slanted his head, reminding her that it was her turn.

Taking a step back, she cleared her throat. "I think Fred and Ginger have the cat's scent. They knew it was here last night. I'll go into town on Monday to see Nick with the state Fish and Wildlife Department. He'll know what to do."

Joel responded with a slight shrug. "I don't have a problem with that." He looked at his watch. "It's still early. Why don't you both come to church with Lori and me? We can go out for breakfast in town afterwards."

Chase shifted his eyes to the ground. "Uh, thanks, but I'll pass."

Jenny's thoughts returned to last night when he'd shared his reasons for rejecting his parents' faith. His admission saddened her, not that there could ever be anything more than friendship between them, anyway. After all, he had an agenda, and it had nothing to do with her.

Joel interrupted her thoughts. "What do you say, Jen? You're not going to turn me down too, are you?"

The two men's expectant gazes burned into her like lasers. "Another time maybe. I've been working so much I've got a long list of things I need to do at home today." She quickly turned to leave.

"Wait." Chase strode up beside her as she neared his SUV. "Hop in. I'll give you a ride."

Without stopping, she tossed him a quick glance. "Thanks, but I'd rather walk."

He touched her shoulder. "Hey, if I didn't know better, I'd think you were running away from me."

She paused, unable to face his questioning stare. "It's a nice day, and I need the exercise."

"When can I see you again?" Anticipation resonated in his voice.

"You're seeing me right now."

He leaned closer. "You know what I mean."

In daylight, his handsome features and magnetism were even more undeniable. Her exit strategy wasn't working, and his persistence only weakened her resolve. She had to nip this in the bud. "I'm only a half mile down the road. We're bound to run into each other sooner or later."

The spark in his eyes faded at her remark as a layer of frost coated his expression. "If that's the way you want it, fine. I'll leave you alone."

She caught his arm when he turned to leave, regret spilling over her. "Chase, wait. We're still friends, right?"

He eyed her with an impatient stare. "*Friends*? Sure, whatever."

As she walked home alone, she had to agree with Chase about one thing. Things sure looked different in daylight.

"That's the fifth livestock killing in the last two months," Nick said after Jenny told him about the sheep incident at Joel's.

She frowned at the news. "All in the same area?"

"Here, I'll show you." The tall, bearded man who had been sitting on the edge of his desk grabbed a red marker and sprang to his feet. He turned to the county map on the wall behind him. "See these four dots?" He pointed to red marks on the chart.

She nodded.

He added a fifth dot for the sheep killed on Joel's property. Then he drew a circle around them all. "It's a cougar all right, and this circle is its territory."

She rubbed her mouth with her finger. "What do we do?"

"We have to catch it before it strikes again."

Jenny left Nick's office still mulling over the cougar attacks. As she stepped into the crosswalk, a young man with shaggy, black hair came out of nowhere on his motorcycle. He swerved, barely missing her.

Recognition set in as he sped away and disappeared around the corner. *Dylan Veracruz?*

Gus Patterson strode up to her. The brawny, middle-aged deputy sheriff gave Jenny a hard look. "You know, young lady, I could ticket you for reckless walking. You almost collided with that motorcycle."

"I thought pedestrians always have the right-of-way."

Gus grinned. "True, but you didn't look both ways before crossing."

She wanted to argue the point, then realized he was kidding. "I guess I was distracted."

"I'll say. So what's the problem?"

"Only a cougar on the prowl. That's all."

"I'd take cougars over co-eds right now."

Jenny gave him a puzzled look. "I thought you'd be happy to have Wendy at home."

"Oh, I am. But it's different now. Since her mother and I split, it seems like she's grown up so fast. Too fast."

"Don't all fathers say that about their daughters?"

"Maybe. Especially if their daughters turn out to be eye-candy for the opposite sex. She's only been home for a few days and already boys have been texting her, wanting to go out." Gus scratched his face. "Hmm. I wonder . . ."

"What's that, Deputy?"

"Could you spend some time with her while she's here? She's always looked up to you. Maybe you could help steer her away from trouble."

"You know I'll do what I can, but she *is* an adult now."

"Age is one thing. Maturity is another. I'm afraid the divorce was hard on her. Maybe it affected her more than I realized."

Jenny noticed the worry lines etched in his face. "What do you mean?"

He flicked a dismissive wave of his hand. "Nothing. I guess I want to protect her from the world, you know?"

Jenny smiled. "She's lucky to have you for a father."

Her comment seemed to perk him up, and he changed the subject. "How's Clint?"

"Grumpy as ever. By the way, have you got any leads on the break-in at Frank Baker's cabin?"

"Not yet, but I suspect it might be one of those teenage boys who hang out at the lake. Mostly, I think they're goofing around, swinging on ropes and jumping off rocks into the water, but I've found empty beer cans, cigarette butts and a few other things that make me suspect they could be up to mischief too."

Gus was probably right, but it didn't bring her any peace. If a few misguided kids started breaking into cabins and stealing hunting rifles, what would they do next?

"Clint told me that Frank is planning to rent the cabin out," she said. "Do you know when it will be available?"

"Why, do you know someone who's interested?"

"Me."

He chuckled at that. "Now why would you want to leave that nice trailer next door to your brother and move into that rundown hunting cabin?"

"For the scenery, of course."

"You better hurry and put your name in. I just spoke to a man who's interested in it."

She frowned. "Really? Who?"

"Some fella, new in town. I gave him the keys to look it over. He's on his way there now. If you hurry, maybe you can catch him and take a look too."

Jenny drove to the cabin as fast as she could without breaking the speed limit. She didn't want to cross Gus again.

When she arrived, she noticed the For-Rent sign with a phone number placed in front of the cabin, and the Audi parked in the driveway. She parked next to the Audi and hurried to the front door.

A nice-looking man with short, reddish-blond hair answered her knock with an inquisitive expression.

"Hi, I'm Jenny. Deputy Patterson told me he gave you the keys to this cabin and suggested I come over and look at it too."

His grip tightened on the door's edge. "Sorry, but you're too late."

She stuck out her hand and wedged in her foot, blocking him from shutting her out. "Do you know who rented it?"

He cracked the door wider and peered at her. "I did."

"I don't understand. Gus didn't tell me it was rented. He said you were only looking it over."

He opened the door again, all the way this time. "I was, but then I called the owner and told him I wanted to rent it. He's sending me a copy of the lease today as we speak."

She studied the man for a moment and withdrew her hand, annoyed that he'd arrived at the cabin first. "How did you find out about it so fast? I came here as soon as I heard it was available."

"There was an online listing, and I responded right away. I've been looking for a place to rent the last couple of weeks."

"Oh," she said, finally conceding the cabin to him. "In that case, congratulations on your new home." Then she waved and turned to leave.

"Hold on," the man called.

Jenny pivoted around.

"I didn't catch your name. I'm Dr. Reggie Grayling." He grinned and extended his hand.

She stepped toward him to shake it. "What brings you to Eagle Valley, Dr. Grayling?"

"I'm starting a veterinarian clinic."

The news boosted her spirits. "Really? We're desperate for a good vet. Where's your office?"

"I have my eye on that small shop near the lake."

"The old bait and tackle shop? It'll need a lot of work to make it usable."

"It's all I can afford right now." He glanced down at her uniform. "And you must be a park ranger."

"The uniform gave me away, huh?" she grinned.

He lowered his gaze and paused. "I didn't know park rangers carry guns."

She glanced at the SIG holstered on her waist. "Unfortunately, not everyone obeys the law these days."

"Even in the parks?"

"Especially in the parks. By the way, did you know this cabin was broken into recently?"

"Yeah. The window is still busted. The sheriff told me kids have been hanging out by the lake, and he thinks they were the culprits."

Jenny suddenly recalled Chase asking her to tell him about anything suspicious in the park. She hadn't considered the cabin incident until now. "Hey, since I'm here, would you mind if I took a look at that window?"

He shrugged and held the door open for her. "Be my guest."

She noticed the shabby couch and armchair when she stepped into the living room.

Reggie followed her. "I told the owner that if he let me move in right away, I'd clean the place out for him."

She glanced at him from the corner of her eye. "No wonder Frank rented it to you."

After navigating the small, wood-paneled room, she stopped at the dusty bookcase. The variety of books on native wildlife and plant species drew her attention.

"The former owner had an interesting collection of nature books."

She picked out one on birds and blew off the dust. "Are these going back to Frank?"

"No, he said he didn't want anything that was left. Would you like them?"

Jenny raised her brow. "Are you sure you don't want them? They may be worth something."

"Hmm, on second thought . . ."

"Oops. I shouldn't have said anything. Now you'll want to keep them for yourself."

He grinned, diffusing her doubts. "No, an offer is an offer. They're all yours. Think of it as my way to make it up to you for depriving you of this place."

"Great, thanks."

"I'm curious. Are you going to sell them online?"

After placing the book back on the shelf, she clapped the dust from her hands. "No, they're good reference books for the park."

"I figured you were already an expert."

She smiled. "There's always more to learn. Unfortunately, I'm running out of space in my trailer." She looked around at the old, run-down furnishings. "Are you going to keep this lovely furniture?"

"Why, you don't like dingy early American décor?"

She made a face and shook her head. "Uh—no."

"I thought I'd start a new trend. Hey, we could go into business together. You could sell your old books, and I'd sell antique furniture."

She pointed out a large rip in the couch. "Better keep your day job."

Turning around, she assessed the entire dismal room. The only things from this century were the flat screen television and DVD player that rested on a stand by the far wall, along with a small boom box.

"Compared to this place, my trailer is starting to look better and better. It's not much, but it's clean." She gazed back at him. "Maybe you should re-think renting this cabin and find another place."

"Do you know of any other rentals in Eagle Valley?"

She considered the question. "No, none that I can think of."

"That's because there aren't any. Consider yourself lucky to have that trailer."

"I am. It's my neighbor who's the problem."

"Who's that?"

"My brother, Joel."

"Ah. A family feud."

She grinned. "Not quite. Do you have family around here?"

"No. Mine is back east." He was facing her and took a few steps backwards toward the window. "So besides your brother, are there any other men in your life?"

Chase entered her mind. The warmth of his smile and the touch of his hand after their stroll the other night stirred up feelings better left alone.

Cocking her head to the side, she gave Reggie a speculative glance. "Well, there's Fred. He lives with me."

"Who's that, a boyfriend or husband?"

She laughed. "He's my dog. I'm sure you'll meet him soon enough."

"I can't wait."

"And Ginger too. She's his sister. Do you have any pets, Dr. Grayling?"

"Unfortunately, no . . . at least, not now. My dog died before I moved out here."

"Sorry to hear that. Where are you from?"

"Atlanta."

"I thought I detected a Southern accent."

Jenny came behind the doctor to the broken window with plywood covering it. She recalled her break-in last night. Could they be linked? Chase might rush to that conclusion, but without proof, she wasn't ready to go there yet. Besides, Gus's theory of a few mischievous kids being the culprits sounded more plausible than an escaped felon hiding out near Eagle Valley.

Something wasn't right—she looked around—the modern

television and boom box were still in the cabin. Having been a youth leader for several years, she knew something about adolescents. What teenager would pass up electronics for a couple of old hunting rifles and cans of food?

She glanced over her shoulder at Reggie. "Other than the broken window, have you noticed anything else unusual about the cabin?"

"Not so far, but you'll be the first to know if I do."

She glanced down at her watch and turned around. "Thanks for the tour, Dr. Grayling. I better get back to work now or Clint will be on my case."

"Wait. There's a box in the kitchen. I'll fetch it so you can take these books with you." He returned with the box and set it beside the bookcase where she was standing.

"This has turned into a profitable trip after all." She quickly filled the box.

As she lifted it, Reggie politely intervened. "Here, I'll get that for you." He escorted her outside to her truck, carrying the books.

She lowered the tailgate, and he set the box down on the bed. "Who's Clint?"

"My boss, but he's really more like an uncle, the way he worries about me."

"Your personal body guard."

"Not exactly. That's more like my brother."

"The one you're running away from."

"That's right, but now that you've rented the cabin, I've got nowhere else to go." She shrugged helplessly then closed the back of her pickup.

"I hope you won't hold that against me."

"It's okay. You've given me a whole new appreciation for my humble abode. Besides, there isn't enough room in that cabin for all my animals."

"Hmm. You do have a point. Maybe I'll get a cat instead of a dog. After all, I am an equal-opportunity vet."

She laughed. "Well, thanks again for the tour and the books, Dr. Grayling."

"Please, call me Reggie, and feel free to stop by any time. No charge."

Jenny started her truck and glanced back at the cabin as she drove off. Having seen it in person, she breathed a sigh of relief that she hadn't rented it. Her trailer suited her much better.

Besides, she couldn't shake the feeling there was something about that cabin that didn't add up.

CHAPTER SIX

WHEN JENNY ARRIVED AT JOEL'S THAT evening to tell him about her meeting with Nick, Lori greeted her at the door. Joel and Chase were busy making repairs to the barn, so Lori invited her to wait on the back porch while she went to fetch a cold drink.

Jenny reclined in a rocker. The warm evening made her glad she'd changed into her T-shirt and cut-off jeans before coming over. She watched Joel's sheep grazing lazily against the backdrop of the mighty mountains as the fresh scent of Lori's roses floated up from the garden. The tranquility of the moment allowed Jenny to relax and collect her thoughts after the busy day.

Having seen the cabin now, she knew it wouldn't have worked for her dogs. They needed plenty of room to roam. Soon they would destroy her trailer. She had to find another solution and fast.

The cougar was another problem weighing on her mind. She knew what Joel's reaction to Nick's news would be. Somehow she needed to convince him to see things her way.

Jenny looked up when Lori returned with two glasses of lemonade. "Where's Adam?"

Lori set the drinks on a small table beside Jenny and smiled. "He's taking a nap. Chase kept him up too late again last night. Adam loves it when he reads him bedtime stories." She gave Jenny a significant look. "We better enjoy this peace and quiet while it lasts. He'll be awake soon."

In her yellow sleeveless shirt and khaki shorts, Lori looked as if she'd come straight off the golf course. She exuded the kind of feminine class men found attractive, yet, despite her beauty,

Jenny's best friend and sister-in-law remained genuine and unassuming, with a heart big enough to overlook Joel's faults, as well as her own.

Jenny glanced down at her own faded denim shorts and T-shirt, suddenly aware of her careless appearance.

Lori sat in the rocker opposite Jenny. "What's wrong?"

"I think it's time I invested in a new wardrobe."

Her friend shrewdly narrowed her eyes. "Hmm. Now why are you so concerned about your appearance all of the sudden, as if I didn't know?"

"What's that supposed to mean?"

Lori shrugged. "You like Chase, don't you?"

Jenny scoffed. "What's that got to do with me needing a new wardrobe?"

"This is Lori you're talking to, Jen. We've been friends all of our lives. I haven't seen you this interested in a man since . . . well, in a very long time."

Jenny knew Lori was thinking of Russ. At least she had the decency not to mention his name.

"Chase is nice," Lori continued, "and he's very attractive. Why shouldn't you be interested?"

"Being nice and attractive isn't enough for me anymore. It wouldn't be enough for you either. Not if he didn't share your beliefs."

Lori fell back in her rocker, resting her head against the chair. "Oh." She turned her head toward Jenny. "You know, Joel and I think God brought him here for a reason."

He's here for a reason, all right. "And what would that be?"

"I don't know, but Joel thinks Chase is tormented by his past." Lori leaned in closer, speaking in a low voice. "Did you know his biological parents were murdered when he was a boy?"

The revelation shocked Jenny, and compassion flooded her heart. "I knew his parents died, but he never told me how."

"He trusts you. Maybe you can help him through whatever it

is he's dealing with."

Jenny shook her head, and her rocking back and forth became jerky. "You're giving me way too much credit. I may know how to treat his bee sting, but only God can heal his soul."

Lori touched the arm of Jenny's rocker and stopped it. "Speaking of souls, what's going on with yours? You never come to church anymore."

"I've been busy," she replied.

Lori's perceptive gaze told her she wasn't buying it. "We've missed you. The truth is, both Joel and I are concerned about you. I know it's been hard since your father passed away. It's been hard on all of us." Warmth radiated through her concerned expression. "I've always thought we were much more than in-laws. You've always been like a real sister to me."

Jenny smiled. "I know. I feel the same way."

Joel appeared with Chase, and they ascended the steps to the porch. "What are you two chatting so seriously about?"

Jenny and Lori shared secret looks. Then Lori smiled back at him. "Why you, of course."

"That's what I was afraid of." He turned to Chase. "See, we can't leave them alone for a minute."

The men's clothes were so dirty and damp with perspiration Jenny couldn't resist ribbing them a bit. "What have you two been doing, digging ditches?"

Joel blew out a breath. "Close. We started with mending the fence and ended with replacing rotting boards on the barn."

Chase raised his finger. "Don't forget all that time we spent fixing your tractor and working in the garden." He smiled at Jenny. "I'm now your brother's personal indentured servant. The things I'll do for a piece of Lori's apple pie."

Lori rose from her rocker. "I'm saving the pie for dessert tonight, but I do have cookies. I'll run in and get more glasses for the lemonade too."

After she left, Joel took out a handkerchief and wiped his brow and hands with it. "What did Nick have to say today?"

Jenny leaned forward. "It turns out your sheep is the fifth cougar kill in two months. He wants to come over tomorrow morning at nine a.m. to see if he can track it down."

"Works for me." He turned to Chase. "Want to join us?"

Chase shrugged. "Sure. Why not?"

"You can't tell Lori though. She doesn't like it when I go hunting."

Jenny bristled. "Nick is bringing a tranquilizer gun. He's not planning to kill it."

Joel pivoted to her. "I'm still bringing my rifle."

"Then I'm coming too," she said.

"Don't you have to work?"

"I'll take the morning off."

"Won't Clint mind?"

"He might, but I have so many vacation days on the books he's practically ordered me to take time off."

"Okay. We'll muster here in the morning."

Jenny stood and cautiously approached her brother. "Joel . . . I want to take my dogs."

He recoiled. "No way."

"But I've been training them to track. If the cougar was here last night, they already have its scent. They could lead us right to it."

Her brother stubbornly shook his head.

Chase spoke up. "Why not give it a try, Joel?"

Joel shot him an annoyed look. "Who asked you for your opinion?"

"What have you got to lose?"

"Yeah," Jenny seconded, delighted to have Chase on her side.

Joel scowled. "Those wolves are more likely to scare that cougar off than track it down."

"It's still worth a shot. And if it doesn't work, you can blame me."

Joel eyed his friend, thinking it over. Then, with an exhale of surrender, he raised his hand. "Okay, whatever."

"Yes!" Jenny jumped and clapped her hands. In her jubilation, she moved in Chase's direction to give him a hug, but stopped herself.

Chase lightened the awkward moment with an amused smile. "Congratulations."

Joel shook his finger at him. "You owe me, buddy."

Chase turned and leaned against the porch railing, facing Joel. "Tell you what, if Fred and Ginger blow it, I'll personally build them a fence they can't escape anymore."

Joel rubbed his chin and grinned. "I'm gonna hold you to that, Matthews."

The two men shook on it.

Jenny glanced around the premises. "Did Shep and Fleece ever come back?"

Joel's expression darkened. "No."

"What on earth could have happened to them?"

"I wish I knew." He turned and plopped into the rocker Lori had vacated, wearing a somber expression. "Without those dogs, my sheep are even more vulnerable to predators. Then there's Adam. He's been calling them all day. I haven't had the heart to tell him they may never come home."

The news distressed Jenny. If something happened to Fred and Ginger, she'd be devastated. "Hopefully, they'll return."

Chase was still leaning against the rail.

Joel gestured toward the porch swing. "Take a load off, buddy. You've worked hard enough today. You deserve a rest."

Chase declined with a slight wave of his hand. His bronzed skin gleamed in the afternoon sun as he turned around and stared at the mountains in the distance.

His pensive expression reminded Jenny of what Lori had told her earlier. She knew the pain of losing one's parents, but she couldn't imagine the agony if they had been murdered. And then to lose his partner like that.

Her mind replayed the ghastly look on his face as he stared at his red-stained shirt at Joel's barbecue. As if he'd seen a ghost

. . .

Or a demon.

Maybe he had.

No wonder he was so determined to find the fugitive who killed his partner.

"I hear you're thinking of moving."

Jenny turned in Joel's direction. "Who told you?"

"Gus stopped by this afternoon and mentioned it."

She sighed. *Can't I do anything without Joel finding out*? "I was. However, someone beat me to the punch."

Joel's brow lifted. "Really? Who?"

"The new vet in town. His name is Reggie Grayling."

Chase turned his head, appearing to take an interest in the conversation.

"That's the first I've heard of it," Joel said. "Where's he going to set up his clinic?"

"At the old bait and tackle shop by the lake."

"In that shack? Wonder why I didn't hear any of this at the town council. Where's he from?"

"Atlanta."

"That's a long way to go to start a vet clinic. Does he have any family around here?"

"No."

"A wife, kids?"

"No, he's single." Judging from Joel's arched brow and Chase's frown, perhaps she'd volunteered the last detail a little too quickly.

Joel squinted at her. "Sounds like he made quite an impression on you."

She laughed. "You're jealous because you didn't know about it first."

"Yeah, right," Joel replied in a dismissive tone. "At least we can cancel posting the ad for a vet now. The town council never could agree on what it should say anyway."

"You never posted the ad?" she asked.

"No, why?"

"I assumed Reggie came here for the vet position, but how would he know about it if it was never posted?"

"Maybe someone in town told him."

Jenny doubted it, but let it go. "The important thing is that we finally have a vet in town." She looked at the sun setting in the western sky. "Well, it's getting late. I need to let Fred and Ginger out or they'll go nuts." She descended the steps.

"Where are you going, Jenny?"

She peered over her shoulder and saw Lori standing at the door with a tray of more refreshments.

"I need to get home."

Lori tilted her head slightly. "I was hoping you'd stay for dinner. I still have apple pie left over."

"Thanks, but I wouldn't want to deprive Chase." She tossed him a teasing glance.

"Don't forget the cougar hunt in the morning," Chase called out.

Jenny stopped and pivoted to see the frown on Lori's face. She knew Joel would be in hot water if Lori thought they were going for a real hunt.

"I'll be here bright and early," Jenny replied. "Oh, and by the way, it's not a hunt, it's an animal rescue mission."

The next morning, when Jenny arrived at Joel's place with her dogs, her brother met her as she got out of her pickup. "What's the matter? You look like somebody died."

He glanced down and blew out a long breath. "After you left yesterday, Chase and I went on a search for Shep and Fleece. We found them both in the canyon about a mile across the road, barely alive. Somebody must have whacked them with a stick or a club, but it seems they put up a good fight. We found a scrap of plaid material nearby that looks like it was ripped from a man's shirt."

Chase appeared from behind the house and joined them.

Jenny looked around. "Where are the dogs now?"

"Lori rushed them to the animal hospital in Watkinsville. Fortunately, the vet says they're going to pull through, but it'll be several days before they can come home."

The lingering tension on the men's faces caused her to be suspicious. "There's more to this, isn't there?"

Joel rubbed his chin. "I did a headcount of my sheep this morning."

"And?"

"Two lambs are missing."

"There's no way a mountain lion did this," she said.

Chase's eyes flashed with speculation. "Whoever injured the dogs must have stolen the two missing lambs."

Jenny looked down and sighed. "I didn't want to say anything until after we found the cougar, but someone came into my trailer a couple of nights ago and stole the money I had in my nightstand."

"What?" Chase and Joel said in unison.

She rolled her eyes at their overreaction. "I wasn't home when it happened. I was having dinner with you and Lori. It was only thirty dollars and the fool's gold coins Dad gave me when I was little." Then she snickered.

"What?" Joel said.

"I was imagining the thief trying to pay for something with that fool's gold. You have to admit, it's kind of ironic."

"This is no laughing matter." Joel closed his eyes and grimaced. "So now we're looking for a prowling cougar and an outlaw."

Jenny caught Chase's enigmatic expression and knew he'd come to that conclusion much earlier. No doubt he thought it was *his* outlaw.

Fred and Ginger pulled Jenny forward as she clung to their leashes. The scent of the mountain lion drove them deeper into the woods.

Chase, who was at Jenny's side, grabbed hold of the restless dogs' tethers to help Jenny restrain them. "Why didn't you tell me about the break-in yesterday?"

"Billy stopped by after you left. There were two sets of footprints outside my window. One of them was Billy's. He's been going through some hard times. I didn't want him to get implicated in this. Besides, it's only $30."

Chase shook his head.

"I know that look, but other than the footprints, there isn't much to go on, and the rain washed them away already. I did get a picture of them, but it's not very clear because it was at night." She pulled her phone from her waist holster and showed him the snapshot. "See?"

"Still, you should have told me. You are going to report it, aren't you?"

"Yes, but it will be hard to track down thirty dollars and a few trinkets. I'm sure Deputy Patterson has bigger fish to fry."

Chase held onto the leashes while Fred and Ginger lurched forward. "They've got the scent," he called back to Joel and Nick.

Jenny glanced over her shoulder. Nick clutched his tranquilizer gun while Joel tightened his grip on his hunting rifle. She turned back in time to see Chase reach for his pistol.

The weapons in the hands of the men made her nervous. With these trigger-happy cowboys along, the situation could easily get out of control.

"Let the dogs loose," Joel shouted above the barking and growling. "We'll follow them."

Jenny hesitated. She didn't want to risk Fred and Ginger cornering the cat and getting into a scuffle with it. Not only could they get seriously injured, but it would be hard to aim the tranquilizer gun. She looked at Nick for confirmation.

He shifted his eyes to her. "They may lose the scent if we hold them back."

She stopped and stooped down to release the dogs from their leashes.

Once freed, they bolted through the woods like a couple of greyhounds toward the finish line.

The hunters tried to keep up, following the sound of their barking.

A half mile later, Jenny spotted her dogs nipping and barking at the big cat. The cougar, ears pinned and teeth exposed, pawed and hissed at the dogs to hold them off. Cornered against a rock wall, there was no way of knowing what its next move would be.

Nick took the tranquilizer gun and aimed. Right as he pulled the trigger, the cat jerked away. The dart missed its target.

While Nick reloaded, the cougar swiped at Ginger, barely missing her.

"Ginger, Fred, come!" The dogs ignored Jenny's command. She snatched the gun out of Nick's hand. "Let me try. That cat will kill my dogs if we wait any longer."

She aimed, but Fred blocked her view. "I've got to move in closer to get a clean shot."

Chase stepped in front of her. "No way. It's too dangerous."

His intrusion angered her. "Back off, Matthews. This isn't your turf."

He stood his ground. "I may not know much about cougars, but I know first-hand how unpredictable people can be when they're cornered at gunpoint."

She glared at him. Who did he think he was, telling her what to do? "That cat isn't one of your escaped felons. I know what I'm doing."

He looked to Joel, who simply shrugged, unwilling to cross his sister this time. Chase finally backed off, giving her space.

Jenny closed in on the cat. The rustle of Chase and Joel's

footsteps in the brush as they followed made her uneasy. She aimed, but her dogs blocked her view. If the first shot didn't hit her target, she might not get another chance. Joel and Chase would never let the mountain lion escape alive if she missed.

She crept closer until she had a clear shot. Her timing and aim had to be perfect or the big cat could leap over her dogs and pounce on her. Like the ticking of a clock, her heartbeat counted off the seconds.

As she pressed the trigger, the cougar lunged. Jenny jumped, snagging her foot on a branch.

A second shot echoed through the fog in Jenny's head as she hit the dirt.

When she came to, Jenny was sprawled on the ground with Fred and Ginger whimpering and nudging her. It took several seconds to collect herself. Then she noticed the cougar's drugged body a few feet away.

Chase reached out a hand to help her up. "Are you okay?"

Annoyed at falling like a lightweight in front of him, she came to her feet on her own. "I'm fine." She teetered off-balance and he caught her before she fell again.

She had no choice but to accept his help this time, as she leaned against his strong body until the blood returned to her head. But being so close to him, made it hard to relax. She needed to calm her heart, not excite it.

When she pulled away, he continued to assist her until she was steady on her feet. The strange conflicting emotions warring within her only added to her bewilderment. "Thanks. I guess I landed a little harder than I thought."

"It happens to the best of us." His easy grin melted her injured pride.

She looked down and slapped the dust off her ranger shorts. Then she headed to Nick, who was inspecting the big cat lying on the ground.

Nick stood when Jenny joined him.

She crouched down and gently ran her fingers along the cat's fur. "She's nursing cubs." After examining the cougar, she shot Nick an urgent look. "Why isn't she breathing?"

Appearing uncomfortable, he skulked away.

Puzzled by his reaction, Jenny spotted the trail of blood underneath the animal.

She fell back on her heels in disbelief.

Chase came beside her. "I'm sorry. I know you wanted to save her."

She glimpsed his rueful expression. "You killed her!" She pounced on him, fists flying. "I had it under control. You ruined everything."

Joel pulled her away from him. "He had to. That cat lunged at you."

She shook her head. "No, I had a clean shot, until your friend decided to play the lone gunman."

"Think back, Jen. The cougar lunged at you after you misfired. Chase is the one who shot it. He saved your life. You said it yourself. There's no tranquilizer dart in her."

Jenny rested her head in her hands. It was all a jumbled blur. She remembered the second shot. She'd dismissed it as an echo.

She shook her hands in the air. "Who said my life needed saving? When are you two going to realize I'm not a fragile china doll ready to break apart the first time I get dropped?" She spun around and stomped away.

Joel raised his voice. "Where do you think you're going?"

Jenny paused but didn't turn around. "There are orphaned cubs out here. Thanks to you two, they'll die of starvation."

"How do we find them?" Chase asked.

"Look for a den. Chances are it's close. The cubs may be hungry, or scared and crying from all the noise, so listen for them." She pointed ahead. "That rock wall over there may have a small cave. I'd start there."

For the next few minutes, they scoured the area, searching for the cubs. When Joel shouted that he had found them, Jenny rushed over and squeezed her head and torso through the small opening in the rock.

Two spotted kittens approximately two weeks old, were crying and shaking inside.

Carefully, Jenny picked them up and carried them with her as she backed out of the narrow opening.

Chase reached out to take one of them.

She hesitated.

"Please," he said.

She finally relented.

He gently took one of the cubs and cuddled it in his hands.

She couldn't reconcile the man who was so gentle and fascinated by the kittens with the reckless killer of their mother. Her head throbbed with the distressing conflict until she couldn't take it any longer.

She retrieved the cub from Chase's hands, then headed for her truck with the two crying kittens, and Joel calling for her to come back.

She should never have allowed Chase to go with them. This only confirmed that he couldn't be trusted. He was a loose cannon, and she couldn't cover for him any longer. It was time to tell Joel the truth.

CHAPTER SEVEN

Jenny rapped on Reggie's door. While she waited, she peered into the small pet carrier. The cubs' mewing grew louder. She would need to feed them soon.

When Reggie opened the door and saw her, he grinned. "You don't give up, do you?"

"Actually, I'm here on official business." She held up the pet carrier. "Your first clients."

He glanced at the small cage. "Well, that didn't take long, but I'm not open for business yet."

"That's okay. They only need a checkup."

"And who are *they*?"

"The two baby cougars I rescued this morning."

"Oh." He eyed her warily. "You know, I'm really not a wildlife expert."

She smiled. "Pretend they're housecats."

A hint of doubt crossed his face. Finally, he shrugged and let her in. "Okay, we'll use the kitchen table."

Jenny followed him inside to the small rustic kitchen with pine-wood cabinets and a faded countertop that had seen better days. The sink was full of dirty dishes.

"Excuse the mess," he said. "I'm still getting organized."

"It's okay. You should see my trailer now that I'm keeping my dogs locked up in it." She set the carrier on the table in the kitchen and opened it.

"Wait." He gestured to the newspaper on the kitchen counter. "Let's put that down first."

She laughed. "Good thinking." She grabbed the paper and found the classifieds. "You don't need this section anymore, do you?"

"I guess not."

She handed it to him and lifted the carrier to let him spread the newspaper over the flat surface.

He glanced at her after covering the table. "How did you acquire two cougar cubs?"

Chase's second gunshot replayed in her mind. "By accident. I was trying to capture the mother this morning. Things got out of control, and she was killed."

"Sounds dangerous. Were you by yourself?"

"No. My brother, Joel, and two others came with me. My dogs tracked the cat, but Chase got trigger-happy and—"

"Chase?" Reggie glanced at her.

"Chase Matthews." She sighed. "He's a friend of my brother's, here on vacation." It bothered her that she was still covering for Chase's ruse. The sooner the truth came out, the better.

She took the cubs out of the carrier and handed one to Reggie. He picked it up and held it at arms-length.

She smiled, amused by his behavior. "Are you sure you're a vet? You're acting like you're holding a baby alien or something."

He placed the fur-ball on the kitchen table. "I wasn't exactly honest when I told you I was an equal-opportunity vet. You see, I'm allergic to cats, and I haven't taken my allergy medication."

"Oh. Maybe I should come back at a better time."

"Don't worry about it. Why were you tracking a cougar in the first place?"

"We've had a few livestock killings in the area, and we think the cougar was responsible. To tell you the truth, I mainly went along because I thought I could save it. I knew if my brother and Chase went without me, she was as good as dead. Unfortunately, she died anyway."

The kitten mewed at the vet.

"They must be hungry," he said.

"I know. Do you have any Esbilac or any other kitten formula I could use?"

Reggie shook his head. "No, I'm afraid not. My supplies are still on order."

"That's okay, I know how to make formula from scratch."

He gave her a curious look. "What are you going to do with the cubs?"

"I'm going to take care of them for now. Long-term, I don't know."

"Do you have the facilities to keep two full-grown mountain lions?"

She frowned, imagining Joel's reaction if she told him she planned to raise the cougars herself. It was bad enough with her dogs. "No. What about you?"

"Definitely not."

She picked up a cub and cradled it to her face. "But they're so cute and cuddly."

"So are raccoons, but I don't want to live with them. Sorry I can't do more for you today."

"What about shots? Shouldn't they get a rabies shot, and maybe one for distemper?"

"Like I said, I don't have my supplies yet. Tell you what, stop by in a couple of weeks, and I'll give them a full workup."

"Okay." She returned the cubs to the carrier. "I can't tell you how much we've needed a real vet around here. Joel was a little miffed when I knew about you before he did. You see, he's on the town council, and they were planning to advertise the vet position, but now they won't need to."

"Big brother, Joel?"

"Yep."

"Glad I could help you get a one-up on him. Are you still planning to move?"

"No. I've decided to stay put for now."

The kittens' crying grew louder.

"I better go home and feed them."

"Here, let me get that for you." Reggie lifted the pet carrier and escorted Jenny to her truck. When she opened the passenger door, he set it on the seat. "Have you read those books yet?"

"No, I've barely had time to unpack them."

A couple riding bicycles sped past them. The young woman suddenly stopped and looked back. "Jenny, it's me, Wendy."

Jenny turned and waved.

The young woman parked and came over.

The man with her got off his bike and followed.

Wendy removed her helmet and shook her head, letting her shiny tresses cascade down her shoulders. She addressed Jenny with a nod in Reggie's direction. "Who's your friend?"

"This is Dr. Reggie Grayling, the new vet in town."

Wendy took a long look at him. "Nice to meet you."

Jenny recognized the young man who strode up to them. "Hi, Sam. Are you enjoying your summer at home?"

"Yeah. I've been helping Dad out with the farm."

She turned to Reggie. "Wendy and Sam went to Eagle Valley High together. Now they're college students here on summer break."

"Ah, those were the days," Reggie said in a wistful voice. "Do you two go to the same school?"

"No," Wendy replied. "Sam goes to Washington State, and I go to USC." Flicking her hair over her shoulder, she eyed him with a curious glint. "Where are you from, Dr. Grayling?"

"Reggie, please. And I'm from Atlanta."

"I like your Southern accent." Wendy gazed at him with a flirty smile.

"We should be going, Wendy," Sam said in a disapproving tone.

"In a minute." Wendy kept her gaze fixed on Reggie.

The vet glanced in Jenny's direction. "How long have you two known each other?"

"Since forever," Wendy blurted before Jenny could reply. "She was my youth leader at church."

Reggie grinned at Jenny. "Well, it looks like you did a good job."

Jenny smiled at his compliment. "Wendy was easy. Now Sam . . . he was a different story." She grinned at the young man to let him know she was kidding.

"Hey, I wasn't so bad," Sam replied, "except for that time I put a possum in the girl's bathroom."

Jenny rolled her eyes. "Don't remind me."

Sam took Wendy's hand. "Come on, Wendy, we need to go." Then he waved at Jenny. "We're meeting friends for a cookout."

"Sounds like fun."

The kittens' high-pitched crying came from the open window in Jenny's truck.

"Wait," Wendy shook off Sam's hand, and she stepped up on the running board to peer inside the truck. "What's in the carrier?"

"Cougar cubs," Jenny replied.

"Sweet." She climbed down and opened the passenger door to get a better look. "They're so cute."

"I wish you could take them back to college with you," Jenny said.

"That would be Sam. WSU's mascot is the cougar."

Sam grinned. "Hey, why don't you bring them to the cookout? My WSU friends will get a kick out of them."

"I don't think so. I need to get them home and fed. That's why they're crying so much."

"What about you, Reggie?" Wendy flicked a lock of hair over her shoulder. "Want to come to the cookout?"

He politely shook his head. "Maybe another time."

"Let's go," Sam took Wendy's hand again and led her back to their bikes.

"Hey, Jenny, let's get together," she shouted over her shoulder. "I'll give you a call."

After they left, Reggie walked Jenny to the driver's side of her truck. "Nice kids."

"Yeah. It's hard to believe they're in college." They stopped at the driver-side door. "Do you go to church, Reggie?"

"Me? No—I mean . . ."

"It's okay. You don't have to explain." She opened the driver's side door and hopped in. "I was just curious."

He closed the door behind her and lingered beside her open window. "You know, I might be persuaded with the right inducement."

She raised her brow at his suggestive tone. "Something tells me I'm not the first woman you've used that line on."

He grinned with a brash gleam in his eye. "Now why do you say that?"

"I've been trained to detect wolves on the prowl."

His smile faded, and he cleared his throat. "I hope you'll drop by again soon."

"I think I'll wait until you're officially open for business."

She started the engine and noticed him watching as she drove away. For a vet, he didn't seem to know much about how to treat cougar cubs—or women.

So which are you, Reggie Grayling, a dog or a wolf?

When Jenny got home, Fred and Ginger weren't happy. Her trailer had suddenly become a three-ring circus. The cubs were crying, the dogs barking and growling, and she was trying to keep the peace.

She locked the dogs in her bedroom while she worked on feeding the cubs, but Fred and Ginger whined and barked non-stop. She removed the band holding her ponytail in place and fidgeted with it. *There's got to be a better way.*

Once the kittens were fed, they quieted down, and Jenny returned them to their carrier.

With everything going on, she couldn't go to work that afternoon, so she called Clint and explained the situation. He must have heard the frustration in her voice because he told her to take the rest of the day and tomorrow off too, if she needed it.

Afterward she went into the bathroom and changed into a comfortable pair of shorts and a T-shirt. As she sat down to eat a snack, there was a knock at her door. *Now who could that be?* When she answered it, she was surprised to see Chase standing on her steps.

"I saw your truck out front. I hope this is a good time."

She stared at his bright orange, University of Tennessee jersey, and wondered how anyone could look so amazing in that color. But then, he always looked good, even with barbecue sauce smeared on his shirt. Running a hand over her free-flowing hair, she wished she had changed into nicer clothes. "It's been a rough day, and I wasn't expecting anyone."

He glanced at her casual attire. "If this is you on a bad day, I should drop by unannounced more often."

She peered at her clothes and flip flops and shook her head. "You don't get out much, do you?"

He smiled. "Do you want me to come back another time?"

She noticed he was carrying a large shopping bag, and her curiosity trumped her vanity. "What do you have in there?"

"I was in town today and found something that will keep your dogs away from Joel's place." He pulled out a big box. "It's an invisible fence."

Looking it over, she was thrilled that Chase had found the perfect solution to her problem. "But you won your bet with Joel. My dogs tracked the cougar, so you don't owe me a fence."

"I know. I want to do it anyway." He folded the empty shopping bag in his hands.

"Here, I'll take that." She took the bag from him and stashed it under her sink for recycling.

"There's one catch," he said from the door. "Fred and Ginger will have to wear special collars."

She rejoined him. "They'll get used to it. You have no idea how crazy my life has been since I brought those cubs home with my dogs cooped up inside."

He glanced over his shoulder at the yard. "I can install it now, if you show me the area you want them confined to."

She gazed at the sky. Clouds were rolling in. "Maybe this isn't the best time."

"The sooner it's installed, the sooner you'll get your life back. If you need to go to work, I can do this while you're gone."

"No, I took the afternoon off."

He smiled. "Great. Then I'll get started."

Fred and Ginger barked from her bedroom.

"I'll be right there, Chase. I want to let my dogs out."

After she released them, the Huskies came with her to the backyard, pacing excitedly as if they knew something was up.

Jenny studied her lawn carefully, then began collecting rocks as she walked along, placing them along the perimeter until she had outlined the entire border for the fence. "Okay. I'm finished."

Chase walked around the large yard to survey the boundary she'd laid out. "Looks good. Do you have any tools I can borrow?"

"In my shed." She gestured toward the small storage building behind her trailer and headed in that direction. "That's strange," she said when she reached the door.

Chase came up beside her. "What is?"

"The lock's been broken." She opened the shed and looked inside.

"Is anything missing?"

She quickly scanned the wooden shelves. "Everything appears to be here—wait! One of my shovels is missing . . . and my axe." She scratched her head and turned to Chase. "Now why would anyone care about that and leave my toolbox and bicycle?"

His eyes narrowed. "My guess is your thief had something specific in mind. It was probably stolen the other night when your money was taken."

Jenny sighed. "At least it's mostly small stuff."

"You should still file a report."

"I will. First thing tomorrow." She picked up the toolbox and handed it to him. "You're welcome to whatever's left."

She went to help install the fence, handing Chase tools as needed. But he obviously knew what he was doing, and she admired his skill at putting it together.

Darker clouds gathered in the sky. By the time he'd finished, it sprinkled.

"We better make a run for it, before we get drenched," she said, ready to head for her trailer.

"You go. I'll put the tools away."

When she came inside, Jenny waited for Chase and her dogs.

Chase hurriedly returned the tools to her shed and closed it. By the time he reached her trailer, the rain was pounding against the roof.

Jenny held the door open for him and her dogs, who rushed in on his heels.

"No!" Too late. Her pets were already soaked.

Fred and Ginger shook themselves off, splattering water all over Chase and her furniture.

Jenny winced, embarrassed by her canine kids. "Oops. Sorry about that."

Chase returned an easy shrug. "It's okay. I was already wet."

"I'll get some towels." She hurried to the linen closet down the hallway and returned a moment later with her arms full. "Here, take one."

He grabbed the top of the stack and began drying off. His damp shirt clung to him, revealing his muscular torso. "What?" he asked when he caught her staring at him.

"Here," she tossed him another towel, "Your shirt is sticking to you like glue."

While he finished, she sat on the floor and vigorously rubbed down her dogs. When Chase was through, he grabbed another dry towel from the stack and wiped off her bookshelf.

She came to her knees on the floor. "Oh, don't worry about

the furniture. I'll get to it in a minute."

He continued with his task. "I don't mind."

"But you already installed the fence. By the way, what do I owe you for that?"

"Nothing."

She pushed to her feet. "I know it wasn't cheap. I insist on paying you for it."

"Consider it a peace offering."

"I don't understand."

He tossed the wet towel he was using on the heap nearby and grabbed a new one from the stack. "We got off on the wrong foot this morning, and I want to start over."

She tilted her head. "Where?"

"How about with friendship?"

"Then what?"

He turned around, his eyes regarding her intently. "That's up to you."

Before she could respond, he turned back to the bookcase and picked out a book. "This looks like an intriguing manual on birds."

"Reggie gave it to me, along with some others that were in the cabin he's renting."

"Reggie?"

"The new vet."

"Oh, him." He eyed her with a raised brow. "He gave them to you, without asking the owner if he wanted them first?"

"Frank already told him he could have anything that was left." Guilt nibbled at her as she watched Chase peruse the book collection. "Now that you mention it, I probably should send Frank a note thanking him for them."

Chase thumbed through the bird book. "This Reggie-person. You like him."

She hesitated. "I hardly know him, but he's been generous."

"Generous with other people's belongings, you mean."

His comment hit a nerve. "Reggie was simply being nice. In

fact, he examined the cougar cubs free-of-charge today."

Chase thumbed through the pages of the book. "I bet he did."

"Why do you have to be so suspicious about everyone?"

He glanced at her. "Occupational habit. When are you going out with Reggie-the-vet?"

"Who said I wanted to go out with him?"

A spark of challenge gleamed in his eye. "Why not? He sounds perfect for you. He gives you free books. You'd have free vet visits. With all your animals, that alone could be worth a small fortune. I assume he also goes to your church."

His comment surprised her. "No. Why would you assume that?"

"I figured that was a requirement."

"Requirement for what?"

"I thought church was important to you."

She crossed her arms. "What exactly are you getting at? You're beginning to sound like my brother."

He paused and rubbed his face. "You know, Joel is pretty concerned that you've dropped out of church."

Her mouth gaped open, furious that Joel had confided in him about her. "I haven't *dropped out* of church." She straightened her spine and jutted her chin. "I'm taking a break, that's all."

"A break . . ."

"Yes, a break. Not that it's any of your business anyway."

"Okay. Forget I said anything." He turned around to place the book back on the shelf.

This was far from over. How dare he drop the subject so easily after filling her head with doubts about Reggie, and then challenging her faith?

Fred and Ginger wandered over and whimpered as if they were the young victims in a domestic dispute.

She bent to pet them. "Now you've upset my dogs."

He glanced at the canine pair and gave them a sympathetic smirk. "You baby them too much. Once you put those collars on them and they get a load of that invisible fence, then they'll really be upset."

Despite her anger, his remark elicited a smile from her lips. "You think my dogs are spoiled?"

"They need to know who's boss. That's all."

"Now you're an animal psychologist."

"There's a lot about me you don't know."

"So I'm discovering."

He picked up a picture of Jenny, Joel, and their father from the shelf. "Is this your dad?"

"Yes." Her heart softened at the mention of her father. "He died a week after that was taken."

Chase gently returned the picture to its place and faced her. "I hope you don't mind me asking, but how did he die?"

She glanced down. "A heart attack . . . It was very sudden. One day he was here, and the next . . . he wasn't."

She gathered the wet towels and carried them to the washing machine in the hallway. "Are you hungry?" she asked when she returned.

He grinned. "Starving. I came straight here after I bought the fence. I didn't have time for lunch."

"I'll make us something to eat."

He raised his hand. "Don't go to any trouble for me."

"It's no trouble." She opened the freezer and took out a box. "It's a frozen pizza."

He shrugged with a smile. "In that case, okay."

She took out the pizza and placed it in the oven, then set the table.

Chase stared out the window. "Looks like the rain stopped already."

"That's the way it is in the Northwest. We get lots of showers, but they don't last very long."

"In the South, it can rain for hours. And storms . . . We have the most amazing lightning and thunder storms. Sometimes, we even get a tornado. Now that's exciting."

"Do you miss it?"

He turned around. "What? Tornados?

"No, silly. Being home."

"I haven't really thought about it. I've been too busy helping Joel and playing tourist."

She gave him a teasing smile. "Are you actually enjoying your vacation?"

He nodded. "More than I expected. I can definitely see why Joel is so happy living here, a stone's throw from the mountains and the great outdoors."

"Now all you have to do is forget about all this business with the fugitive."

He peered at her. "I'm not giving that up. I'm just taking a little break from it right now."

She sighed. "I can't keep covering for you with Joel. You owe him the truth."

"I know. And it's not fair to you or Joel, but until I have hard evidence that Jim's killer is actually here, it's only a theory. There's no point in getting everyone upset if it turns out I'm wrong."

He crossed the living room and relaxed on the couch. A magazine was lying on the end table next to him, and he flipped through it.

When she'd finished in the kitchen, she came and sat beside him. Reaching under the end table, she retrieved a large photo album from the bottom shelf. "Here." She handed it to him. "You might enjoy looking through this. They're pictures of Joel when he was a kid. I also have a few from when he was in the Army."

Chase spent the next few minutes perusing the photos. He pointed to a picture. "Who's this?"

"That's my mother and me."

"Nice picture. You favor her."

"You think so? I've always thought I took more after my dad. My mother was so pretty and feminine. I've always been such a tomboy and . . ."

He glanced her way. "You're pretty too, you know."

The intensity of his gaze quickened her heart as he leaned closer.

Ginger barked, and Jenny jumped. Her nose collided with Chase's, thwarting his kiss.

"Ouch." She sprang to her feet and held her nose. "Are you okay?"

"I don't think anything is broken," he said, rubbing his face. "Where are you going?"

"The pizza should be ready now. I'll go get it."

"Right," Chase murmured as she sprinted toward the kitchen.

She took the pizza out of the oven and cut it into wedges. After carrying the plates to the small kitchen table, she paused.

Chase was roughhousing with Fred and Ginger on the floor.

She smiled. "They like you."

"They're good dogs. Aren't you guys?" The playful canines barked and wagged their tails, wanting him to tussle with them longer. "Sorry, but I gotta eat."

He rolled over and hopped up. "I need to wash up first."

"The bathroom is down the hall."

By the time he returned, Jenny had filled both of their glasses with water. She turned to sit and realized he was standing behind her, holding out her chair. "After you."

She glanced at him and smiled. "I never know what to make of you, Chase Matthews."

He sat across from her. "Good. I like to keep you guessing."

"But is the real Chase the charming Southern gentleman, or the ruthless lawman?"

"Why does it have to be one or the other? Why can't I be a lawman and a gentleman at the same time?" He sniffed the pizza. "Mmm, that smells really good. I guess I was hungrier than I thought."

Bowing her head, she stopped and stared at Chase as he lifted a piece of pizza with his fingers and raised it to his mouth.

He took a bite, then focused on her. "Why aren't you eating?"

"I always pray before I eat."

"Really?"

"Why do you sound surprised?"

"I don't know. I thought maybe since you were taking a vacation from church . . ."

Vacation from church! She'd only missed a few Sundays. And, Chase, of all people. Who was he to be casting stones?

After considering it more, she raised her chin. "So what if I don't go to church?"

"I thought you didn't want to discuss it."

"I changed my mind. Now answer my question."

"It's really none of my business whether you go or not." He took another large bite and chewed for a long time before swallowing. "This is delicious."

"You're taking a break from your job. I'm taking a little break from . . ."

"God?"

"It's not like that at all."

"Then what is it like?"

She couldn't think of an adequate rebuttal. "Let's drop it."

"Fine by me."

Their temporary truce was broken when Fred and Ginger rushed to the door, barking and growling. Jenny groaned. "Not again."

"What's with them?"

"I wish I knew."

She pushed herself away from the table. The noise from their barking made finishing dinner impossible.

Chase shouted over the dogs. "Another cougar?"

"I don't think so." She clapped her hands. "Fred and Ginger, stop it!"

The revving of a car engine brought Chase to his feet. "That's no wild animal."

Jenny followed him outside in time to see his SUV speeding

down the road until it vanished out of sight.

CHAPTER EIGHT

AFTER CHASE TOLD THE DEPUTY SHERIFF about his stolen SUV, Gus handed him a clipboard with a blank document attached.

"Fill this out, and I'll call it in," Gus said.

"A paper form?"

"Our computer is down. We don't have much of an I.T. budget around here."

Carrying the clipboard, Chase took a seat in a nearby chair.

Gus stood behind the front desk, chomping on a stick of gum. "You know, car thefts don't happen a whole lot around here. Have you notified your insurance company yet?"

Chase grabbed the pen dangling from the clipboard by a chain. "I did that right away."

"You said you were at Jenny Snowfeather's place when it happened?"

Chase nodded. "I was there yesterday installing an electronic fence for her dogs. I'm here on vacation, visiting her brother. Joel and I served in the Army together."

The deputy's eyes widened with interest. "Is that right? I've known her family all my life. Their father was a fine man. Shame he died so sudden."

Chase glanced up. "Speaking of Jenny, yesterday she discovered her shed had been broken into and a couple of things are missing. Some cash in her nightstand was taken too."

"Sounds like someone is targeting her. She filed a report about the thefts this morning and left right before you arrived. You just missed her."

"Really?" Chase wished he'd come earlier.

"The other deputies and I will drive by her place more often to keep an eye out."

"Good idea." Chase turned to his form. "You should talk to Joel too. Someone seriously injured his dogs and stole a couple of lambs."

"Jenny mentioned that. I'll give Joel a call." Gus frowned. "It's one thing to steal, but when somebody maliciously hurts a dog, that really galls me."

"I know what you mean," Chase replied. "Have you had any other thefts in the area lately?"

"Hmm. Now that you mention it, we had a break-in at a hunting cabin a little over a week ago."

Chase stopped writing and peered at him. "Do you think it might be connected with the theft at Jenny's?"

Gus eyed him with a raised brow. "For someone on vacation, you sure ask a lot of questions."

Chase returned an amiable grin. "Comes with the territory. I'm in law enforcement too."

"Which branch?"

"Marshal."

The look of doubt on the man's face prompted Chase to pull out his badge.

Gus grinned as he handed it back. "Well, I'll be . . . like Wyatt Earp."

Smiling at Gus's reaction, Chase leaned back in his chair. "Not exactly. First of all, I'm a deputy marshal. And, second, a lot has changed since the days of Wyatt Earp. Our horses are better trained, for one."

Gus gave Chase a double-take. Then he erupted in a deep belly laugh. "Our horses are better trained," he repeated. When he had composed himself, he came around the front desk, dragged a chair over to Chase and straddled it. "What do you want to know about the break-in?"

"What was taken?"

"Hmm. I better get the file." Gus jumped up and disappeared into the back office. A moment later, he returned with a folder and pulled out the report. "Says here that two hunting rifles, some cartridges, cans of food and a fishing pole were stolen. "You know that cabin is occupied now. The new vet in town rented it out."

Reggie strikes again. "Are there any other unoccupied cabins in that area?"

"Only one that I can think of this time of year."

"Can you tell me where it is?"

Gus laid out a large area map on the front desk.

Chase rose and met him there, his eyes tracing the invisible line on the map from the deputy sheriff's office to where Gus's finger rested.

"I figured it was delinquents. You think they stole your car? Is that why you're so interested?"

"That, and I'm concerned about Jenny and Joel, if they're being targeted." Chase had to be careful how much he told Gus. He scratched his face. "You know how it is, being a lawman yourself. You can't turn it off, even on vacation."

Gus leaned forward, resting his forearms on the desk, squinting at Chase. "Are you and Jenny seeing each other?"

Surprised by the question, Chase played it cool. "I told you, I'm a friend of her brother's."

A knowing grin appeared on Gus's face. "But you like her, don't cha?"

Chase focused on the form. "Sure. She's nice."

"Yeah, you like her." Gus chuckled. "That Jenny sure has a mind of her own, but she's also got a heart of gold. My daughter Wendy thinks the world of her."

Chase glanced up. "I met your daughter the other day. You must be happy to have her home this summer."

"I am, but she's a pistol, that one." Gus peered at him. "Do yourself a favor. Don't have any daughters if you can help it. You'll live a lot longer."

"I'll keep that in mind," Chase said with a smile.

"Want some more advice?"

He didn't, but needed to stay on good terms with the deputy, so Chase laid the pencil on the clipboard to give him his full attention. "Okay. Let's hear it."

"If you want to win Jenny's heart, you need to take an interest in the things she cares most about."

"And what would that be?"

Gus pointed a finger at him. "That's for you to figure out. But it's got to be sincere, mind you. Women know when men are putting on an act."

"I don't know if that would work with Jenny. Besides, I think she may be interested in someone else."

"Then what have you got to lose? Take it from me, if I had made a real effort to show an interest in what was important to Wendy's mom, maybe I wouldn't be divorced right now."

Chase smiled politely. "Thanks for the advice, Deputy, but like I said, Jenny and I are only friends." He ignored Gus's skeptical look and finished filling out the form.

When he'd completed it, Chase stood and handed the clipboard to the deputy.

"I'll keep you posted if anything comes up regarding your SUV," Gus said.

"Sounds good . . . I'd appreciate hearing any new developments on the other thefts too."

Gus eyed him with a sly grin. "I thought you were on vacation."

After leaving Gus, Chase headed to the sweets shop to get an ice cream. The new information about the cabin break-in had supercharged his mind and his appetite.

He glanced up and spotted Jenny in her ranger uniform coming out of the post office across the street.

When she saw him, she stopped and crossed the road. "Chase? What are you doing here?"

"I filed a report for my stolen SUV," he said. "Looks like

Eagle Valley is experiencing something of a crime wave. Gus told me about a cabin break-in too."

"Oh, that."

"You knew?"

She nodded. "Clint, my boss, mentioned it to me right before Joel's barbecue. That's the cabin Reggie is renting."

"So I hear."

"Did Gus find out who did it?"

"No. He suspects it was kids."

He caught the flicker of doubt on her face. "You don't agree?"

"I checked out the cabin. A flat-screen television and a boom box were left by the previous owner. I can't imagine kids stealing rifles and food but not electronics."

Another possibility entered Chase's mind.

She placed a hand on her waist, her eyes flashing. "I know what you're thinking, but it doesn't mean it's your fugitive, Chase."

He decided to drop the subject. "How's that dog fence working out?"

She rested her thumbs in her pockets. "Fred and Ginger are not so happy, but I love it. Especially getting my trailer back. It was turning into a real circus. Where are you headed now?"

"I'm waiting until Joel returns from the hardware store. He's giving me a ride to Seattle so I can rent a car. How about keeping me company over an ice cream?"

She pulled her phone from her pocket and scanned it. "Okay, but I can't stay long. I dropped something off at the post office for work and my lunch hour is almost over."

They strode to the sweets shop a few doors down from the sheriff's office, and Chase held the door open.

Jenny turned to him. "Thank you, but I can get the door myself."

"Indulge me. I'm a Southerner. It's in my DNA."

She laughed. "If you insist. Actually, I like being spoiled."

"Good. You'll have to come to Tennessee sometime and see

how we do things in the South."

"Is it that different?"

"Not really," he replied as they walked to the counter to order. "But it is hotter there right now. I'm amazed how cool it is here for July. I still can't believe Joel doesn't need air conditioning."

"You should have been here last winter. It was one for the record books with so much cold and snow. But at least we're not having a drought this summer. Then we'd have to worry about wildfires."

They looked at the menu posted on the wall behind the counter.

Chase ordered a cone with two scoops of mint chocolate chip ice cream.

Jenny ordered a chocolate shake and pulled out her wallet to pay.

"I've got this," Chase said, handing the clerk the money. He glanced at Jenny. "My treat."

"Chase, you already bought and installed the fence, and that wasn't cheap."

"I was pretty tough on you at dinner last night."

"Is this another peace offering?"

"More of a bribe."

She gave him a doubtful look. "What do you want in return?"

"The pleasure of your company for a few minutes."

She glanced down, smiling. "You don't need to bribe me for that."

They headed to an empty table nearby and sat across from each other.

She stared at her milkshake. "Since we're making amends, I was pretty hard on you for killing the cougar. I heard the second shot, but I didn't want to believe that I missed with the tranquilizer gun."

"I'm sure it all came as quite a shock after you fell."

She nodded. "You see, I've spent my life trying to save and

rehabilitate animals. When I lose one, it's personal."

"You have to believe that I wouldn't have killed it if your life wasn't in danger."

"I know that now. Sorry I took it out on you." She took a sip of her drink and pointed to her cup. "This is really good. Feel free to bribe me with chocolate shakes anytime."

He chuckled at her last remark. "Gus told me you filed a report about the stolen money and tools. For a sleepy, little town, Eagle Valley seems to be having more than its share of crime lately."

A frown replaced her pretty smile. "I have to admit; it is starting to sound more sinister than petty theft and vandalism. I can't imagine who would harm Shep and Fleece. Even with the invisible fence, I plan to bring Fred and Ginger inside at night."

"That's not a bad idea. Had I known there was a thief in the area, I wouldn't have left my keys in my car. I guess I didn't expect to be there that long."

"Do you regret you stayed for dinner?" she said with a subtle grin.

"Definitely not. That was the best frozen pizza I've ever had. You'll have to give me the recipe."

She laughed. "Too late. I already recycled the box."

"In that case, how about going to dinner with me this Saturday?"

"Sorry," she said in a muted tone. "I already have plans."

"Oh," he replied, somewhat deflated.

"I promised Wendy I'd do something with her Saturday night."

"What about Friday?"

"I thought Joel was taking you backpacking."

"Oh, yeah. I forgot."

She glanced at her watch. "Well, I really need to get back to work." She rose from her chair. "Thanks for the shake."

He stood. "Maybe we can do it again sometime."

"I'd like that." She hesitated before leaving. "Well, see you around."

He watched her walk away. It bothered him not knowing when he'd see her next. With the recent crime spree, he didn't like her being alone. *Too bad I can't protect her with an invisible fence.*

Jenny finished feeding the cubs and tucked them into their cozy carrier for the night. Soon they would be too big for the small cage, and she couldn't continue to rely on Lori to come over and feed them every day while she was at work. It was too much to ask. She needed another solution, and soon.

Maybe Chase could install another invisible fence for them. She smiled at the thought. It probably wouldn't be very well received by her neighbors to see cougars roaming free. Joel would be livid.

Fred and Ginger's sudden barking and growling ended Jenny's momentary peace. Remembering what happened to Shep and Fleece, she went to her bedroom to get her gun.

She slowly opened the back door, wielding her weapon in front of her. It was dark and rainy outside. She descended the steps and swept the area behind the house.

The dogs growled and paced behind their invisible wall near Jenny's trailer.

"Who's there?" Jenny called.

The sound of movement came from the side of her trailer, and she hurried in that direction. Peering around the corner in the dark, she saw a faint figure pawing through her trashcan.

Jenny pointed her gun. "Stop!"

The figure turned and ran.

CHAPTER NINE

The Avalanche Grill, the town's only nightspot, was crowded even for a Saturday night. Jenny sat across from Wendy at a table close enough to watch the band, but far enough away to conduct a conversation.

Wendy, bobbing her head in time with the music, glanced at Jenny. "Thanks for coming here with me tonight. I thought you might have a hot date with that cute vet."

Jenny sent her friend a dry look. "Yeah, right. Speaking of dates, how come you're not out with Sam tonight?"

"He's getting too serious. He wants us to see each other exclusively."

"And you don't."

She glanced down and played with her shiny bracelet. "He's a great guy and all, but we're only nineteen. In a few weeks, we'll both go back to college and won't see each other again for months. I'm not ready to get tied down with one guy yet. I want to have a good time, no strings. You know?"

A harried waitress appeared at their table and handed them menus without looking up. "What can I get you two?" she asked as she readied her pen to take their order.

"Hi, Sue," Jenny said.

The woman took a break from her notepad and smiled. "Well, hi there, Jenny. I'm surprised to see you. So sorry about your dad. I would have come to the funeral, but I had to work."

Even in the dim lighting, Jenny's former high-school classmate looked pale and tired. Jenny gestured to her young friend. "You remember Wendy, don't you?"

"Oh, yeah. You're all grown up now, and so pretty. I'd give

anything to have hair like that."

"Thanks." Wendy said, beaming.

Jenny noticed the size of Sue's swollen belly. "When is your baby due?"

"Only one more month to go."

"It must be hard standing on your feet all day."

"Now that Butch has the new convenience store, we're hoping we can afford for me to quit and stay home with the baby for a few weeks. Then I'll help him out with the store."

"Is his business going well?"

"Well enough. You know, we've had a real hard time making ends meet. We sunk our entire savings into the Trail Break, but now it's beginning to pay off. It helps that we're located on the highway, so we get lots of tourists dropping by. Your brother Joel comes every now and then to gas up his truck. You should stop by too. Our gas prices are lower than in town."

Jenny nodded. "Thanks for the tip. I'll get my next tank-full there."

Sue covered her mouth, sharing a secret. "But don't tell Lou I'm promoting my own business."

"My lips are sealed."

With her pencil raised, Sue stood ready to take their order. "Now what can I get for you two ladies tonight?"

"Lemonade for me, please," Jenny replied.

Wendy, who had been listening to the music, shifted her eyes to Sue. "I'd like a beer."

Jenny shot Wendy a surprised look.

Sue responded to Wendy's request with a stern expression. "I'll need to see your ID first." The girl grabbed her purse to take out her wallet while Jenny and Sue exchanged doubtful glances.

Jenny put her hand over Wendy's. "What are you doing? You and I both know you're underage." She glanced back at Sue. "She'll have a root beer."

Wendy pouted. "Diet root beer."

"And please bring us an order of onion rings."

After Sue left their table, Jenny pounced on Wendy. "What in the world was that all about?"

"It's no big deal."

"What were you planning to show for ID?"

Wendy hesitated, then took out a card and handed it to her.

Jenny scrutinized it. "This is a fake. Where did you get it?"

Wendy shrugged matter-of-factly. "All the kids at college have one."

Jenny huffed. "Well, this kid doesn't anymore." She put the card in her pocket.

"Wait a minute! You can't do that. I paid a lot of money for that card."

"A lot of your father's money, you mean. Wendy, this isn't like you. What's going on?"

"You're not going to tell Dad, are you?"

"Not if you tell him first."

The color drained from the young woman's pretty face. "I can't tell him. He'd be so disappointed in me."

"You have to tell him, Wendy. You owe him the truth."

"I thought you were my friend."

"I am. That's why I have to tell your father about this if you won't do it yourself."

Wendy pleaded. "Please don't tell him, Jenny."

Jenny pulled the ID from her pocket and gave it back. "I'll give you a week."

A male voice interrupted them. "Looks like my lucky night. Two lovely ladies, and no men around."

"Reggie!" Wendy cried.

Still irritated at her young friend's behavior, Jenny glanced up and saw Reggie with a drink in his hand.

His eyes focused on Jenny. "Did I interrupt something?"

Wendy didn't give Jenny a chance to respond. "No, nothing at all. Please sit with us. This place was getting boring until you showed up."

"Maybe another time. I don't think Jenny is as happy to see

me as you are, Wendy."

Jenny decided she could use the diversion too. "No, it's fine. Please join us."

Reggie slid into the seat beside her, across from Wendy.

Sue stopped by their table and dropped off a heaping pile of onion rings. "What can I get for you?" she asked Reggie.

He pointed to his drink. "I'm good."

Wendy leaned in his direction. "It's funny you showed up here. Jenny and I were just talking about you."

"You were, huh?" His gaze briefly darted to Jenny. "If I'd known you two were here, I would have come earlier. I don't know all the nightspots yet."

Wendy scoffed. "It's a pretty short list. There's this place and the Eagle Valley Lodge restaurant. That's about it."

He grinned. "Wendy, I should have consulted you instead of searching online for a place to eat. To tell you the truth, I'm surprised to see you both here. I figured you mostly hung out at church."

"*Church*?" Wendy made a sour face. "I don't go anymore. It's so passé."

Jenny turned to Wendy. "Since when did you stop going to church?"

Wendy giggled uncomfortably and grabbed an onion ring to munch on, avoiding eye contact.

The band started playing a love song and Reggie turned to Jenny. "How about a dance?"

"Thanks, but I'm not much of a dancer."

"I'll go," Wendy hopped off her chair and tugged his arm. "Come on."

He slowly got up and set his drink on the table, giving Jenny a helpless shrug as Wendy pulled him to the dance floor.

After they left, Jenny snatched an onion ring and bit into it, relishing the comfort only fattening junk food could bring.

Billy Norton appeared at her table. "Hey, Jenny."

"Hi. What are you doing here?"

He shrugged. "Hanging out. What about you?" His zombie T-shirt glowed in the dim lighting.

"I'm here with Wendy." She rested her chin on the palm of her hand. "How's the job search going?"

"I got a job."

She raised her head. "Really? That's great. Where?"

"At the Eagle Valley Lodge. I'm a waiter there. I start tomorrow."

Jenny gave him a warm smile. "I'm so happy for you."

He stared at her for an awkward moment. "Uh—would you like to dance?"

She'd always considered Billy an old friend, nothing more. Still, she tried to let him down easy. "I don't think so, Billy, but thanks."

His downcast expression made her more sympathetic. "Why don't you have a seat?"

He took Reggie's chair next to her then pushed Reggie's drink away. "Hey, there's a good horror movie at the drive-in. How about going with me next weekend?"

Jenny decided it was time she was honest with him. "How long have you been asking me out?"

He shrugged. "Since middle school."

"Then why do you keep asking me out?"

"I don't know." He grinned. "Maybe one of these days you'll say yes?"

She sighed, giving him a compassionate look. "You're a great guy and a good friend. That's why I think it's time we were frank with each other. As much as I like you, I'm not going to go out with you."

"You're telling me this because you're seeing that guy you were with at the barbecue."

"Chase has nothing to do with this. Look, you deserve someone who will appreciate you for who you are. You and I don't even like to do the same things. You're into hunting, I'm into saving wildlife. You're into horror movies, I'm into classic movies. You're into tattoos, I'm into books . . ."

"Yeah, yeah, but you're forgetting something. We both have pickups."

She shook her head. "Billy . . ."

The dim lighting seemed to cast an angry shadow across his face. "I saw how lovey-dovey you two were when he walked you home last weekend."

"You were watching us?"

"He doesn't belong here. He's just using you."

Her mouth fell open. "This isn't like you, Billy."

He jumped up. "I gotta go."

"Billy, wait!"

Chase came to the bar and found a seat where he could scan the Avalanche Grill without being noticed. He spotted Jenny sitting at a table with Billy Norton, not far from the stage.

He watched them from a distance, recalling how she'd gently brushed Billy off at the barbecue. *Relax, Matthews. They're only old friends.*

The bartender came over. "What'll you have?"

Chase kept his eyes on Jenny. "Ginger ale, please,"

"Coming up." The bartender quickly filled a chilled glass with the soda and handed it to him.

Chase glanced at the man. "Thanks."

"My name's Lou if you need anything else."

Chase gave him an amiable nod as Lou set the drink in front of him. "By the way, I'm Deputy Marshal Chase Matthews." He removed his badge and showed it to Lou.

The man took a step back. "Hey, I don't want any trouble."

"Don't worry. I need your help with something." Chase reached for his wallet and pulled out a photo, placing it on the bar. "Can you tell me if you recognize this man?"

Lou took the picture and studied it. "You know, he looks familiar. I think I have seen him in here before, but I'm not sure."

Lou handed the picture back.

Chase opened his wallet and put the photo away. Then he pulled out a card with his name and cell number. "Call me if he shows up here. Okay?"

Lou read the card and nodded. "Sure, will do."

Chase swiveled around in his chair in time to see Billy bolt for the door, leaving Jenny all alone.

Jenny glanced at her phone to get the time. She turned her eyes back to the crowded dance floor, searching for Wendy. Finally, she spotted her with Reggie. Jenny frowned at how close they danced together.

Chase slid into the chair beside Jenny, startling her.

"Have a seat, Chase," she said, mocking his uninvited move.

"Thanks, I did." He set his ginger ale on the table. "What made Billy run out of here like that?"

She rolled her eyes. "You don't want to know." Then she smiled. "What brings you here tonight?"

His sheepish expression gave him away.

"Ah, still chasing ghosts."

He shrugged. "It keeps me busy when your brother's not working me to the bone. This afternoon, I helped him with his fence and discovered how stinging nettle got its name."

She thought of his bee sting allergy, but after he'd ignored her previous reminders to see a doctor about it, she decided not to mention it again. As long as he was so obsessed with capturing the fugitive, everything else would take a back seat, including his health.

He looked at the dance floor and pointed. "Isn't that Wendy out there?"

"Yeah."

"Who's that man she's with?"

"Reggie."

"Not Reggie-the-vet." Chase eyed her with an exaggerated

expression.

Irritated by his ribbing, Jenny glanced away at Wendy. "Yeah, that's him."

"From the way he's ogling her, Wendy better watch her step." Chase grabbed an onion ring and started munching on it. "And why is he dancing with her instead of you?"

"I declined."

His pleased expression brightened the darkly-lit room.

"Why are you grinning?"

"His loss is my gain."

She deflected his remark and noticed he was still wearing his windbreaker. "Isn't it a bit warm in here for that jacket?"

He leaned closer and nudged her. "Actually, I was thinking it's a little chilly."

She broke down and smiled at his ribbing. "How was your backpacking trip with Joel yesterday?"

"Okay, at first. Unfortunately, the weather turned, and it snowed, so we decided to come home early."

"That's too bad, but it's good you're getting out and exploring the mountains."

"Maybe I'll come back for a real vacation."

She sighed. "Why can't you simply relax and make *this* a real vacation? You should be enjoying yourself while you're here."

"Who said I wasn't enjoying myself?"

Jenny shrugged off his flirting.

"What did you do last night while I was freezing?"

"I had a visitor." She filled him in on the garbage invader.

Chase frowned. "Have you told Gus?"

"No. It was dark and rainy, and I only caught a glimpse of something moving. I would have suspected a bear, except that my trashcan is bear-proof." She sighed. "I wish I'd been able to get a better look at whoever it was."

"But it was a man."

"It's not your fugitive, Chase."

"If you didn't see him, how do you know?"

"Hey, maybe Big Foot is responsible for the recent crime spree," she said in a lighter tone. "Have you thought of that?"

He returned a dry look. "Nice try, but I'm sticking to the fugitive theory, not Sasquatch."

Jenny rolled her eyes then looked back at Wendy slow-dancing with Reggie. "If I had enough money, I'd pay the band to eliminate all the love songs from their playlist."

He chuckled. "You don't like seeing the two of them together, do you?"

She sipped her lemonade. "He's too old for her, and she barely knows him. I'm worried about her. She's changed since she went away to college."

"Doesn't everybody?"

"Well, I don't like *these* changes."

"Such as?"

"She tried to order a drink tonight with a fake ID."

Chase frowned. "That is a problem."

"And now, this infatuation with Reggie."

"She probably wants attention. Didn't Lori say that her parents went through a difficult divorce recently?"

"Yeah. It was really hard on her, but either college or the divorce has affected her more than I realized. I don't want to see her make choices she will regret for the rest of her life."

Chase nodded in agreement.

"Tonight, she told me she's stopped going to church." Jenny glanced at Chase. "I know what you're thinking."

"You do?"

"Maybe you're right. How can I blame Wendy for turning away from her faith when I haven't exactly embraced it lately? Sometimes it's difficult to believe, especially when life is so painful."

"Like when your father passed away."

She nodded.

He wiped his fingers with a napkin. "Look, I'm the last person who should be counseling you about faith, but it seems to me that it's in the darkest times when faith would provide the most comfort. Even if you don't understand why, you know that someone is in charge and there is a plan."

She stared back at him in amazement. "You're full of surprises, aren't you?"

"Chase," Wendy cried when she came back to the table with Reggie. "When did you get here?"

"In time to see you cut a rug out there on the dance floor."

Wendy gushed at having the attention of two attractive men at her table.

Jenny gestured to Reggie. "Chase, this is Reggie. Reggie, Chase,"

Reggie eyed Chase with a shrewd smile. "You must be the trigger-happy friend of Jenny's brother."

Chase's gaze shifted to Jenny long enough for her to regret that she'd told Reggie about the cougar hunt.

He looked back at the vet. "Jenny tells me you've come all the way out here from Memphis to start a vet clinic."

"Atlanta," Reggie corrected.

"Oh, right. That's a long way to go to find sick animals. Is there a shortage in Birmingham?"

"Atlanta," Reggie repeated.

"Atlanta. Right." Challenge flickered in Chase's eyes. "Is there a shortage in Atlanta?"

Reggie's lips tightened. "A shortage of what?"

"Sick animals."

"That's not the reason I moved here. I've always loved the mountains in the west."

Jenny, who'd been listening, remembered what Joel had said earlier. "Reggie, I'm curious. How did you know we needed a vet?"

Despite his carefree smile, his eyes narrowed slightly. "I thought I told you. I saw an ad."

"My brother Joel said the ad for the vet position was never posted."

"Oh, right. I was thinking about the cabin. I heard about the vet position from the owner of the cabin."

"Frank? I wonder how Frank knew."

Reggie shrugged. "Small world, I guess."

Chase shook his head. "That's a pretty big gamble, moving all this way without a job waiting for you."

"I had money set aside to tide me over for a while."

"It sounds so exciting," Wendy exclaimed. "Like living on the edge."

Reggie rewarded her with an indulgent smile.

She gazed back, clearly enamored.

Wendy turned to Chase. "Would you take our picture?" She dug her cell out of her purse. "Rats. I forgot to charge it and now the battery's dead."

Chase reached for his phone. "It's okay. I'll take it with mine and send it to you."

She smiled. "Would you?"

"Sure. No problem." He stood and aimed the phone at the three of them.

Reggie moved to the far side of the women, trying to get out of the picture. "You should take Wendy and Jenny together."

"Come on, Reggie," Wendy begged. "Don't go shy on me."

Chase snapped the image before Reggie could slide out of the frame. "Got it."

"It's been fun, but I have to run," Reggie said. He downed the last of his drink.

Wendy pouted. "Oh, no, it's still early, Reggie. You can't leave yet."

He shrugged. "You'll have to enjoy yourselves without me. See you around."

After Reggie left, Jenny noticed Chase checking messages on his phone. "What is it, Chase?"

"I'll be back in a minute." Chase set the phone on the table and rose, looking around the restaurant.

"Hey, you, stop!" Lou yelled from across the room.

Jenny turned as Chase strode in that direction.

The smack of fists and bodies crashing against tables erupted from the bar.

The crowd seated in the restaurant jumped up to see the brawl, blocking Jenny's view.

"Don't let him get away!" Lou shouted.

A loud commotion erupted, and Jenny glimpsed a man knocking over chairs and shoving people out of his way as he bolted for the door.

Chase reached for his gun, zigzagging through the obstacle course the man left behind, and following him outside.

Jenny, stunned by the chaos, glanced at Chase's phone and read the text.

He's here. --Lou

Jenny dropped cash on the table and rose from her seat.

"Where are you going?" Wendy asked.

"Stay here, Wendy." She grabbed Chase's phone and headed for the door.

Outside, Jenny found Chase holding his gun at arm's length, searching the parking lot. "Chase?"

He spun around, lowering his weapon when he saw her. After clicking the safety on, he slipped it back in its holster, hidden under his jacket.

She strode to him and handed him his phone. "I read Lou's text. It was your fugitive, wasn't it? He was here."

"I didn't get a good look at him before he bolted. From the way he flew out of here, he must have recognized me." Chase growled and kicked the tire of a car parked next to him. He glanced at Jenny with a look of pain and chagrin as he hobbled on one foot.

The music had stopped playing from inside. Wendy wandered outside with Sue, Lou and a half dozen patrons. She ran up to Jenny. "What happened?"

"Nothing. Let's go. It's getting late."

"It's not *that* late."

"It's late enough. I need to get up early in the morning to go to church." She caught the surprise on Chase's face. "Vacation is over," she said as she headed for her truck.

When Jenny dropped Wendy off at Gus's, she was tempted to tell him about the incident at the grill but decided to keep it to herself. After all, Chase was a professional. He should be the one to inform the authorities.

But she couldn't shake the feeling that Chase wanted to go it alone, and now that he had his fugitive in his sights, he would stop at nothing to catch him, no matter the consequences.

Driving home, Jenny glanced in her rearview mirror. Headlights moved up fast and shone in her eyes.

She turned the corner and they followed her.

She sped up and they stayed with her.

Sweat broke out on her brow as she glanced in the mirror. The menacing headlights stared back, mocking her.

The Trail Break, Butch's convenience store, was ahead. Peeling off the road, Jenny darted into the parking lot before the other driver could react.

She glimpsed the reckless vehicle as it sped away in the dark. There was something disturbingly familiar about it. Then she realized, it looked like Chase's stolen SUV.

CHAPTER TEN

JENNY ARRIVED EARLY AT CHURCH THE next morning. Nestled against the wooded landscape, the small, gray-stone building with stained-glass windows opened a floodgate of memories. She clutched the small cross around her neck. After so much time spent there with her father, it would never be the same without him.

Yet coming back again brought her unexpected comfort. Though bittersweet now, most of her memories were happy ones.

She took a deep breath and entered through the main door. As people filled the sanctuary, Jenny looked around for a seat. She felt someone touch her arm and turned around.

It was Wendy, standing there with her father. "Are you all right, Jenny? Dad told me someone followed you on the way home last night."

"Yes, I'm fine," she gave Wendy a bright smile. "I'm sure your father will find whoever it was soon enough."

Jenny shifted to Gus. "I hope I didn't wake you when I called last night."

"You didn't. I stayed up waiting for Wendy to come home." He eyed his daughter with a teasing glint.

"Have they found Chase's SUV yet?"

He shook his head. "I hope you stayed at Joel's last night like I suggested."

"I appreciate your concern, Gus, but Joel is the last person I want to know about this. Besides, whoever followed me last night knows I got a good look at his SUV. He'd be crazy to try anything now."

Gus frowned, clearly not happy that she'd ignored his advice. "Wendy tells me there was a commotion at the Avalanche Grill last night."

Jenny glanced at Wendy. She didn't feel it was her place to say too much.

"I told Dad about Chase trying to catch that guy," Wendy said.

Jenny wondered how Chase's foot was today, and his pride. "Unfortunately, the instigator outran Chase."

As Gus moved to find a seat, Wendy gestured for Jenny to follow. "Come sit with us."

They headed to a row in the middle, and Jenny seated herself beside Wendy.

Wendy glanced around the church. "I've been away from church for so long it feels kind of strange to be here."

"I know what you mean, but it is good to be back."

Happy memories of her father surfaced in Jenny's mind as they sang familiar worship songs. She could almost hear him singing in his deep bass voice next to her.

Then Pastor Mark's message on the hope of eternal life spoke directly to her heart, soaking in like rain in the desert. The reminder that she would one day be reunited with her father and mother again buoyed her heavy heart. All God's promises suddenly resonated like a balm for her pain and grief, and gave her hope again.

At the end of the service, girls from the youth group Jenny had led swarmed Jenny and Wendy to welcome them.

It warmed Jenny's heart to see the young women again and catch up on their lives.

Pastor Mark came to greet her too. Having served at her church for the past twenty years, he was like a member of the family. "I'm glad you came, Jenny. We've missed you."

They chatted for a few minutes until the pastor had to excuse himself to greet more people.

Soon Jenny was surrounded by old friends she'd lost touch

with after her father passed away. The happy reunion with her long-lost church family made her realize what she'd missed, staying away so long. She remained and visited with them until the church began to clear out.

After her friends departed, Jenny turned to leave too.

"Aunt Jenny," Adam called.

She stopped and saw her nephew, who ran into her waiting arms. His sweet, innocent smile filled her with happiness as she lifted him up. She playfully scolded him, shaking her finger. "Young man, don't you know you aren't supposed to yell and run through church."

He giggled and grabbed at her finger that she kept barely out of his reach.

When Jenny looked around for Joel and Lori, she paused.

Chase stepped in front of her with a tentative look.

She greeted him with a smile, impressed at how magnificent he looked in a suit and tie. "I'm surprised to see you here."

The corner of his mouth curved into a wry grin. "Not as surprised as I am to be here." He edged closer. "You look beautiful."

Unexpected shyness flushed her face. "You don't look so bad yourself."

He straightened the knot at his neck. "Joel loaned me his suit and tie. He warned me it was overkill, but I'm used to dressing up for Christmas and Easter."

She started to tell Chase about her run-in with his stolen SUV, but Joel and Lori joined them, and she decided to wait. There was no point in worrying them.

She gave Adam a peck on the cheek and put him down. He went to stand beside Chase, staring at him with a proud look.

"How are the cubs?" Lori asked.

Jenny's gaze lingered on Chase for a moment longer before she pivoted to her sister-in-law. "They cried a lot last night, so I stayed up late feeding them. I thought they'd never go to sleep."

"It's like having a new baby in the house," Lori said,

laughing.

Jenny sighed. "Twins. The good news is I think they're going to make it."

Joel's genial mood suddenly vanished. "I hope you're not planning to raise them, Jen."

"What else can I do? I can't let them die."

Joel raised his voice. "Those cute little kittens are going to turn into big wild mountain lions."

"No kidding," she shot back. "Look, I don't want to discuss this right now, especially at church. If you'll excuse me, I need to get back and feed those man-eating cubs I've adopted."

Chase watched Jenny as she brushed past her brother and left in a huff. She definitely had spunk, but mostly she had heart. If she could care for him half as much as she did her animals, he could almost imagine a heaven on earth.

Gus's advice echoed in his mind. *Take an interest in what she cares about.*

Chase glanced over his shoulder at the large cross at the front of the church. Though she'd taken a brief vacation from it, he knew how important her faith was to her, more than any man could ever be.

His phone rang. He sent Joel and Lori an apologetic look as he pulled it from his belt to answer it.

"We'll wait for you outside," Joel told him.

Chase waved to them as they left. "Matthews," he answered in an impatient tone.

"And I thought vacations were supposed to make people happy," Kate Phillips said.

He raked a hand through his hair. "Sorry. What's up?"

"It's about your fugitive . . ."

His pulse accelerated as he moved into the church foyer. With a quick furtive scan, he confirmed the coast was clear. "What have you got?"

"I know I'll regret telling you this, but a man matching his description was sighted yesterday at a truck stop along Highway 20 in Washington State. We think he may be heading for the Canadian border. They've alerted the border patrol and the marshals up there."

His mind processed the new information.

"Chase? Are you still there?"

"Yeah . . . Hey, thanks for the info." He pulled his phone away to kill the call.

"Wait!"

At the sound of her voice, he pressed the phone back to his ear. "Yes?"

"You've been away for two whole weeks. When are you coming back?"

"I was told to take a long vacation, and that's what I'm doing. Besides, this place is starting to grow on me. Maybe I'll stay and take up mountain climbing."

"I hope you aren't getting too settled there. You still have a life back here, you know."

He grunted. "Some life. For all I know, I may not even have a job to return to."

"I'm sure whenever you're ready, you'll still have a job if you want it. Don't forget your friends at home, okay?"

"How can I?" he said in a dry tone. "You won't leave me alone."

"Seriously, take care of yourself. Okay?"

"Always do. Hey, Kate, before you go, I have a favor to ask."

"Name it."

"I need you to do a background check on someone."

"What's the name?"

He glanced around the room once more. "Dr. Reggie Grayling."

"Do you have a photo?"

He smiled, recalling the snapshot he took last night. "Yeah, I'll send it to you from my phone."

He heard her chuckling on the other end. "I knew it."

"What?"

"Vacation, my foot. You're still on the hunt, aren't you? What's this Dr. Grayling done?"

"Nothing that I know of."

"What do you suspect him of?"

"I'm not sure."

"But you want me to check if he's got a rap sheet?"

"That's right."

"What makes you think he does?"

"Call it a hunch. He's hiding something, and I want to know what it is."

There was an audible silence on the other end. Kate finally spoke. "All right, on one condition."

"What's that?"

"Don't do anything crazy without talking to me first."

Eagle Valley Lodge, a quaint two-story log cabin with a beautiful mountain setting, was known for having the best restaurant near the park. Its exceptional food, good service and warm atmosphere drew locals and tourists alike.

Jenny ascended the steps to the large front porch where several patrons relaxed in rocking chairs, whiling away the evening in casual conversation.

The owner greeted her when she came inside. "Hello, Jenny. Are you here for dinner?"

"Hi, George. I want to order something to go."

A familiar male voice surprised her. "You know, it's not healthy to eat alone."

Jenny spun around. "Chase? What on earth are you doing here?"

He shrugged. "Same as you, to eat."

Realizing how abrupt she must have sounded, she glanced down and touched her brow. "Sorry, I didn't mean it like that.

I'm just surprised to see you here."

"Don't worry, I'm not following you. We passed this place on the way home from church, so I decided to come and give Joel and Lori an evening alone. Besides, I've been meaning to check it out anyway. Before the cougar incident, I was planning to take you here. If you aren't busy, why not join me for dinner now?"

Jenny considered his offer, noting how handsome he looked in his red golf shirt and black trousers.

Before she replied, George came up to them. "A table for two?"

Chase appealed to her with an inviting grin. "What do you say to two friends having dinner together in a nice restaurant?"

She playfully responded, "I say . . . there's a grilled salmon with my name on it."

Chase turned back to George. "You heard the lady, a table for two, please."

George nodded obligingly. He led them to one of the more secluded tables near the big fireplace in the back, tucked away from the direct lighting of the wagon-wheel chandeliers in the large open dining room.

"He's a lucky fellow to be having dinner with Eagle Valley's most eligible female park ranger," George said in Jenny's ear as he seated her.

Jenny peered over her shoulder. "It's not what you think, George."

"That's what they all say, and the next thing you know they're renting this place out for the wedding reception."

Chase took his seat across from Jenny.

George handed them their menus before discreetly disappearing from their table.

"A friend of yours?" Chase asked.

"An old friend of the family, actually. Joel and I used to come here with my father every Sunday night."

"So we're keeping the tradition alive."

She whisked her napkin in her lap. "Yes, I guess in a way we are."

The sight of Billy Norton heading their way elicited a groan from Jenny's throat. So much for a pleasant evening.

"Uh-oh." Chase said when he saw Billy.

Jenny tried to be amiable. "Hi, Billy."

Billy cast a suspicious glare at Chase. Then, addressing Jenny, he jerked his head in Chase's direction. "I thought you said you weren't dating him?"

"This isn't a date. We ran into each other and decided to have dinner together. That's all."

"That's right, Billy," Chase said with an easy grin. "It's not like we prearranged to have dinner together . . . It just happened."

Billy's face reddened, and his nostrils flared.

Jenny leaned forward. "Chase, please. You're not helping."

Billy turned on Chase. "Yeah, why don't you go back to wherever you came from?"

Chase moved to get up, but Jenny shook her head to dissuade him, and he backed down.

She opened her menu and pretended to be reading it, hoping to dismiss the whole matter. "Billy, could you please ask our waiter to come and take our order?"

"I am your waiter."

His snarky tone generated a weary sigh from Jenny. "Of course you are." She glanced down at her menu. "I'll have the special."

Billy snatched her menu from her and put away his pen.

"Hey, what about me?" Chase said as Billy turned to leave. "I haven't ordered yet."

Billy paused impatiently, refusing to look at him.

Chase read from the menu. "I'll have the special, with a baked potato, and . . ."

Billy cut him off. "Got it." He left without so much as a stroke of his pen.

Chase leaned in Jenny's direction. "Either he can read my

mind, or I'm not going to get what I want to eat."

"My guess is the latter."

"Great." Chase slammed his menu closed. He studied Jenny for a moment. "It's all your fault, you know."

"My fault?"

"Yeah, you've been trying to let him down easy, but instead, you give him mixed messages. No wonder he's frustrated. If you're not interested in him, you should let him know in no uncertain terms."

She had to restrain herself. "For your information, that's exactly what I did last night. That's why he's so angry. I can't help it if he refuses to take no for an answer."

Chase grinned, his eyes flickering in the candlelight. "That's why he stormed out last night. He's obviously jealous of our relationship."

"What relationship?"

He stared at her with a penetrating look. "Billy thinks you're attracted to me."

Jenny scoffed. "That's ridiculous."

"Hey, for all I know I'm intruding on his turf, and I don't particularly like claim-jumping another man's girl. We men have a code of honor, you know."

"You make it sound like I'm a piece of property or bargaining chip for men to fight over. Don't I have a say in the matter?"

His eyes twinkled at her reaction. "No need to get all worked up."

"I'm not worked up," she continued. "You obviously don't need a woman in your life, or you'd be married by now. Well, I'm no different."

"Are you finished?"

She pressed her back against her chair and jutted her chin. "Yes."

"For someone who barely knows me, you sure have made a lot of bad assumptions. For instance, I'm not opposed to marriage. I've just had too many other things going on in my life. The truth is I would like to be married someday, to the right woman. I really want the kind of life Joel and Lori have. So there."

Jenny stared back at him. The last person she expected to hear extolling the virtues of matrimony was Chase Matthews.

Seeing Billy arrive with their dinner brought a welcome distraction from Chase's latest revelation.

Jenny reared back as Billy shoved her plate in front of her. At least she'd gotten what she requested.

Chase eyed the liver and onions on his plate with revulsion. "This isn't what I ordered."

Billy took out a crumpled piece of paper from his pocket. "It says here liver and onions." He looked down at Chase's plate. "Looks like liver and onions to me."

Jenny interceded, feeling as if she were talking to a child. "Billy, cut it out and give Chase the special like he ordered."

"Why should I?" Billy spat.

"Because it's your job."

"Not anymore. I quit!"

George quickly came over and cast Billy a suspicious glance. "Is there a problem?"

Chase looked past Billy to George. "I didn't get what I ordered."

Billy tossed his pen and pad on the table. "I'm outta here."

Jenny jumped up and called after him, but he was gone.

"Please accept my sincerest apologies," George said as he gathered the pen and paper from the table. "Dinner is on the house tonight."

"Thanks, but that's not necessary," Chase replied.

"I insist. Now what did you order?"

Jenny lifted her finger to get the owner's attention. "It's okay, George. Everything is fine."

He nodded and quickly departed.

Jenny sat down again, thinking out loud, "That's not like Billy at all. I've never seen him so angry. I must have really hurt him."

"Don't blame yourself. He's the one with the problem."

"But he needs this job. I don't want him to lose it because of me."

"He should have thought of that before he decided to be so rude. I detest liver and onions. Why didn't you let me reorder?"

She raised her plate to trade. "Here, take my salmon. I happen to like liver and onions."

"Are you sure?"

She nodded.

He exchanged his plate with a relieved smile. "Thanks. I'm starving."

After swapping meals, Chase devoured his food as if it were his last, washing it down with his entire glass of water. "At least we don't have to leave a tip, not that he'd get one from me anyway."

She laughed, seeing humor in the situation now that Billy was gone and she was full. She poured water from her glass into Chase's.

He gave her a curious look. "How many other jilted men are in your past?"

She smirked in jest. "Too many to count."

"That's what I was afraid of."

He wiped his mouth with his napkin and rested his hands on the table, lightly tapping his fingers on the wood. "You know, after I got home last night, I had a really strange dream."

"What kind of dream?"

"It was weird. You're gonna think I'm nuts if I tell you."

"Too late. I already think you're nuts, so you may as well tell me anyway."

"Is interpreting dreams another trait you inherited from your ancestors?"

She shrugged. "You brought it up, not me."

He paused and stared at his glass, his mood more subdued now. "I have this recurring dream—or nightmare. It's like I'm watching my friend, Jim, from a distance, but he doesn't know

I'm there. He's in danger, and I call out to him, but he can't hear me. I'm stuck behind a sort of barrier I can't break through."

"Like the invisible fence?"

He glanced up. "Yeah. Something like that. But last night the dream was different." Chase's eyes were glazed and dark. "Usually, at the end of the dream I hear a loud gunshot. Then I see Jim, lying in a pool of blood."

"You were reliving that same nightmare at Joel's barbecue, weren't you?"

His mouth twisted into an awkward grin. "I've never done that before. Maybe it's good my boss put me on leave."

"You've been through a lot, Chase. It's going to take time for you to recover."

He held her gaze for a moment, then glanced down and started playing with the salt shaker. "It's strange, but before Jim died, I used to have the same dream when I was little. Except it was my parents lying there in a pool of blood instead of Jim."

She recalled what Lori had shared with her earlier about his parents being killed. "Your biological parents?" she softly asked.

He nodded without looking up.

"You never told me how they died, Chase."

He shrugged. "It's not a pretty story." He lifted his gaze to hers to confirm she wanted him to continue.

She gave him a small smile, encouraging him to go on.

"I was only six, not much older than Adam when it happened. A man had escaped from a prison not far away. He broke into our home and robbed my parents, and then killed them both."

"Where were you?"

"Up in the loft where I slept, hiding. I saw everything though. I wanted to scream, but nothing came out. All I could do was watch."

She shuddered at the vision of the boy helplessly watching his parents' murder. The silent scream tore her heart in two. Gently, she touched his fingers, and he stopped fidgeting with the shaker. "You were only a boy. There was nothing you could do."

He put down the salt and managed a weak smile. "Enough of my happy story. How did we get on this subject anyway?"

"You were telling me about your dream."

"Oh. Right."

She gave his hand an encouraging squeeze before releasing it. "What was different last night?"

He hesitated. "After the gunshot, I looked for Jim's body as usual, but this time he wasn't there. Then someone tapped my shoulder, and I turned around. It was Jim. Alive again, standing right next to me. He smiled and said, 'It's okay, buddy. I'm home now.' Then he was gone. When I woke up, I felt this tremendous sense of peace. I've never felt anything like it before." Chase looked at her. "Bet you never thought a heathen guy like me could have such a spiritual dream, huh?"

"You and Jim were close?"

"Like brothers. I always knew he had my back. Know what I mean?"

She thought of her brother Joel. "Yes, I do."

"You would have liked him. He was a good Christian husband and father." Chase gave her a small, wistful smile. "We used to have long talks about faith. Though we didn't always agree on everything, I respected him. He used to say, life only comes around once, so you'd better make the most of it. And that's the way he lived his life, making every moment count. Even right before he died . . ." Chase's voice faltered, raw with emotion.

"It's okay," Jenny said.

Chase cleared his throat. "Jim was more concerned about me than himself. He knew I'd want justice, so he made me promise not to avenge his death."

Shadows darkened Chase's face. "I should have been the one who took that bullet, not him. He didn't deserve it. He had so much to live for with a family and a ministry . . ."

Compassion flooded Jenny's heart. "I know what you mean."

He looked up, surprised. "How's that?"

"When my father died, I was so angry and confused. It seemed so wrong. I didn't understand why God had allowed it to happen. And yet I know he's okay."

She reached out her hand, and Chase took hold of it. "What matters is that Jim knew you were there for him, and now he's with the Lord."

Chase gave her a skeptical look. "How can you be sure of that?"

"Faith," she replied with an easy shrug.

He released her hand, frowning at the word. "Then why did you take a vacation from it?"

The directness of the question hit her hard. But after he'd been so painfully honest with her, she owed him the truth. "I blamed God for letting my father die, and my anger blinded me to His love and grace. It doesn't take much faith to believe when everything is going well. It's when things don't make any sense that our faith is tested the most. I guess I failed the test."

"Don't be so hard on yourself. You're only human."

"I'm telling you this because you helped me see the truth about myself. I gave my anger over to God this morning. I've finally made peace with my father's death."

A reluctant smile tugged at the corners of Chase's mouth. "Then I'm happy for you."

"Something tells me I'm not the only one who's been struggling with God lately. He's obviously reaching out to you too."

"I don't know about that."

"Why not?"

He shrugged. "Look, faith for you is black and white, but it's not that simple for me. Not that I don't want to see Jim again. I do. And it's not like I have anything against Jesus, or church, or anything like that."

"Then what is it?"

"It's not as easy as you make it sound. Not for me anyway."

She paused, surprised by his statement. "You've obviously given this a lot of thought."

He didn't respond. Jenny knew better than to pressure him, but a sense of urgency pestered her. "What are you going to do?"

"Nothing."

"What do you mean nothing?"

"If God really wants to reach me, He's going to have to send me a clear sign. Something tangible, not a crazy dream. I'm a hands-on kind of guy. I deal with the here and now. The spiritual world is too subjective for me."

"I see. So you want to be struck by lightning."

"That's one way to put it." A mischievous grin came to his lips. "Of course, I'd want you there to resuscitate me so I wouldn't die."

"That's not funny, Chase."

"Sorry. I guess that was a bit irreverent. Maybe a burning bush would be a better choice."

She shook her head at him as if he were a petulant child.

"I see that look in your eye. You think I'm hopeless."

"Not hopeless, but stubborn. Be careful what you ask for. You might get it." She glanced at the candle flickering on the table, reminding her of the headlights from last night. "I almost forgot to tell you. Someone with an SUV like yours was following me home last night."

"What?"

"I notified Gus right after it happened. I meant to tell you at church this morning, but I didn't get a chance."

"You should have called me. Something could have happened to you."

She looked away. Why did men always think they needed to protect her? "It's getting late. I'd better go."

"Wait. Forget what I said. It's clear you can take care of yourself, but I can't help being concerned. Guess I'm old-fashioned that way."

"It's okay. But I really do need to get back and feed the cubs." Something caught her attention as she started to get up.

"What is it?"

"Wendy. She's here with . . . Reggie." Jenny watched George seat them both at a table not far away. "They look like they're on a date."

Chase rose and offered her his hand. "Come on."

"Where are we going?"

"To find out what's going on." Before she could refuse, he was leading her to their table.

"I don't think this is such a good idea." She dragged her feet, but it was too late. Wendy had already spotted her.

Guilt colored her young friend's expression. "Jenny."

Chase exuded all the confidence of a professional date-crasher. "We saw you come in and stopped to say hello."

Reggie eyed Jenny and Chase, then stood and smiled. "Would you like to join us?"

Jenny hung back, scrutinizing Reggie. *What was he up to?*

Chase answered for them both. "Thanks, but Jenny and I have already eaten."

Reggie gave Jenny an engaging grin. "Too bad we didn't know you were coming. We could have made it a foursome."

"Maybe next time." Jenny took Chase's arm.

He raised a brow at Jenny's arm linked with his.

Jenny looked at her young friend. "Wendy, it was good to see you and your father at church this morning." She glanced at Chase and tugged his arm. "Come on, let's go."

Chase played along and waved to Wendy and Reggie. "Enjoy your dinner."

Jenny led him to the door. Outside, she let go and began pacing the parking lot.

Chase inspected his arm. "What was that all about? I think your fingerprints are permanently branded in my flesh."

She ignored his remark. "Do you think I should call Wendy's father and tell him she's here with Reggie?"

"They're only having dinner."

She shook her head, waving her arms. "No. He's up to something. I know it." It was dusk, but there was still enough light to see the skeptical flicker in Chase's expression. "You don't think so?"

"I'm wondering if you're upset with Reggie for Wendy's sake, or because you're jealous that he was with her instead of you."

She glared back at him. "I don't believe you said that."

Chase followed her as she stormed away toward her truck. "Which is it? Are you jealous of Wendy?"

She halted and spun around, nearly colliding with him. "You're crazy."

The colors of sunset reflected in his eyes. "Maybe. But I'd still like to know how Reggie fell off his white horse overnight."

She poked her finger at him. "I don't know what you're talking about."

"So you're not jealous?"

They were standing toe-to-toe with enough charged energy to trigger an explosion if someone lit a match. "No, of course not. My only concern is for Wendy."

His closeness drove everything else from her mind. "I'm afraid she's in way over her head."

He inched closer. "She's not a child anymore. She's a grown woman." The light in his eyes flickered like candles.

"She's playing with fire." The words from her lips reminded her that Wendy wasn't the only one.

Tearing her gaze away from his, she reached for the keys in her pocket. "I've got to go." She turned around to open the door of her truck.

He touched her arm from behind. "I want to see you again."

She didn't look back. "I don't think that's such a good idea."

"Why not?"

His phone rang, piercing the moment. "I have to get this. Please don't leave."

She took advantage of the interruption and hopped in her truck. After rolling down her window, she waved. "Goodnight, Chase."

Without looking back, she revved the engine, kicking up gravel as she sped away.

Chase moved aside to avoid the rocks flying from Jenny's back tires. "Yeah?" he barked into the phone as he watched Jenny drive off.

No answer.

"Who is this? I know you're there."

Click.

He stared at the phone and checked caller ID, but it was unavailable. The sensation of being watched by a million unseen eyes sprung the hair from the back of his neck.

Reaching for his gun, he mentally kicked himself when he remembered he'd left it locked inside the glove box of his new rental. With his guard up, he strode toward the Mustang convertible he'd parked under a street light.

He approached the driver's side of the car and froze. Scribbled across the window, in what appeared to be blood, was a warning.

Stay away from Jenny.

CHAPTER ELEVEN

JENNY HAD IGNORED CHASE'S TEXTS AND phone calls all morning. She didn't like putting him off last night and this morning, but her feelings for him had crossed the friendship boundary into uncharted territory and she wasn't ready to go there. At least, not yet.

Seated on a bench by the edge of the scenic Gorge Lake, her thoughts turned to Wendy and her involvement with Reggie. Last Saturday, at the Avalanche Grill, she could have dismissed them as simply two people hanging out and having fun, but at the lodge last night, Reggie and Wendy were clearly on a date.

Or had Chase's opinion of Reggie clouded her own objectivity? No, there were enough missing pieces to make her suspicious too, like that shady story Reggie told concerning the vet position. The ad was never posted. And how would Frank know about it when he was in Seattle?

Maybe all was fair in love and war, but not where her young friend was concerned. The prospect of Wendy being taken advantage of poured acid into an old wound.

Chase had been right to confront Reggie and Wendy at dinner. No doubt Wendy wouldn't have called and invited her to lunch today to *explain things* if Jenny and Chase hadn't seen her with Reggie.

Jenny looked up. Wendy was headed her way, carrying a small sack.

"Thanks for meeting me here for lunch," Wendy said in a tentative voice.

"Have a seat." Jenny slid down the bench to create more space.

After sitting, Wendy opened the bag. "I stopped by the Trail Break and bought us a couple of sandwiches." She handed Jenny hers with a drink in a paper cup.

"Thanks." Jenny removed the straw from the wrapper and pierced a hole in the lid with a single jab.

Wendy cleared her throat. "I think I owe you an explanation."

Jenny unwrapped her sandwich and took a bite of it. Her eyes stayed focused on the teal-colored lake. "For what?"

"I should have told you I was going out with Reggie."

Jenny gave her a sidelong glance. "Why?"

"I don't know. You met him first. I thought you kind of liked him."

A tiny morsel stuck in Jenny's throat as she swallowed, and she coughed. "Is that why you went out with him, to make me jealous?"

The sparkle in Wendy's blue eyes dimmed. "No." She finally opened her sandwich wrapper and paused. "Are you mad at me, Jenny?"

The vulnerability in her friend's youthful face softened her disappointment. "No, I'm not mad. Only concerned."

Wendy looked surprised. "Concerned? You don't need to be. I know what I'm doing."

"Do you, Wendy? How well do you really know Reggie?"

"Well enough. He's a veterinarian from Atlanta, and a good dancer." Seeing Jenny's serious expression, Wendy shrugged. "It was only dinner. It's not like I'm marrying him or anything. You were out with Chase. How well do you really know him?"

"I wasn't *out* with Chase. We ran into each other at the restaurant and ate together. That's different."

"Then you're not dating him?"

"No."

Wendy's face lit up. "He's fair game then."

Jenny rolled her eyes. "You know, there's more to life than men."

"Like what?"

"Like friends. Why aren't you spending more time with your girlfriends while you're here?"

"I don't have much in common with them anymore. Most of them didn't go away to college and their parents are still together. All they know is Eagle Valley. I don't expect you to understand. You may be content to stay here in this Podunk town, but I'm not."

"This may come as a shock, but I do understand, more than you know." Jenny affectionately swept a stray lock of Wendy's hair over her shoulder. "That's why I'm concerned, because I don't want to see you hurt."

Wendy looked down and nibbled on her sub as if she'd lost her appetite.

Jenny's cell rang. She pulled it from her belt and saw the number on the caller ID. "I better get this."

"It's Joel," her brother said when she answered. "The Trail Break was robbed a few minutes ago. Butch was shot."

A small gasp escaped Jenny's lips as her thoughts turned to Sue and their baby. "Where is he now?"

"At the hospital in Watkinsville."

"Who shot him?"

"They don't know yet. The sheriff's office put out a BOLO."

"What happened?" Wendy asked when Jenny hung up.

"Somebody tried to rob the Trail Break."

"Oh, no!" Wendy covered her mouth. "I was just there."

"Did you see anything suspicious?"

"Not really."

"Who else was there?"

"Only Butch and me. There was someone in an SUV in the parking lot, but he never came in."

"Did you see his face?"

Wendy shook her head "It was a man, but I couldn't see him very well."

"Do you remember what the SUV looked like?"

"It was blue. I don't know which brand."

Jenny immediately thought of Chase's stolen vehicle, and the one that followed her to the Trail Break. Was it the same SUV Wendy saw before the robbery?

She wrapped up the rest of her sandwich and rose to her feet. "Thanks for lunch, Wendy. I really need to get back to work now. Promise me you won't forget what I told you, okay?"

Wendy got up. "I won't."

Jenny smiled and gave her a quick hug. "Be careful. They haven't found whoever robbed the store yet. Your father is looking for him."

Wendy offered her the empty sack. "Here, take the rest of your lunch with you."

Hands full with her lunch and drink, Jenny hiked to the road.

The squeal of tires from behind stopped her, and she peered over her shoulder.

A blue Grand Cherokee swerved dangerously close.

Jenny dove for the ditch as the front bumper brushed past.

Catching her breath, she pulled out her phone. As she called Gus, she watched the SUV zip down the road.

"Did you see the driver?" Gus probed after she told him what had happened.

"No, but I got a good look at the plates. It was Chase's SUV."

"The same one that followed you the other night?"

"I think so." While she talked, she headed toward the ranger station, toting her sack lunch under her arm with her drink in her free hand. "There's something else. Wendy was at Butch's store this morning right before the attempted robbery. She saw a blue SUV in the parking lot. The driver never got out. She didn't see him well, but it was a man."

Jenny turned her head at the sound of a car approaching.

A red Mustang convertible pulled up beside her. Chase rolled down his window. "Want a lift?"

Giving the sporty car a double-take, she raised her hand for him to wait until she was off the phone. "I've got to go, Gus. I'll call you back if I think of anything else."

She tucked the phone away and jogged to the other side of Chase's car.

After she hopped in, he cast her a sidelong glance. "You know, you're a hard person to track down. I've been trying to reach you all morning."

"Why?"

"I wanted to make sure you got home all right."

Surprised and touched by his concern, she gave him a warm smile. "Of course, I did. Why wouldn't I?" Her eyes scanned the black leather interior and fancy dash. "This is your rental?"

He nodded. "They were out of SUVs. What do you think?"

"It'll do." She shot him a teasing glint from the corner of her eye. "Do you mind if I finish my lunch on the way?"

"Go ahead."

After fastening her seatbelt, she took out her soda and sipped through the straw. "Speaking of SUVs, your stolen one just drove by."

Chase mashed his foot on the gas and took off.

She caught her cup before it flew out of her hand, then she grabbed the handle above her seat. "What are you doing?"

"Maybe we can catch him."

"You're kidding, right?"

Sporting a pair of stylish sunglasses with his hair blowing wildly in the wind, Chase grinned as he sped down the road. "Relax. I've been driving since I was a teenager."

"You mean driving like a teenager. Now slow down or I'll call Gus and have you arrested."

He sighed and decelerated. "I didn't know park rangers were such wimps."

"I didn't know marshals were such speed demons."

"How do you think we catch our escaped felons?"

"I thought maybe you told them they won the lottery."

"Hey, that's not a bad idea. Do you have any big lotteries in Eagle Valley?"

"No, but we do have bingo on Saturday nights. I doubt the

jackpot is big enough to entice your fugitive to come out of hiding though."

She pointed ahead. "Look! There it is."

Chase sped up and closed the gap. "That's my Grand Cherokee, all right. It has the same plates." He glanced in the rearview mirror. "Uh-oh."

"What?"

"I think I'm busted. There's a sheriff's car behind me with his lights on."

Jenny peered back and called Gus on the phone. "Gus, Chase's stolen SUV is right in front of us. We're tailing it."

Gus's deputy car passed them on the left with his lights and siren on.

Chase glanced at Jenny. "Thanks. If I'd gotten a speeding ticket on top of a stolen car all in the same week, I'd probably have to mortgage my condo to pay my car insurance."

"Speaking of which, Wendy saw a blue SUV like yours in the Trail Break parking lot right before it was robbed."

"Robbed?"

"Yeah. The owner, Butch Hopkins, was shot."

Chase grimaced and shook his head as he followed in his Mustang a short distance behind Gus. "This has got to end."

When the road straightened, Jenny could see the SUV further ahead. By now, Gus had closed in enough for the driver to see his lights and hear his siren.

The SUV made a sharp right onto an old logging road.

Gus swerved and continued to tail it.

Soon Chase and Jenny were careening along a spiraling descent through the forest. The force from the tight bends pressed Jenny against the door as she peered down into the deep hollow below.

She spotted Gus and the SUV on the switchbacks. "Careful, Chase. This road is really steep."

Chase hugged the corners, barely missing rocks and trees along the edge.

Jenny caught a glimpse of something poised by the side of the road. "Stop, Chase!"

He slammed on the brakes, causing them both to lurch forward. A deer darted out in front of them.

Jenny blew out a deep breath. "That was too close."

"Do you see Gus below us?" Chase asked.

"No. We lost him."

The deer disappeared into the woods, and Chase took off again. A couple of miles down the road, at the junction where the old logging road met the main highway, they came upon the deputy's parked car. Gus was crouched beside it, inspecting his rear tire.

Chase pulled up behind him on the shoulder of the road.

Jenny jumped out and hurried to Gus. "What happened?"

"I hit a rock and blew out my tire," he said, his voice gruff.

After parking his Mustang, Chase strode up to them. "Need any help?"

Gus straightened and turned to address them. "Nah. Unfortunately, I lost that SUV." He looked at Jenny. "By the way, I got an update on Butch. His arm was injured, but it's not life-threatening. He's expected to make a full recovery."

Jenny closed her eyes. "Thank heavens."

Chase leaned forward with heightened interest. "Did the robber take any money?"

"No. Butch managed to set off the security alarm after he was shot, and the thief bolted."

"Did anyone get a good look at him?"

Gus shook his head. "He was wearing a bear mask, and no one else was in the store."

"A bear mask? Sounds like someone with a sick sense of humor." Jenny glanced at Chase, whose jaw was set with determination.

"Where do you think he's headed?" he asked.

"Probably Canada. Hopefully, the state troopers will catch him before he crosses the border." Gus got on his knees to take a closer look at the tire.

Chase joined him. "Let me give you a hand with that."

Jenny waited while Chase helped Gus change the tire. After they'd finished and Gus drove off, Chase stared into the distance, his jaw muscles flexing.

"You don't know it was your fugitive."

He turned and walked her to his car. "It fits the profile. He's getting desperate now. I've got to find him."

His intensity made her uneasy. "Now that there's a BOLO out on him, it's only a matter of time," she said as he opened the passenger door for her.

"Maybe. But he's not stupid. He's slipped through our fingers before. Let's hope no one else gets hurt before he's caught."

When Chase drove to the ranger station entrance to drop Jenny off, she grimaced at the clock on his dashboard. "What's wrong?"

Her pretty brow creased with dread. "I'm so late. What am I going to tell Clint?"

"Tell him you had a date with me for lunch and it went long."

"I'd rather tell him the truth."

"He'll never believe you."

She gave him an ironic glance as she exited his car. "I think I'll take my chances."

A man dressed in a ranger uniform with a Smokey-the-Bear Stetson appeared. "I was beginning to wonder if you got lost." The man's grumpy tone matched his expression.

Jenny turned around. "Sorry I'm late, Clint. Something unexpected came up."

He put his hands on his hips and eyed Chase suspiciously. "So I see. Aren't you going to introduce me to him?"

She gestured to Chase. "Clint, meet Chase. Chase, Clint. Now you've been introduced."

Chase raised his sunglasses and smiled. "Is she always like this?"

"Afraid so. At least you don't have to work with her."

"Okay, guys. That's enough." She turned to her boss. "I really do have a good explanation for why I'm late."

He squinted in her direction. "It better be good."

Chase turned off his engine and exited his car. "I want to hear this too."

She eyed him with an arched brow. Then she turned back to Clint. "Well, first of all, I was almost run off the road by a stolen SUV driven by a robbery suspect. That's when Chase drove up and offered to give me a lift back to work. Then Deputy Patterson's car passed us and we got in a car chase, and—"

Clint raised his hand. "Stop. I've heard enough. You don't need to concoct some lame story because you had a long lunch date."

Chase smiled. "That's what I told her."

"But it's true," Jenny insisted.

"It's okay. With all the extra hours you put in, you're entitled to a romantic lunch now and then."

Chase grinned. "See, Jen, I told you."

She waved him off. "Don't listen to Chase. I'm telling you the truth."

Clint's radio went off with a static-laced voice. "Avalanche reported on Spider Mountain. Two people missing."

Jenny shot Clint a serious glance.

"Roger that," he said into the radio. "We'll be right up. Over." Then Clint turned to Jenny. "Let's go. We don't have long to find them."

Chase touched Jenny's arm. "I'd like to help."

"Clint," Jenny called out, "I'm going with Chase. We'll meet you there."

Clint nodded. "I'll get the packs and take the truck. See you at the ridge."

After Chase and Jenny hopped back in his Mustang, Chase

gunned his car across the parking lot.

Jenny gestured toward the exit. "I know a shortcut. Go out the way we came, and we'll find an old mining road that will take us up the back side of the mountain."

While Chase drove, Jenny alerted the first responder search and rescue team on her cell. Then she pointed to an old dirt road ahead. "Turn there."

Chase swerved, turning right on the rugged trail, and they ascended the mountain along steep switchbacks. The car shook and rattled over the ruts in the dirt. "Now I really wish I had my SUV."

She held the handle above her seat as the car bounced around. "Your rental car company will blacklist you after this."

He stared at the clock on the dash, wishing he could go faster. "How long can people stay alive under all that snow?"

"Thirty minutes max. With every minute, the odds of survival get less and less."

Chase was silent the rest of the way. He navigated his sports car over the rough terrain like a race car driver in the Yukon outback. With the lives of two people at stake, he knew the time it took to reach them might very well mean the difference between life and death.

At the end of the snow-covered road, he parked the car, and they jumped out.

"This way," Jenny shouted. "We'll hike the rest of the way on foot."

They jogged across the glacier fields on the back side of the mountain until they made it to the top of a ridge. The jaunt left Chase breathless. His heart felt like it would explode.

Jenny looked down, shielding her eyes from the sun. She pointed to the small group of people below. "There they are!"

She began a controlled skid down the slope to the others and followed suit, descending over the fresh avalanche powder like a snowboarder. They met up with five male teenagers, dressed in T-shirts and shorts, with gloves and knit caps covering their hands and heads. They had abandoned their skis to dig for the victims.

"How long have they been buried?" Jenny asked the one closest to her.

"About twenty minutes."

"Are they wearing avalanche beacons?"

He looked down and shook his head.

Chase felt for the young man, who obviously regretted their impulsive ski adventure now.

She turned and addressed the group in a loud voice. "Listen up, everyone, I need you all to follow my instructions. Gather up all the ski poles and bring them to me."

Chase raced with the young men to get the poles lying in the snow and ran back with them.

"Now everybody take one."

Lifting her pole, Jenny plunged it into the snow. "Without the beacons, we'll have to find your friends the old-fashioned way. We'll use these poles to probe the snow."

Chase spotted Clint on the ridge. The seasoned ranger quickly slid down the hill and slung off his pack.

"They don't have beacons, Clint," Jenny said to him in an urgent tone.

"You start probing. I'll assemble the longer poles from the pack and join you."

She nodded and then addressed the others. "Okay, everyone, take your ski pole and flip it over so the handle is pointing down. Now, I want you to form a line at the bottom of the slide where those rocks have blocked the snow. We're going to probe the area together and then move up the slope in unison. We'll keep doing this until we've searched the entire area. Understand?"

They nodded and lined up.

Chase positioned himself next to Jenny in the center of the line.

Clint joined the line and handed the taller poles he'd assembled to Jenny and Chase, keeping one for himself.

The next five minutes seemed like an eternity as Chase and the others probed the snow. He knew time was running out as Jenny and the makeshift rescue team called the names of the missing skiers while carefully and systematically poking the snow with the poles.

Finally, Chase's pole met with resistance. "I found something." He dropped to his knees to dig.

Clint rushed over with his small, collapsible shovel. Together, they plowed the snow to the side until they uncovered the body of a young man, deathly pale.

After feeling for a pulse, Clint addressed Jenny and Chase. "His heart has stopped. I'll do CPR. You two keep searching for the other boy."

One of the young men shouted. "I got something!"

Chase scrambled over with Jenny and started to dig. They quickly uncovered a face.

The deathly pallor and bluish lips of the victim sunk Chase's hopes.

"Dylan?" Jenny's face had turned whiter than the snow.

For a moment, Chase thought he'd have to perform CPR on her. "Jenny, are you okay?"

She sucked in a deep breath. "I know him. He's Dylan Veracruz. He was in my youth group at church." Pressing her finger to the boy's neck, she felt for a pulse.

Chase glanced at her, prepared for the worst. "Is he—"

She didn't let him finish. "He needs CPR."

Chase swept the snow away from Dylan's body, while Jenny leaned over and began pumping his sternum with straightened arms in a firm, rhythmic motion.

After a few reps, she bent her head to listen for a breath. "It's not working. I need to give him mouth-to-mouth. Chase, take over the chest compressions."

He nodded and pressed his palms against the young man's chest, waiting while she performed mouth-to-mouth resuscitation. When she'd finished, he started pumping. They repeated this procedure for what seemed like hours but was only a few minutes.

The boy jerked and convulsed.

Chase drew back, surprise and relief washing over him. "He's alive."

"He's breathing, but he's still unconscious. He needs to get to a hospital."

Chase glanced over his shoulder at Clint.

The senior ranger stopped CPR on the other victim and looked their way, his face grim. "It's too late. He's gone."

The news hit Chase like a sucker punch. When he turned around, Jenny's pained expression mirrored his emotions.

She dropped her head and closed her eyes.

Chase thought she might cry.

He started to reach out to her when voices from the ridge prompted him to look up.

The first responders had arrived and began a controlled slide down the mountainside to where they were. They brought rescue sleds with them and went to work harnessing the other victim's body in one of them.

Chase got up and watched them strap Dylan in.

Jenny's stricken face as she clasped her hands together over her chest tugged at his heart.

He came and stood beside her.

A rueful smile touched her lips as she swept away a stray tear from her eye. "A few days ago, Dylan almost ran me off the road with his motorcycle . . ."

"He's going to be all right." Chase wrapped his arm around her shoulder.

She gazed at him, the light returning to her lovely eyes. "Dylan's had it tough. He comes from a troubled home. Some people think he's a lost cause, but I've always seen the good in him."

Her words brought to mind Chase's own troubled youth. As he watched the young man being attended to by the rescue workers, it was suddenly like seeing himself. If not for Hal and Sarah, his adoptive parents, who knew where he would be right now? Perhaps, in prison or . . . dead.

"Where will they take him?" he asked.

"They'll medevac him by helicopter to the Seattle trauma center." She looked back at Chase and dealt him an affectionate punch in the shoulder. "Hey, you should be proud of yourself. You helped save a life today. Good work."

He smiled at the compliment. The ordeal had shaken him a bit, and, like the bee sting, he was once again struck by how precious, *and fragile,* life really was.

CHAPTER TWELVE

WHEN JENNY ARRIVED AT WORK WITH her pet carrier on Tuesday, Clint was waiting for her with his hands on his hips.

"Let me guess. Cougar cubs."

"I didn't feel right asking Lori to take care of them anymore. You don't know anyone who has the facilities to raise them, do you?"

He scratched his chin as he thought it over. "Well, there is that wildlife refuge about an hour from here. You might try them."

"That's a great idea." Her mood lifted at the notion that there might be an alternative to her running a zoo.

"Meanwhile, you can keep 'em in the back, and we'll help take care of them during the day."

Jenny smiled with relief. "Really? That's so nice of you. Thanks."

His grumpy façade returned. "I'm not that nice."

Jenny shook her head at Clint's remark and turned her attention to the back wall where the latest park announcements were posted.

Clint moved beside her and pointed out a new alert. "Numerous thefts have been reported by backcountry campers in the Cascade Pass and Horseshoe Basin area. At first, it appeared random, but since they're all in that general area, it's looking more like a pattern."

"You're kidding." She glanced back at him. "What was stolen?"

"You name it, money, food, backpacks, even a sleeping bag."

"Doesn't sound like a bear, does it?"

Clint eyed her significantly. "It was canned food. A hunting knife was also stolen." He moaned. "Looks like we've got ourselves a thief. By the way, the park superintendent closed the trails until further notice."

"What a shame. That area is only open a couple of months of the year. So many people will be disappointed."

"I know, but we can't risk people going there if there's a thief on the loose."

After breakfast and the morning chores, Joel, Lori, and Adam left to visit Lori's parents for the rest of the day. They invited Chase to join them, but he declined. Instead, he spent most of the afternoon finishing the home projects he had been helping Joel with.

While taking a break on the back porch, Chase flipped through Joel's Bible. He couldn't shake Gus's advice to him concerning Jenny.

If he was to take an interest in what Jenny cared about, he'd better brush up on his Bible. Maybe if he knew it better, he'd find something to win her over, despite their differences of opinion about faith.

Then again, maybe she was better off without him. Before he came to town, Jenny was safe. Now she'd been robbed and tailed by a man in a stolen SUV, not to mention the anonymous graffiti warning Chase to stay away from her.

When he glanced up, he was surprised to see Jenny at the bottom of the steps.

"Someone is home. I tried knocking, but no one answered."

"They all went to visit Lori's parents. What are you doing here?" He sounded more abrupt than he intended.

"Clint must be rubbing off on you." Her eyes lingered for a moment on the Bible in his hands. "Sorry, I disturbed you. I'll come back later." She turned to leave.

"Wait!" Her startled look softened his tone. "I mean . . .

please wait."

She paused and turned around.

He set the Bible on the table beside his rocking chair and gestured to the empty rocker. "I'd like you to come and join me."

She hesitated at first, then ascended the steps and took a seat. As she rocked back and forth, her eyes subtly turned to the book on the table between her and Chase.

His eyes followed her gaze. "I was looking up a verse."

"Really? Which one?"

"John 11:35." It was the first verse that came to mind.

She stared back at him with a raised brow. "Jesus wept?"

He shrugged, wishing he'd thought of a more impressive passage. He stood and leaned against the porch rail directly across from her.

Mercifully, she changed the subject. "Actually, I want to discuss something with you. Remember when you asked me to tell you if anything unusual happened in the park?"

Chase's mind shifted back to business. "Yeah?"

She told him about the trail closures due to thefts in the Cascade Pass and Horseshoe Basin area. "I'm beginning to think there might be a connection between the crime spree around here and the thefts in the park."

"So you're starting to take my theory seriously now."

She sighed. "Until the cabin break-in, the only crime we had in Eagle Valley was feeding the wildlife."

He glanced down, his mind quickly analyzing all possibilities.

She stopped rocking. "Chase, I don't like that look on your face."

He shifted his eyes to her. "What?"

"You can't fool me. You're plotting something."

"Don't you want to put an end to all this crime?"

"Of course I do, but until we know who's responsible, how can we stop it?"

"Exactly."

"You have a plan?"

"I'm working on it."

"You know, if it is your fugitive and he's hiding out in the mountains, then he has the advantage."

Chase eyed her, puzzled. "What do you mean?"

"If he knows the mountains, then you'll be hunting him on his turf. You can't go into that wilderness by yourself."

He scratched his face. "You have a point. I may need a guide."

"How about me?"

An unexpected surge of emotion invaded his rational mind. "No way! I couldn't put you in that kind of danger."

"Chase, listen to me. I know those mountains backwards and forwards, and I don't have a husband or kids to consider."

He struggled with how to respond to her sensible argument. "Joel would have my hide if anything happened to you. I can't take that chance. It's too dangerous."

She sprang from her chair, her chin lifted in defiance. "Forget my brother. I'm not a delicate flower that wilts if it gets too cold. And I can outshoot any man in the state. If you're going to outsmart this felon, you need someone who knows those mountains better than he does."

"True, but maybe I don't need to go into the mountains to catch him." A sly grin came to his lips as an idea formulated in his mind.

Facing him now, Jenny took a few steps backward and leaned against the porch rail. "What are you thinking?"

"Let's say these events are connected. If it's the same person doing all this, he'll need more provisions soon."

"So?"

"Since the trails are closed, he'll lay low for a few days, but then he'll make his move."

"He's running out of options."

"Exactly. What's his least risky next move?"

"He could hunt or fish if he's living in the mountains."

"I don't think he'll use his rifle. It would draw too much

attention. Besides, he goes for the easy targets, and something, *or someone,* is drawing him to Eagle Valley."

"In that case, he could steal from another campground."

Or another cabin.

Jenny eyed Chase with a cautious glance. "Don't forget, he stole rifles and ammo. If you go looking for him, he'll be armed and dangerous."

"Don't worry. I know what I'm doing."

"Whatever you're planning, I hope you know better than to go it alone. Isn't there someone you can call in Tennessee who can come out and help you catch this guy?"

"I don't need to call them. I can handle this on my own."

"Look, I'm not a marshal, but in the park service, we're always in contact with the main office, and we don't intentionally set out on dangerous assignments alone. I'm sure the marshals' service is no different." She studied him for a moment. "What's the real reason you don't want to call them?"

He didn't respond.

"Chase?"

He lifted his eyes to meet her questioning stare. "If I tell you, it doesn't go any further."

She returned a slow nod.

"My boss put me on leave because he thought I was under too much stress after Jim died."

Jenny put her hands on her hips. "If you pursue this fugitive, you'll be disobeying a direct order. Don't you think it's time you checked in with your office before you get in any deeper?"

Her last comment riled him. He rose from his chair. "I think we're done here. Thanks for the tip on the thefts at the campground."

She reached out and stopped him as he turned to go inside. "There's something else, isn't there? Something you're not telling me."

He stopped and glanced at her. "What makes you say that?"

"It's written all over your face."

He turned and searched her eyes, tormented by the truth he'd withheld from her. A truth that could devastate her.

"I'm going away for a few days. I want you to stay with Joel and Lori while I'm gone."

"What?"

"Please don't argue with me about this. You have to trust me."

She put her hands on her hips. "Trust you? Why? What are you keeping from me? If I'm in danger, I have a right to know everything."

Blowing out a deep breath of frustration, he crossed the porch to the railing. "All right, but first sit down."

She lowered herself into a rocker. "What on earth is going on?"

He closed his eyes and leaned against the rail. "The other night at the lodge after you left, I walked back to my car and there was a message written on the window . . ."

"What kind of message?"

"It said, 'Stay away from Jenny.'"

She stared at him for a moment. Then she laughed.

"What's so funny?"

"That's what's got you so worried? It was probably Billy trying to get back at you after he quit."

"Jen, the message was written in something meant to look like blood." He took out his phone and showed her the disturbing image he'd taken.

The color drained from her face as she studied it. Then she handed it back to him. "It's probably fake. It could still be one of Billy's pranks."

"What about the person who followed you after you left the Avalanche Grill?"

She bit her lip. "What are you saying?"

"The same thing you've been saying. What if all these incidents are connected somehow?"

"I don't understand. What does that have to do with me?"

As much as he wanted to avoid hurting her, he couldn't keep it from her any longer. She had a right to know. "I was hoping not to put you through this. I thought I'd catch him and then tell you everything. It would be easier on you. But since you're bound and determined to know the truth, I have no choice but to tell you. The man I'm after—the man who killed my partner—is the same man who robbed the bank in Langston when you were sixteen. It's Russ Webb."

Late that night Jenny sat in bed. She ran her silver cross back and forth along the chain that circled her neck. Chase's stunning revelation unleashed a storm inside her that was years in the making. The truth still stared her in the face. Russ had never loved her. He'd only used her to get what he wanted.

And now he was back to torment her again.

If he broke into her shed and later stole Chase's SUV, he must have been watching her for weeks. A chill shot up her spine.

She reached in her nightstand and pulled out her gun. "This time I'll be ready for you, Russ."

CHAPTER THIRTEEN

TIME PASSED SLOWLY AS CHASE WAITED behind the unoccupied hunting cabin, betting his man would strike again. In the silence of night, the high-pitched hum of the pesky mosquito swarming around him seemed as loud and annoying as an air raid siren. For three nights he'd staked out the cabin in the rain and had nothing to show for it but a dozen mosquito bites and a serious case of sleep deprivation.

He regretted not telling Joel and Lori where he was. When he told them he was going camping for a few days, they assumed he'd be in the mountains. He'd never actually said where he was going but didn't correct their assumption either. The way he figured it, the best way to reward his friends for their kindness was to rid Eagle Valley of the scumbag who had killed his partner.

The roaring of his empty stomach was louder than the mosquitoes now, and the bulletproof vest under his jacket made him sweat. But being hungry, miserable, and living in the rain gave him a taste of what it felt like to be on the run. And the more he understood the man he was after, the better the chance he had of anticipating his next move.

He considered telling Gus his plan, but he might contact Chase's home office and blow his cover. Jenny's disapproval of his plan to do this alone added to his frustration and impatience. What if she told Gus? No, she wouldn't do that. She knew it could ruin his career, such as it was.

Recently, he'd found himself re-thinking his modus operandi. He'd always done whatever was necessary to get the job done. He figured the end justified the means, but he knew

Jenny wouldn't agree. Doing wrong, even for a just cause, would never fly with her values.

His thoughts turned to his old partner. Jim would never have disobeyed a direct order from the boss. He was a stand-up guy. The kind of person you'd want on your team if you were going on a mission to save the world. He was loyal, honest, and responsible.

Chase wished he had told Jim how much he looked up to him. Instead, he poked fun at him for being too much of a straight-arrow and too soft-hearted. They weren't supposed to get emotionally involved with the criminal witnesses they were protecting, but Jim took an interest in their lives. He wanted to help them leave their life of crime and better themselves. Yet, he managed to maintain a professional distance, never crossing the line.

Despite everything, Jim had kept his humanity. Chase admired him for that. He never could balance work with life. His life *was* his work.

The crash of breaking glass rattled the quiet night from its slumber.

A shadowy figure climbed through the window a few feet away.

Chase crept closer, wielding his gun in front of him. He skulked to the broken window and followed the intruder inside.

Once he cleared the broken glass, he slipped off his shoes and laid them aside. In the dark, he crept along the hallway in his sock feet and clicked off the safety on his gun.

The floorboard beneath him creaked.

He winced and froze in place.

No sound.

Continuing on, he made it to the kitchen. From the doorway, he heard a noise and glimpsed something move. He ducked behind the door, barely escaping the searching beam of a flashlight that would have given him away.

Holding his breath, he inched closer and found the light

switch. Only a couple more steps.

One.

Two.

He planted his feet, aimed his gun, and flipped on the light. "U.S. Marshal. Hold it right there."

A flicker of movement caused Chase to shift as a whirling knife hummed past his ear and stabbed the door beside him.

A large can of tomatoes launched from across the room crashed into the overhead light, shrouding the kitchen in darkness again.

Chase's eyes were still adjusting when the force of a foot struck him, knocking his gun out of his hand. He pounced on the shadowy figure, wrestling him to the ground. As he tackled the man, the stench of sweat, smoke and filth assaulted his nostrils.

The trespasser was strong and slippery, like a human reptile.

Finally, Chase pinned him down with the man's back to the floor. "Got you."

Two beams of light from the window over the sink blinded Chase as the loud putter of a truck engine revved from the driveway outside. The intruder head-butted Chase and punched him in the chest, knocking the wind out of him.

"Wrong again, Marshal."

They dove for the Glock on the floor at the same time.

Chase beat him to it. Then something hard struck Chase's skull, followed by a sharp bolt of pain that knocked him to the floor. When he opened his eyes, a haze of spots and stars clouded his vision as he caught a fleeting glimpse of the man running for the door.

Chase struggled to his feet, but a wave of dizziness forced him back to his knees. The headlights from the truck outside sharpened the ache in his head.

Mercifully, someone shut the engine and lights off.

After putting his gun away, he grabbed the handle of the nearby refrigerator to pull himself up.

When he heard footsteps, he reached for his weapon again. The beam of a flashlight pierced his eyes. Shielding them with his hand, he squinted at his tormentor. "*Jenny*? Are you crazy? You could have been killed!"

"You're the one who's crazy. I just saved your career, and maybe your life."

Returning his gun to its holster, he grumbled. "I had him, Jen. I had him right where I wanted. Thanks to you, he's gone."

"You *should* be thanking me. What if you had caught him? How would you explain to your boss that you deliberately disobeyed his orders and took the law into your own hands? How do you think that would go over?"

Chase fumed. He didn't know if he was angrier at her because she'd thwarted his plan, or because she was right and had probably saved his job—assuming he still had one. "First, your headlights and now your flashlight. If your goal is to blind me, you're doing a really good job."

She clicked off the light. When his eyes recovered, he noticed her shapely silhouette bathed in moonlight. It was hard to stay angry at anyone so beautiful, even now when he was ready to explode.

He staggered over to the counter and leaned against it for support, rubbing the bump forming on his crown. "How did you find out where I was?"

She moved toward him. "It wasn't hard. When Joel told me you'd gone camping for a few days, I put two-and-two together."

"He was here, exactly like I said."

She remained unimpressed. "Being right doesn't mean a whole lot if you're dead."

He twisted his torso in her direction, his hand still gripping the counter.

Her keen eyes assessed his condition. "What happened to you?"

He grimaced from the pain throbbing in his head. "I got

whacked with a flashlight when you drove up."

"What were you thinking coming out here on a stakeout by yourself? You could have at least asked Gus to come with you."

"I couldn't risk getting anyone else involved. If you hadn't shown up, I would have caught him tonight."

She pointed her finger at him. "Or he might have killed you."

A grenade exploded inside of him. "Get this straight, Jenny." He wagged his finger at her. "Despite your interference, I'm not giving up. I will find him if it's the last thing I do."

"The way you're going, it may very well be the last thing you do. Now get in my truck before I personally call the deputy and turn you in myself."

He glared at her one last time before grudgingly following her outside. The constant drizzle of rain had finally let up. His head throbbed and his feet stung from rocks and sticks poking through his wet socks. But it was nothing compared to the frustration of failing to get Webb again.

Jenny glanced over her shoulder as he strode to the driver's side. "What are you doing? Get in the truck."

"I have my car. It's right up the road."

"Okay. Then get in and I'll drop you off." She climbed into her seat and slammed the door.

He tapped on her window.

She unrolled it. "What now?" she snapped.

"I'm the one who should be angry. Why are you so upset?"

She huffed and looked away. "I'm not upset."

"Yes, you are."

Both of her hands clenched the steering wheel. "Okay. How's this, for starters? You kept the truth from me about Russ being your fugitive. You're staying with my brother and his family under false pretenses. You didn't even tell him where you are right now. And you've made me an accomplice in your little scheme. I don't like deceit, Chase."

Her honesty landed a hard punch to his heart. No wonder she was furious with him. Everything she said was true. And yet, she'd still come to his rescue. "You're right. I should have been straight with you from the beginning, but I didn't tell you about Russ for your own protection. After you told me your history with him, I was afraid if you knew, it might devastate you."

Her lips tightened as she looked away. "Just like my brother. Always thinking you know what's best for me."

He clutched the side of her pickup. "Like I said, I was wrong."

She glanced back at him with a flicker of concern in her eyes. "What now? How much longer are you going to play the lone marshal?"

"As long as it takes."

"Even if it kills you or puts other people in danger?"

He gazed down. "I know what I'm doing. If you hadn't played mother hen tonight, I would have caught him, and we'd both be free from that menace."

"Then you should know I can't stand by and watch you throw your life away over this crazy obsession."

He pushed off the side of her truck. "It's not crazy. If you thought I had a screw loose, you wouldn't have come out here tonight. You came because you thought I was in danger. Admit it, you were worried about me."

She started up the engine, threw the truck in reverse, and jerked out of the drive without him, wheels spinning.

Chase ran and leapt onto the running board as she turned to drive away.

He hung on for dear life while she sped down the dirt road. When they reached his car, she slammed on the brakes, lurching him forward until he nearly fell off.

"This is your stop," she said through the open window, without looking at him.

Chase stepped off the truck. "Uh, thanks. Hey, Jenny, about what I said—"

"Save it. I think you've said enough for one night, don't you?"

He watched the taillights of her truck disappear down the road. Then he stared down at his feet and groaned. He'd forgotten his shoes.

While Jenny drove away, she thought of Chase standing outside in his sock feet and laughed. It served him right. How dare he try to make her concern for him something more than it was. Okay, maybe he was right. Maybe she did care more about him than she wanted to admit. If he knew she prayed for him every day, he'd really rub it in.

Seeing him at church last Sunday had thrown her for a loop. The next day, she'd found him reading the Bible. Encouraging signs, but she would refrain from celebrating until he showed a real change of heart. Tonight only proved he was still obsessed with avenging his friend's death.

Jenny braked at the four-way stop and noticed the lights at Reggie's cabin ahead. Easing her foot off the gas, she slowly approached. Was that Wendy's car parked in his drive?

The sound of angry voices rippled through her open window. She strained to see who was yelling in the darkness. The shadowy figures of a man and woman in the front yard came into view.

The man grabbed the woman's arm. "You'll be sorry!"

The woman jerked free and raced to the car and jumped in. The car pulled out of the drive and peeled out.

Jenny followed it to Gus's house. His motion-sensor light came on and illuminated the driveway enough for her to confirm it was Wendy who got out and went inside. Jenny wondered if she should go in and make sure Wendy was okay, but since she was already safe at home with her father, she decided against it and drove on.

A few minutes later, Jenny saw the lights from Joel and Lori's place. She still needed to pick up the cougar cubs she'd dropped off with Lori after work, telling her she had an errand to run. She'd have to collect the cubs and get out of there before they asked too many questions concerning where she'd been and why she was so late.

Through her rearview mirror, she spied headlights. Goosebumps pimpled her flesh at the memory of the SUV following her the other night. She pulled into Joel's drive and parked, ready with her SIG in hand in case Russ decided to pay her a visit.

Her tension eased as Chase's red Mustang turned in and parked beside her truck. After securing her weapon in the glove box and locking her pickup, she joined Chase on Joel's front porch. "You're lucky you didn't get a speeding ticket for driving so fast. What happened to camping?"

He shrugged. "After living in the rain the last three nights, I decided I could use a good night's sleep on a real bed. Hopefully, Joel and Lori won't mind me dropping in this late."

He'd left his jacket and Kevlar vest in the car. Despite his unkempt appearance, the moonlight accentuated his handsome features as he stood with his backpack slung over his shoulder.

"That explains why you look so scruffy."

He stroked the shadow of beard on his chin. "I figured you'd like my mountain man look."

She glanced at his feet and snickered. "Oh, so you found your shoes."

He looked down. "I'm surprised you noticed. You were in such a rush to get away." He leaned against the outside wall while she rang the doorbell. "Why are you here at this hour?"

"To pick up the cubs." She studied him for a moment, concerned by the way he was rubbing his scalp. "You have a bump on your head?"

"More like a grapefruit."

"Here, let me see."

He inclined his head, and she gently inspected it.

"That's quite a welt you've got. Now, look at me."

He lifted his head and obediently turned his eyes toward her.

She shone her flashlight in them.

"Hey! Stop that."

"Good," she said, as she turned the flashlight off. "Your eyes aren't dilated, but you probably have a mild concussion."

He grimaced at her. "What is it with you and flashlights?"

She ignored his remark. "Take Ibuprofen and see the doctor first thing in the morning."

"Don't worry. I have a hard head."

She sent him a dry look. "In more ways than one."

"Ouch. That hurt more than the whack on my head."

"Sorry. I couldn't resist."

"Like you couldn't resist checking up on me tonight." His knowing gaze locked with hers, sending a flash of heat rushing to her face.

She averted her eyes and focused on the door. "I wonder what's keeping them." She banged her fist against the wood.

"Maybe they're busy," he remarked.

She caught a glimpse of him smirking. "What's so funny, Matthews?"

"Beating on the door won't make them come any faster."

She huffed. "Well, no one asked you for your opinion, thank you very much."

Joel finally answered the door; a mix of curiosity and amusement sparkled in his eyes. "For a moment, I thought there were two wildcats fighting out here. I've never heard so much growling and hissing."

He frowned at his sister. "Jenny, where have you been? Lori's been trying to call you."

"I'm sorry. I lost track of time." She ducked past Joel in the doorway.

"So I see."

His tone stopped her. She peered over her shoulder at her brother's smug grin. He obviously thought something romantic was going on between her and Chase.

"I'm surprised to see you, buddy," Joel said. "We didn't expect to see you until tomorrow at the earliest. How was the camping?"

Jenny glanced over her shoulder again, relishing that Chase was now in the hot seat. Maybe he'd distract Joel long enough for her to fetch the cubs and be on her way.

As if reading her thoughts, Chase discreetly looked at her before answering Joel. "I hope you don't mind me showing up like this. After three days in this rainy weather, I could use a good night's sleep."

Joel welcomed him inside. "Adam will be thrilled. By the way, you look like death warmed over."

It seemed Joel, like Jenny, was no longer surprised by anything Chase did. But how would he react if he knew what Chase had been up to? She saw the pet carrier by the door and stooped down to look inside. Empty. "Where are the cubs?"

"In the den where Lori and Adam are spoiling them rotten." Joel led them along the hallway. "I'm waiting for Lori to put them in diapers next."

Lori met Joel at the entrance to the den. "Who was at the door—" Her gaze went to Jenny. "Oh. I'm glad you're all right." Like any true friend, she started probing. "When you didn't answer your phone, I was beginning to worry. Where were you?"

Jenny thrust her hands in her pockets. "Sorry, Lori. I should have called to let you know I'd be late."

Her friend's worried expression subsided. "It's okay." She gave Jenny a warm hug, then glanced at Chase, casting him a curious stare. "Well, hello, Chase. I'm surprised to see you back so soon."

"I've had enough of camping in the rain. I hope you don't mind?"

She gave him the once-over.

He attempted to re-tuck his rumpled shirt under his belt. "Sorry for my appearance. This is what happens to me when there's a shortage of your apple pie."

"Nice try." Lori flicked her wrist. "I'm teasing, Chase. You know you're always welcome."

"Thanks. I'll go put my backpack away."

Lori turned to Jenny and escorted her into the den. "The cubs kept us entertained all night. Turns out these little kitties are night owls."

Jenny laughed. "Tell me about it." She crouched next to Adam, who was playing with the live fur balls on the large, braided-yarn rug. "And what are you still doing out of bed at this hour, young man?"

Lori stood over them. "Oh, he's had a fun time with the cubs, haven't you, Adam?"

The boy nodded with a wide grin. "Can I keep them here with me?"

Jenny sat beside him on the rug. "I wish you could, but they're not pets, Adam. They're wild animals, and eventually they'll get homesick for the mountains, exactly like you'd get homesick if you were away from home too long. We need to help them get strong and healthy so they'll be able to take care of themselves soon."

A wistful look touched Lori's face. "Aunt Jenny's right, Adam. She can't keep them much longer, or they'll never be able to go back to their real home. Now that she's here to pick them up, why don't you run along and get into your PJs? It's getting late."

After Adam left, Chase returned and stood across the rug from Jenny. Lori eyed them both with a speculative glance. "Out with it. What's going on with you two?"

Joel moved in behind his wife, resting his hands on her shoulders. "Yeah, don't keep us in suspense."

Jenny looked at Chase.

He grinned back, but his eyes were wary. They both knew she could blow his cover, not to mention tarnish a cherished friendship between him and Joel.

She shifted her gaze to the cubs, stalling. This was Chase's mess, and he should be the one to clean it up.

"It looks like you've already made up your minds," Chase

finally replied. "You wouldn't believe us anyway."

Jenny did a double take.

His intent gaze told her to trust him and play along.

She arched a brow, warning him he was on notice.

Joel and Lori eyed them with doubtful looks. Thankfully, Lori got the message. "Joel, honey, what do you say we drop it and let it be their little secret?"

Joel sent Chase a sly grin. "All right. I guess everyone is entitled to a secret or two."

Chase's gaze darted to Jenny with a silent thank you.

Adam rushed in, wearing pajamas with little footballs, baseballs, and basketballs printed all over. "Look, Uncle Chase, come see my new pets."

Uncle Chase? Jenny had to admit he looked the part when he sat on the floor, opposite Adam, cupping the little fur balls in his large, protective hands. Who knew the tough marshal was capable of such tenderness? It was a side of him hard to discount, yet contrary to the man who was so driven.

"Do a marmot, please," Adam cried.

The awkward look on Chase's face revealed an appealing touch of bashfulness. "I don't know, Adam. I'm not very good."

"Please."

"A marmot?" Jenny remarked, suppressing a laugh.

He lifted one cub off his leg, extracting the kitten's claws from his jeans. "We've been practicing animal sounds."

She smiled. "I'd like to hear this myself."

He gave her a reluctant shrug. "Remember, you asked for it." After handing the cubs to her, he straightened, sucked in a deep breath, and emitted a high-pitched chirping noise.

Jenny giggled.

"I told you I wasn't any good."

She petted the cubs in her lap. "Actually, you're not bad. Joel and I are probably the only ones who could tell that wasn't a real marmot. They have a slightly higher pitch, but it's a subtle difference."

Adam rocked back and forth excitedly. "Do an owl next."

Chase cleared his throat and began to hoot.

Lori tilted her head. "That's pretty good. Of course, no one does an owl better than Joel."

Joel sat in the chair across from them. "Drum roll, please."

Adam, Chase and Jenny drummed their palms on the floor.

Joel's unblinking eyes became two large circles as he panned his head back and forth in an owl-like manner and hooted.

They all erupted in laughter. Jenny laughed so hard her stomach hurt.

Adam, still giggling from his father's antics, tugged on Chase's shirt. "Do a hawk."

Chase pursed his lips and blew several long, plaintive whistles in succession.

Jenny raised a brow. "Impressive. But can you do an American Dipper?"

"Is that a bird?"

"Yes, it's an aquatic bird in the North Cascades."

"What does it sound like?"

She whistled its intricate tune. When she'd finished, they all applauded.

Chase smiled. "You're much better at this than I am."

She whistled the bird song again.

He gave it a try.

"That's pretty good. You were only off in a few places."

Adam yawned and rubbed his eyes. Chase touched him on the shoulder. "Looks like somebody's getting sleepy."

Lori smiled at her son. "Come on, Adam. It's time to go to bed."

"Aw, Mommy, I want to play with the cubs."

"No, dear, it's way past their bedtime, and yours. They need sleep too, you know. It's not fair to keep them up all night. They'll be tired and cranky the next morning."

Lori excused herself to tuck Adam in, glancing at Jenny and Chase. Then she took her husband's hand, prompting him to get up. "Joel, why don't you come with me?"

Confusion surfaced on his face until her hint registered. "Oh." He waved to Chase and Jenny. "We'll be back in a bit."

"Uncle Chase?" Jenny repeated when they were alone.

"Adam asked me if he could call me that since he doesn't have any uncles. Does it bother you?"

She leaned against the couch behind her, stroking the kittens as they curled up to sleep in her lap. "No, but I never thought of you as the uncle type."

"Oh? And what type am I?" He moved closer with an intriguing smile.

"I'm sorry," Lori said with an apologetic look.

Jenny and Chase glanced up.

"Adam is insisting that Chase read him a story, but maybe this is a bad time."

Chase's eyes lingered on Jenny a second longer. "No, it's fine. I'll go right in to see him."

He came to his feet and glanced at Jenny. "Hey, Jen, why don't you join me?"

She smiled at the offer. "Okay. I'll be there in a minute, after I put the cubs in the carrier."

A few minutes later, when she entered Adam's room, Jenny found her nephew sitting in his bed, picking through a stack of books. He handed one of them to Chase. "Read me this one, please."

Chase glanced at the cover and showed it to Jenny, who nodded her approval. "Okay, but I think I already know how it turns out. I saw the movie with Charlton Heston."

Jenny sat at the end of Adam's bed and listened as Chase read the story. Adam's eyes grew wide, and his mouth fell open when he read about all the Israelite baby boys being killed by the evil Pharaoh, and Moses' mother saving him by putting him in a basket and sending it down the Nile where the Pharaoh's daughter found it.

Jenny became lost in the story as Chase told it. He made it

come alive with his animated voices and expressions. When he finally reached the end, Adam had drifted off to sleep.

Chase quietly closed the book and got up. "Looks like I've lost my captive audience," he whispered, his eyes twinkling in the dimly-lit room.

Jenny smiled at her nephew and tucked him in. She kissed him on the forehead while Chase waited for her at the door.

Lori met them in the hall. "Is he asleep?"

Chase nodded. "Out like a light."

"He's become quite attached to you, you know. It'll break his heart when you leave."

The sudden mention of Chase's eventual departure dampened Jenny's mood. She pivoted toward the door. "It's late. I need to go home."

Lori and Chase came with her down the hall where Joel joined them. He handed her the pet carrier. "You'd better find a home for these critters before Lori and Adam turn them into housecats."

"I'm working on it." Jenny gave Lori a big hug. "Goodnight."

As she turned to leave, Jenny bumped into Chase. For an awkward moment, she wasn't sure how to part company with him.

"I'll walk you to your car," he said.

She spied Lori and Joel's curious looks. "Thanks, but that's not necessary."

"I insist." He waved to Joel and Lori. "I'll be back in a few minutes."

Once outside, Chase firmly shut the front door behind him and Jenny. "There's something I want to show you." His voice was low and serious.

Intrigued, she let him escort her to the passenger side of her pickup where he took the pet carrier out of her hands so she could unlock and open the door. He set the carrier on the seat and closed the door.

"What is it?" she asked.

"After you dropped me off and I had to walk back to get my shoes, I did a quick search of the cabin and found something. It's in my car."

She followed him to the Mustang. When he opened the trunk, she peered inside. "That's my axe!"

"It was used to break the window at the cabin tonight. Our thief forgot to take it with him when he ran away."

"You really think it was Russ who broke into my shed and who's been breaking into the cabins?"

"I can't say for sure yet, but it fits his M.O. I'd like to keep the axe for evidence."

"Sure. What are you going to do now?"

He leaned forward and thrust his hand in his pocket. "I've been thinking about what you said. Maybe it is time I called my boss for backup."

A sense of relief washed over her. "Good. It's the right thing to do."

He shrugged. "We'll see." His gaze rested on her. "I can't let Webb get away again, or let you risk your life to save me."

She smiled and glanced down. "It's very late. I really do have to go, or I'll be a zombie at work in the morning."

"On a Saturday?"

"It's the peak season, and we're shorthanded."

He walked her back to her truck and opened the door for her.

"Well, goodnight." She reached to touch his head. "Don't forget to have a doctor look at that bump tomorrow."

"I'll think about it."

She doubted he would, but at least he didn't say no.

He surprised her with a warm hug that left her teetering slightly off balance. "Goodnight, Jen. Thanks for keeping our little secret tonight."

Slightly dazed, she got into her truck, and he closed the door behind her. She glanced at him through the open window. "I won't keep it forever."

He leaned against the door. "You won't have to."

CHAPTER FOURTEEN

AT SUNRISE SATURDAY MORNING, JENNY PARKED her pickup at the gas station in Eagle Valley. Already dressed in her ranger uniform, she hopped out of her truck. The aroma of coffee prompted a caffeine craving.

Chase approached with two steaming cups. Clean-shaven, he appeared surprisingly fresh and awake, considering they were up so late. "Thanks for coming. I hope it wasn't too much trouble to stop by on your way to work."

"No, but I was surprised when you called me at the crack of dawn. You could have at least told me what's going on. Now I'm in suspense."

"I didn't know myself when we spoke. Gus had called me and told me to meet him here. There's a new development in the search for my stolen car. I thought you'd be interested." He handed her a coffee. "Here, you might need this."

"Thanks." She took a sip and read the brand on the cup. "Cascade Java. My favorite. How did you know?"

"Lucky guess?"

"It's also the only barista in town."

"That too."

Chase escorted her to the deputy sheriff's car.

Jenny's curiosity grew with the adrenaline rush of the morning caffeine when she noticed the blue SUV parked beside Gus's car. "Chase, is that what I think it is?"

Gus walked over. "Hello, Jenny. It's been a busy morning."

"So I see. Looks like you found Chase's SUV. Did you catch the thief who stole it?"

"He's in the car."

Jenny headed that way.

Chase touched her shoulder and stopped her. "Wait. It's not who you think. It's the boy we rescued from the avalanche last Monday."

She stared back at him, surprised. *"Dylan?"*

He nodded.

His serious expression filled her with dread. She inhaled deeply and braced herself as she came around to the driver's side of Gus's car and peered inside.

Dylan Veracruz was slumped in the back seat, staring at the floorboard as if his life was over.

Jenny frowned at the handcuffs around his wrists.

Gus approached her.

"I don't understand. What does Dylan have to do with Chase's SUV?"

"He was driving it when I caught him early this morning."

She addressed the boy through the open window. "Hi, Dylan."

He peered at her as if interrupted from a nightmare. Then he turned away.

"You're looking pretty good for someone who barely survived an avalanche five days ago. When were you released from the hospital?"

He stared out the opposite window. "Thursday."

"What were you doing with a stolen SUV?"

Grimacing, he shut his eyes. "I didn't steal it."

"Then what happened?"

"I found it last night and took it for a joyride, that's all. I was returning it to the place I found it this morning. That's when the sheriff arrested me."

Gus interrupted. "Jenny."

She turned her head in his direction.

He gestured toward the stolen truck. "Chase confirmed this is his SUV that was stolen at your place. Does it look like the one that ran you off the road on Monday?"

She nodded.

"It also matches the description of the vehicle spotted leaving Butch's store right after the attempted robbery."

Dylan turned around. "I told you, I found the SUV, and I didn't rob any store."

Chase joined Jenny at the window. "Where did you find it, Dylan?"

The boy looked at Chase. "In the parking lot at the Cascade Pass trailhead. I was hanging out with my friends."

"Did you break in?"

"No. It was unlocked."

"Was there a key?"

He nodded. "I found it in the glovebox. I wasn't planning to keep it. I swear."

Despite the sunny day, a bitter cold numbed Jenny's soul. All the hopes she'd had for Dylan's future were flittering away.

The boy craned his head in her direction, his eyes pleading. "Please. You have to believe me. I didn't rob that store."

She stared at him, seeing the boy who faithfully rode his bike to church and youth group, though his family never attended, and, who, despite his troubled home life, had overcome so much. Somewhere deep inside that boy still existed, and she wouldn't give up on him any more than she would give up on Wendy or any of the others she'd shepherded. "I believe you."

His eyes brightened. "You do?"

"Yes, I do," she replied with a compassionate smile. Then she pivoted to Gus. "I want to post his bail."

"I haven't charged him with anything yet, but I've got to keep him in custody until we rule him out as a suspect for the robbery and check out his story about the SUV."

"But he's still a minor."

Gus ushered Jenny and Chase away from his car and led them out of earshot from the boy. "You really think he's telling the truth?"

"Yes, I do."

He rubbed his brow, obviously conflicted. "I've known that boy all of his life. I've been called out to his house numerous times for domestic disputes. It's a shame Dylan's father died so young, and his mother married that bully. I'll grant you that boy's had more than his share of tough breaks, and I'd like to give him the benefit of the doubt. But the fact is he was found in possession of the stolen SUV that was used as the getaway car for the robbery."

He pushed up his hat with his finger. "On the other hand, from Butch's description, the robber was taller than Dylan. It's possible after the botched robbery, the perp ditched the SUV at the trailhead parking lot, and Dylan found it like he says."

Chase spoke up. "Did you find anything unusual inside the SUV?"

"Not much, but I did find a hunting rifle cartridge. Do you hunt, Chase?"

"No, but I'm betting that cartridge was stolen from the cabin Reggie Grayling is renting now."

Gus rubbed his chin, his eyes narrowing at Chase with a shrewd stare. "And I'm betting you know more than you've told me."

Chase's jaw tensed as he glanced at Jenny.

"Tell him, Chase."

Gus planted his fists on his hips. "Somebody better start talking."

Chase blew out a long breath and turned back to Gus. "A fugitive wanted for killing my partner may be hiding out somewhere in the area."

Gus's brow popped up. "And how long have you suspected this?"

Chase hesitated. "Since before I arrived."

Glaring, the sheriff muttered a few choice words.

"I wanted to keep a low profile until I was sure. I didn't see the point in alarming the whole town with a theory. Besides, I'm technically on vacation."

Gus crossed his arms over his chest. "And you think your fugitive could be the one responsible for the attempted robbery and cabin break-in?"

"And the thefts in Eagle Valley, and near Cascade Pass," Jenny added.

Chase addressed Gus's question. "It's possible, but I think he'll be making himself scarce in Eagle Valley for a while."

Gus scoffed. "Oh? And why is that?"

"He tried to break into the cabin I was staking out last night."

The deputy shot Chase an incredulous look and raised an accusing finger at him. "Let me get this straight. You've been doing stakeouts without my knowledge."

Chase grimaced. "In retrospect, I probably should have told you about this sooner."

Gus paced and grumbled. He stopped in front of Chase and thrust his finger at him. "What were you thinking, Matthews? This is my jurisdiction. I'm the law around here, not you. Marshal or not, I'm going to report this. You're a loose cannon."

Jenny stepped in between the two men. "Please don't do that, Gus. He's being honest with you now."

"You knew about this too?"

She returned a reluctant nod. "I didn't want to keep it from you, but I also didn't want to create a fuss for nothing. I didn't believe Chase's theory at first. And we still don't know for sure if the same person is responsible for all these crimes."

Gus squinted at her. "This is a fine mess you two have cooked up." His eyes shifted back to Chase, who was staring at the ground. "What's your plan, Wyatt?"

Chase raised his head, shifting to a more serious, professional stance. "I think our thief has gone deep into the mountains to lay low for a while. Other deputy marshals are staking out the Washington-Canadian border in case the fugitive tries to flee the country. I want to organize a small team to conduct a search in the mountains. If we find evidence that someone is hiding out there, we'll expand the search and call in a task force."

"I'm going with you," Gus said in an adamant tone.

"Of course," Chase said. "I'll keep you posted as things develop."

Jenny gestured to the deputy's car. "What about Dylan? What are you going to do with him?"

Gus gave a weary sigh. "Right now, I have no choice but to charge him with theft for stealing the SUV. I'll have him held in the youth detention center in Watkinsville until I can sort this mess out."

"May I speak to him before you leave?"

"Go ahead."

When Jenny came to his window, Dylan looked up. "What's going to happen to me?"

"It'll be all right. Gus has to take you to a detention center until he can clear everything up. You're going to get through this, Dylan. I'll come visit you when I can. Now I want you to have faith and stay strong, okay?"

He nodded, his eyes turning red and watery. "Sorry, Jenny. I let you down."

"You let yourself down, Dylan, but God still loves you. He didn't save you from that avalanche for nothing, you know."

A small smile broke through his dark expression at her last remark. "I never thanked you for rescuing me that day."

She glanced at Chase, who was standing nearby. "I had some help. You're quite a fighter, you know. I figure if you can survive an avalanche, you can pretty much get through anything."

The boy shrugged with slight grin. "Except maybe Calculus."

Chase walked Jenny back to her car. "You were great back there with Dylan."

"Thanks. It helps to know Gus will do everything he can to see that he gets a fair shake."

"Speaking of Gus, I don't think he's too happy with us right now. How do you think Joel will react when I tell him everything?"

She stopped in her tracks, imagining her brother's reaction.

"It won't be pretty. But you two have a bond from your Army days. He'll get over it."

When they reached her truck, Chase gazed at the clear, blue sky. "Nice day, huh?" Flecks of brown and amber glimmered in his eyes from the sunlight.

The fresh scent of pine trees from the nearby woods floated through the air. She'd been so upset by Dylan's arrest, she'd barely noticed. "Yes, it is. What are you going to do with the rest of it?"

He took a long breath. "Unfortunately, I've got to make a few calls and try to get a search team together."

"My offer to be your guide still stands."

"Thanks, but it sounds like you've got more than enough to deal with at work. Hopefully, it'll be an easy day for you, and you can catch up on your sleep tonight."

The corner of her mouth turned up. "I doubt it. Since I brought the cubs home, I've forgotten what it's like to get a good night's sleep. My house has become a twenty-four-seven nursery. I need to get them to a wildlife refuge soon."

Concern registered on his face. "It'll break Adam's heart when you do."

"That's one of the hardest lessons in life, isn't it?"

"What's that?"

"Saying goodbye. Adam's pretty attached to you too. He'll miss you when you leave."

He shrugged. "He'll get over it."

All this talk of saying goodbye made her sad. "Well, I guess we both have a busy day ahead of us. We better get to work." She turned to leave.

"Jen . . ."

She tossed him a curious look. "Yes?"

"Do you have to work tomorrow?"

She turned around. "No. Why?"

He appeared tentative. "How about going to church with me?"

Church?

His shining eyes regarded her as he waited for her answer. "There's no rule against two friends going to church together, is there?"

She smiled at the question. "None that I can think of."

As Jenny drove to the ranger station, she passed Reggie's cabin and recalled the argument she'd witnessed between Wendy and him last night. After she'd followed Wendy home, Jenny had been unable to shake the uneasy feeling that her friend was in danger.

She decided to pull over and contact her. When she picked up her phone, she noticed the new text from Wendy:

Reggie and me r over

Jenny breathed a little easier. That must have been why Wendy was at Reggie's cabin last night. She remembered Reggie grabbing and shouting at Wendy. He was obviously angry about the break-up. But in the heat of an argument, people said things they didn't mean. Still, his words, *You'll be sorry*, still echoed in Jenny's mind.

CHAPTER FIFTEEN

JENNY ANSWERED HER DOOR ON SUNDAY morning, wearing her favorite yellow sundress.

Chase responded with an admiring whistle. "Wow. And I thought you looked good in a ranger uniform." In his blue sport coat with dress shirt and slacks, he looked particularly dashing.

She gave him a nod of approval. "And you've upgraded from scruffy to classy."

He glanced down at his clothes with his hands hidden behind his back. "Joel deserves the credit. I borrowed clothes from him again. If I'd known I'd be dressing up this much on vacation, I would have packed differently."

Jenny eyed him with a suspicious look. "What are you hiding?"

With a dramatic flair, he revealed a bouquet of pink roses. "I thought maybe sweetheart roses would be safer than red. Otherwise, it might look like a date."

She laughed as she admired the delicate, beautiful flowers, inhaling their sweet scent. "They're lovely. I'll go put them in a vase. Be back in a sec."

When she returned, he held out an arm to escort her down the steps.

Fred and Ginger followed them to their invisible fence border.

She glanced at the dogs. "They're never this quiet. I don't think they recognize us."

An ironic smile passed Chase's lips. "I don't recognize us."

Thirty minutes later, when they arrived and entered the church together, Jenny noticed the number of heads that turned their way as Chase escorted her to empty seats near the front.

He whispered in her ear. "Your reputation will never be the same after this."

She looked up and saw Adam running down their row with a big smile. He proudly sat beside her. "You look pretty, Aunt Jenny."

Lori and Joel joined them on the same row.

"When Adam saw you both together, he ran up here before we could stop him." Lori gave them an apologetic look. "I hope you don't mind if we sit with you."

"Of course not." Jenny smiled at Chase giving Adam a secret handshake. It occurred to her as she looked around that Wendy and Gus weren't there. She took her cell from her purse to check her messages. Wendy still hadn't responded to her text sent yesterday.

The worship music began and Jenny silenced her phone. Maybe, after the service, she could convince Chase to stop by Deputy Patterson's place to see Wendy.

Chase admired Jenny as she sang. She'd never looked more beautiful. The yellow dress brought out her feminine side, which he found irresistible.

After the song ended, the pastor read from the gospel of John. When he'd finished, he gazed into the congregation and preached his message from the text about Jesus in the Garden of Gethsemane when the Apostle Peter cut off the ear of the high priest's servant.

"Instead of rewarding Peter," the pastor said, "Jesus told him to put the sword away then healed the man's ear. Later, that very night, Peter—the bold disciple who'd attempted to avenge Jesus by cutting off the man's ear—denied even knowing him—not once, not twice, but three times!

"I'm wondering how many of us are like Peter. Maybe a loved one was harmed, and you're filled with hatred for the person responsible, or maybe you're afraid of the personal cost of knowing Jesus.

"I've got good news for you. The Apostle Peter struggled with these same issues, but eventually become the bold and courageous leader of the early church.

"What's keeping you from God? Will you trust Him with whatever it is?"

Chase looked down and picked up the church bulletin beside him, pretending to read it, a futile attempt to brush off the pastor's penetrating message.

He glanced at Jenny, who was gazing up, listening intently. Her lovely face appeared so serene and luminescent, like an angel.

He, on the other hand, fumed in silence. The last thing he needed right now was a guilt trip from the pulpit. This was all Gus's fault. He shouldn't have listened to his advice. *Take an interest in what she cares about.* What did Gus know, anyway?

The pastor moved on in his message while Chase squirmed in his seat, his eyes searching for the nearest exit. Where was God when Jim needed him?

Did you hear me, God? If you're so fair and just, why did you let a good man like Jim die, and the dirt bag who killed him get away?

After the service ended, Jenny noticed Billy Norton's mother coming toward her. Her puffy eyes and anxious expression alarmed Jenny. "What's wrong, Mrs. Norton?"

"Jenny, have you seen my Billy?"

A sinking feeling plagued Jenny as she glanced at Chase. "The last time I saw him was a week ago. Why?"

The middle-aged woman who shared Billy's freckles and pale blue eyes wrung her hands. "He came home Sunday night, fit to be tied. I've never seen him so upset. I asked him what was wrong, but he refused to tell me. He started packing his camping gear. Said he was going on a backpacking trip through Cascade

Pass. I asked him when he would return, but he wouldn't tell me. It's been almost a week now, and I still haven't heard from him."

"Has he gone off on his own like this before?" Jenny asked, concern gripping her heart.

"Once or twice, when he was really angry, but never for this long. He doesn't like it when I ask when he'll be home. He thinks I'm treating him like a child. He resents living at home still. I know he's grown and all, but . . ." Tears welled in the woman's eyes.

Jenny gently touched her arm. "I'll ask around and see if anyone has seen him on the trail. Don't worry, Mrs. Norton. He knows those mountains. I'm sure he's fine."

"Thank you. I wish you could talk some sense into my boy when he comes home." Her eyes darted to Chase and back. "He's always liked you, Jenny, ever since you two were in grade school together."

Chase walked Jenny to his car. "How does lunch sound?"

Her mind had been exploring possible reasons why Billy left so suddenly without telling his mother when he'd return. Did it have anything to do with her having dinner with Chase? "Umm. Not today. But, if you wouldn't mind, I'd like to go to the Cascade Pass trailhead parking lot and then stop by and see Wendy on the way home."

"I know what you're thinking, and it's not your fault."

She looked up at him, only half-listening to what he'd said. "What's not my fault?"

"Billy getting angry and going AWOL."

She shook her head. "He was so hurt last Sunday. What if I sent him over the edge?"

"Like you said, he knows the mountains. He's probably on his way home as we speak." Chase opened the door for her, and she got in.

"I hope you're right."

When Chase drove into the lot for the Cascade Pass trailhead, he had his choice of parking spaces. The normally-crowded lot had been vacated, except for one beat-up Chevy pickup.

"That's Billy's truck!" Jenny pointed.

As soon as Chase parked his car, Jenny jumped out and headed in that direction, while he went to check the info board at the trailhead.

"Find anything?" he asked when she appeared beside him.

"I looked inside, but only saw a pair of old sneakers, nothing else. At least we know Billy made it to the trailhead."

Chase gestured to the sign on the board. "Why is this trail closed? Avalanches?"

"No. This is one of the trails with the recent reported thefts. Clint told me they closed the trail last Tuesday. I should let him know about Billy and see if any of the rangers remember seeing him up there." Her eyes focused on the trail.

Chase didn't like the intent look on her face. "What are you thinking?"

She shifted her gaze to him. "How would you like to go for a hike this afternoon?"

He frowned. "I don't think that's such a good idea."

"Why not?"

"First of all, the trail's closed. And, second, I need to organize a search, remember? Besides, this is the same parking lot where Dylan claims he found my SUV. If Dylan's telling the truth, then whoever stole it may be up there too."

"Oh." She frowned. "What if Billy ran into Russ?"

"Let's not get ahead of ourselves. In a couple of days, I plan to check out the area with my team, and we'll find out what's going on. But for now, I don't want you up there alone. Understood?"

She crossed her arms in protest.

Chase edged closer and softly lifted her chin with his finger.

"Promise me you won't do it. Not only will you be putting yourself in danger, but it'll jeopardize our search."

She met his warning with a defiant look.

"Promise me," he repeated.

With a sigh, she relented. "Oh. Okay."

"Good." He removed his hand from her face.

"I won't be alone because I'm going *with you*."

He did a double-take. "What?"

"As your guide."

Chase shook his head emphatically.

"You need a guide."

He stared at her. "I know, but I can't let you take that risk."

"No offense, but you don't stand a chance in those mountains without me. So there's no use trying to change my mind."

His cell went off. Quickly glimpsing Kate's number on the caller ID, he held up his hand. "I need to get this, but we're not finished."

Pressing the phone to his ear, Chase answered the call. "Good timing, Kate. I was going to call you this afternoon. What's up?"

"Remember when you asked me to check out Reggie Grayling to see if he has any priors?"

Chase watched Jenny from the corner of his eye as she wandered back to his car. In her yellow summer dress and heels, she looked like an exotic flower. "You got something?"

"First of all, his name isn't Reggie Grayling. It's Henry Cooper."

"I knew he wasn't for real."

"Hold on. It gets crazier. He was practicing medicine in New Orleans without a license. It all came out when he was sued after several botched procedures. He fled, and no one's seen him until now."

"I owe you one."

Jenny's curious gaze shifted in Chase's direction.

"Look, I've gotta go, Kate. I'll call you back later today."

"Sure. Oh, Chase, be careful."

Jenny watched Chase as he hung up. "Who is Kate?"

"A friend," he replied succinctly. "Come on. Let's get going."

"Where?"

"Back to town. I need to see Gus."

On the way to the deputy sheriff's office, Jenny wondered what on earth the woman on the phone had said that had gotten Chase so worked up. She was still recovering from the wild ride over when Chase parked his Mustang and jumped out.

She exited the car and nearly tripped on the heels of her sandals as she followed him up the wooden steps to the door. "What's wrong with you? Why won't you tell me why we're here?"

He repeatedly knocked on the door. "You're about to find out."

Finally, Gus answered. He looked like he hadn't slept in weeks.

"Are you okay, Deputy Patterson?" Jenny asked.

Chase didn't give him time to answer. "Sorry to bother you, but there's something important I have to tell you."

Gus squinted at him. "This better be good."

"Reggie Grayling is an imposter. His real name is Henry Cooper."

Gus rubbed the crevasses in his forehead. "I know." His voice sounded tired and ragged.

Jenny stared at them both, astonished by the revelation.

"You *know*?" Chase exclaimed.

"As of an hour ago."

"Did you also know that he's not a real vet, and he's wanted for practicing medicine without a license?"

"Yeah. That too. I spoke to Frank Baker on the phone last night. He mentioned he still hadn't rented his cabin yet and that tipped me off. I did a search and found a BOLO for a Henry Cooper, who matches Grayling's description. Guess Reggie had us all fooled."

"Did you arrest him?"

"I tried, but by the time I got to the cabin, I was too late. He'd already skipped town. The place is completely cleaned out."

Gus turned to Jenny, his eyes sad and swollen. "Have you seen Wendy? She left the house yesterday evening and didn't come home last night."

"No. She sent me a text yesterday morning, and I tried to call her but she didn't answer, so I texted her back. Wait a minute!" Jenny pulled out her phone and opened the text.

"What is it?" Chase asked.

"What if the text was a ruse to throw us off Wendy's trail? What if it was all part of Reggie's plan for her to run away with him? I should have seen this coming. Chase suspected Reggie was a fake from the beginning, and he was right."

Chase appeared rueful. "Now I wish I'd been wrong."

"I tried to warn her . . ."

Gus shook his head. "Would somebody please tell me what's going on? What does Reggie have to do with my Wendy?"

If only she had told Gus about Wendy and Reggie earlier. Now it weighed on her heart like a giant mountain. She looked at Chase, who sent her a nod of encouragement to continue.

Jenny turned back to the deputy. "Chase and I saw Wendy and Reggie having dinner together a week ago. Then I saw them together again Friday night at his cabin. They were arguing outside. She got into her car, and I followed her to your house. I saw her go inside, and I left. I should have stopped and come in, but it was late, and I figured she was safe at home with you."

Gus anxiously rubbed his mouth, the lines on his tortured face deepening. "She never told me who, but since she broke up with Sam, I suspected there was someone else. I just hope and pray she's all right." He stared at the floor, appearing lost and forlorn.

Chase's tone was soft with sympathy. "Did you update the BOLO for Reggie yet?"

Gus didn't bother to look up. "Yeah, a few minutes ago. I alerted the border patrol too, in case he heads for Canada. Now, I guess I need to add Wendy to the BOLO." Finally, he raised his head. "I won't be able to go with you on your search, Chase. I can't leave with Wendy missing."

"I understand."

"Make sure you coordinate with Clint Newman and the park service on the hunt."

"Will do."

Torn between helping Gus find Wendy and going with Chase to search for his fugitive, Jenny wrestled with what she should do. She'd made a commitment to Chase, but her heart was breaking for the deputy and Wendy. "I want to go with you, Gus."

He gave her a sad smile. "I know, but you're needed in the park. Besides, I'll have every lawman in the state looking for that no-good impostor before the day's out. Rest assured, we'll find him one way or another, and if he's hurt my baby girl, heaven help him."

CHAPTER SIXTEEN

JENNY SUPPRESSED A YAWN AS SHE tried to focus her bleary eyes on the computer screen at work. After she and Chase spent the previous night searching for any trace of Wendy and Reggie, Chase brought Jenny home at midnight. But her troubled thoughts kept her up.

First Billy.

Now Wendy.

What was happening to Eagle Valley?

The thought of Wendy on the run with that imposter tormented Jenny to no end. All she could do now was pray for God's protection and to bring her home safe and sound.

Now that Clint knew about Wendy and Reggie's disappearance, Clint's crankiness reached a whole new level. He and Gus were not only professional peers, they were old friends, and Wendy was like a niece to Clint.

Jenny finally mustered the courage to interrupt Clint in his office where he'd barricaded himself behind the door. First, she tried knocking.

No response.

She cracked the door open. "Clint, I need to speak with you."

He peered up from his computer screen. "What is it?"

She winced at the gruffness of his voice, but entered anyway, closing the door behind her. "Can you check with the other rangers to find out if anyone remembers seeing Billy Norton around Cascade Pass?"

"Why?"

"I saw his mother at church yesterday. She said Billy left for a camping trip in that area last Monday and hasn't returned."

"When did he say he'd be back?"

"That's the thing. He didn't give her an exact date. I stopped by the trailhead parking lot yesterday, and his pickup is still there."

"Why don't you see if he got a permit?"

"He didn't. I already checked."

Clint pushed away from his desk. "Great. If it's not one thing, it's another. Are you saying we have a missing hiker now?"

"I'm afraid so. I was going to hike there myself yesterday, but Chase wants me to wait until his search party is organized . . ." As soon as the words slipped out of her mouth, Jenny closed her eyes and winced.

"*Search party*? For what?"

She sighed. It was going to be a very long morning.

By the end of the day, Jenny needed a vacation. She'd told Clint about Chase's theory that the recent crimes might be connected to the man who killed Chase's partner, and the plan to conduct a search for him in the mountains.

Clint didn't take it well. In fact, he ordered her to close his door on her way out and not to disturb him for the rest of the day. He was so upset, she was surprised he hadn't fired her on the spot. She wouldn't have blamed him if he had.

She'd spent the rest of the morning and afternoon taking care of the administrative work at the rangers' office, a job Clint hated to do. Afterward, she drove into town to mail business letters on her way home.

As she left the post office, she spotted Lori and Adam on Main Street. Adam ran to her, lifting her spirits. She snatched him up in her arms until they were eye-to-eye.

"Where's the cubs?" he asked.

"They're in the back of my truck. You know, Adam, I'm planning to take them to a wildlife refuge where they can be raised in their natural habitat."

He pouted. "I want to keep them."

"I know, but this is what's best for them. God didn't create cougars to be raised by people. I don't want you getting too attached to them. Do you understand?"

He nodded with a sad expression. "Maybe I can visit them at the refuge."

"That's a great idea."

"Maybe Uncle Chase will take me there."

Lori touched Jenny's arm. "Speaking of Chase, he was gone before Joel and I got up this morning. He left us a note that said he was going to Seattle to pick up a friend at the airport and wouldn't be back until this afternoon."

Something caught Lori's eye. "Hey, that's him coming this way now."

Jenny turned her head to see.

"There's a woman with him."

Jenny spotted Chase crossing the street with an attractive blonde, dressed in a white, button-down shirt and black pants. She looked young, in her mid-twenties. They appeared deep in serious conversation as they headed her way.

Adam smiled and pointed in the direction of the young woman. "She's pretty."

The temptation to leave before they saw her crossed Jenny's mind, but she ignored it. She could handle this. After all, hadn't she told Chase to get back-up from the home office? Only she hadn't expected his back-up would be so young and pretty.

Chase strode over with the woman and greeted them with a friendly nod. "Hey, Lori. Jenny."

Adam squirmed in Jenny's arms. "I want to see Uncle Chase." He protested until she finally let him down.

The boy pointed at the young woman. "Who's that, Uncle Chase?"

Chase smiled. "This is Kate Phillips. Kate, I'd like you to meet Adam, Lori, and Jenny Snowfeather." He shifted to Lori. "I hope you got my note. Kate texted me late last night to tell me she was taking the red eye out this morning, so I went to pick her up in Seattle."

Kate extended a hand to Lori. "Nice to meet y'all."

Jenny raised a brow at Kate's charming Southern accent while she discreetly sized her up.

Fit and slender, with cropped, shoulder-length hair and a round, cherub face, Kate looked like she could be one of Wendy's classmates. Yet, despite her girlish appearance, her confident, street-smart manner seemed more like a cop.

Kate didn't fit at all into Jenny's preconceived notion of Southern girls with big hair and lots of makeup, who prided themselves on their looks. Her guileless, down-to-earth personality was instantly likable.

"Your son is adorable," Kate said to Jenny. "I had no idea Chase had a sister, much less a nephew."

Jenny and Lori exchanged glances.

"Adam is Lori's son," Jenny clarified, "and neither one of us are related to Chase."

"Adam calls me uncle, but I'm not really his uncle," Chase explained.

Kate laughed and sent Lori and Jenny a conspiring smile. "If he did have a sister, she'd disown him, don't you think?"

Jenny gave him a speculative glance. "Definitely."

Chase arched a brow at her remark. "Kate works with me back in Tennessee."

The news instantly set Jenny's mind at ease. At least someone from his home office had come to check up on the man. She should be happy about that. She decided to show more courtesy to Chase's colleague and put aside her previous reservations. "Are you a deputy marshal too, Kate?"

"Yeah." The blonde pulled her badge from her pocket and showed it to Jenny. "I finished my training a year ago, right after college. Chase has been mentoring me."

Jenny extended her hand. "Nice to meet you."

Kate returned a warm handshake. "Thanks. When Chase told

me his plan to conduct a manhunt in the mountains, I thought he was crazy, but now that I see how beautiful it is here, I'm kind of excited."

"A manhunt?" Lori cried.

Chase deftly herded the group toward the sweets shop. "Why don't we discuss this over ice cream?"

After purchasing their treats at the counter, he led them to a table in the back, far away from the other customers.

Lori took a seat directly across from him and leaned forward. Before Chase could taste his ice cream, she grilled him for answers. "Now what's this business about a manhunt?"

Adam looked up from his milkshake.

Jenny knew the determined expression on her friend's face. She wouldn't give up without an answer.

Chase raised his hand in retreat. "I should have told you and Joel about this sooner, Lori. I wasn't completely honest when I said I came out here for a vacation. I mean, that was partly true, but I came for another reason too."

He explained about Jim's murder and his theory that the recent crimes were all connected to the fugitive, who he believed was hiding out in the mountains.

Lori shuddered. "This has always been such a quiet, peaceful community. It's hard to believe someone like that would come here."

"That's why it's the perfect place. No one would suspect it."

Appearing somewhat mollified, Lori's features softened. "I guess I see your point, but you should have been honest with Joel from the beginning. He's your friend. He'll be disappointed that you kept something this important from him."

"I know. I'll tell him tonight at dinner. Now that Gus is on board, I'm working with the local authorities, but it's very important that no one else knows."

Jenny spoke up. "I told Clint today."

Chase's eyes widened. "How did he respond?"

"Let's just say I'm not expecting a pay raise anytime soon.

Have you talked to your supervisor yet?"

Kate, who had been listening, took a break from her hot fudge sundae. "I told Mack, our boss, about Chase's suspicions. That's why he sent me out here. Two local marshals will be coming tonight."

Jenny gave Chase a subtle smile. "Sounds like your boss has a lot of confidence in you."

"I'll say." Kate turned to Chase. "You should have seen the look on Mack's face when I told him I was afraid you'd want to stay here and never come back from your vacation. He wants you back to work ASAP, but first he expects you to assist in organizing this search, once he sorts it all out with the local authorities."

Chase's expression brightened a bit. "Maybe I still have a job after all."

Joel exploded at dinner that night. "Are you out of your mind, Jen? You're not going on a manhunt."

Jenny cringed as she sat next to Kate at the table. At least Adam wasn't there to hear Joel's rant. Lori had offered Adam's room to Kate for the night and dropped her son off at her parents' home before dinner.

For Kate's sake, Jenny tried to tamp down her brother's temper. "Calm down, Joel. Chase needs a guide, and I'm the logical choice. It's that simple. I'll be fine."

Chase, who was seated at the opposite end of the table from Joel, intervened. "I won't let anything happen to her."

Joel glared at him, clearly upset that he hadn't come forward with this sooner. "And why should I believe anything you say? Coming into our home, acting like my friend, so you could stake out the area to catch your fugitive."

Chase glanced down, his face penitent. "You're right. I didn't handle things as well as I should have." He peered up again. "But I am your friend. I didn't want to keep this from you."

Gripping his fork and knife, Joel sliced the steak that he'd grilled for dinner, his knife grating against his plate. "I'm not sure what to believe anymore."

Lori appealed to him in a persuasive tone. "Honey, I don't think Chase meant to be dishonest with us. But he didn't know how to tell us what was going on without compromising his mission."

"What mission? He didn't have a mission," Joel barked with a wad of meat in his cheek. "He's been here on independent ops. If he had alerted the authorities earlier, maybe Butch wouldn't have gotten shot."

"But he wasn't even sure if the escaped felon was here."

"Quit defending him, Lori. He not only kept things from us, but he lied to us about being on a camping trip in the mountains, when all the time he was here on a stakeout."

Chase lifted his hands from the table. "Technically, I didn't say I was going camping in the mountains . . . Look, I agree that I should have told you everything sooner, but I thought if I did, you'd want to get involved, and I couldn't let you do that. I couldn't put you and your family in danger."

Joel shifted his eyes to Jenny. "What do you have to say in his defense?"

Jenny drew back. "What is this, a trial?"

"I want to know what makes you think you can trust him."

Her gaze drifted to Chase's unguarded expression as she considered the question. During her time with him over the last three weeks, she'd come to admire his courage and dedication. But he was far from perfect. He still had serious issues where Russ was concerned. But who was she to judge him for that? Hadn't she kept a loaded gun in her nightstand every night since Chase told her Russ was his fugitive?

Her thoughts traveled back to the cougar hunt, the second shot echoed in her memory. "Because he saved my life."

Joel's brows lifted. "Oh, all right," he finally conceded. "If you and Lori think I should give Chase the benefit of the doubt,

I'll try."

"That means a lot to me," Chase said, sending Jenny an appreciative glance.

Joel shrugged. "Brothers in arms, and all that." He turned to Kate. "I'm sorry you had to hear all that. It's not every day I learn that a manhunt is being planned in my own backyard *and* my sister wants to join the war party."

The reality of Joel's words shot a cold chill up Jenny's spine. This was no longer a theory. It was real. Russ wasn't only a thief, he was a murderer now, and they were planning to hunt him down like that cougar.

Kate smiled. "It's okay."

Lori smoothly changed the subject. "How did you become a marshal, Kate?"

"I was living on the street when I met Jim Tucker, Chase's partner. He and his wife, Rose, were doing volunteer work at the shelter where I was staying, and we got to know each other there. They invited me to come and live with them, on the condition that I would go back to school. One thing led to another, and I became a marshal. It was a natural thing for me to do, I guess."

At the mention of his friend, sadness darkened Chase's eyes.

Jenny longed to reach across the table to touch him, but Kate was closer to him, and she knew his grief better than anyone.

Kate teared up. "There's no telling where I would be right now if it hadn't been for Jim."

Jenny marveled at how God had surrounded Chase with so many good people who cared about him. If only he could see God's hand in it too. Now she knew she needed to be on that manhunt, no matter how much he protested.

"I'm going with you, Chase," Joel uttered as he chewed on his dinner roll, drawing a stunned look from everyone at the table.

Chase gave him a humble smile. "That means a lot to me, buddy, but I can't let you do that. You have a family to think of, and this is a dangerous mission."

"We've been on dangerous missions together before, remember?"

Jenny knew he was referring to their time fighting overseas, but Chase was right. Things were different now. Joel needed to think of his family.

"True," Chase replied, "but we didn't have a choice then. Now you do. I couldn't sleep nights knowing I was putting your life in danger with Lori and Adam waiting at home for you to return."

Jenny spoke up. "That's why I'm the perfect choice. I've got no husband or kids, only my animals. I know you'll take good care of them, won't you?" She waited for Lori and Joel's confirmation.

Her brother finally gave a slow nod. "We'll look after them, Jen, but are you really sure you want to do this?"

"Positive. In fact, I've made a list of essential items we need to pack for the trip." She handed the list to Kate.

Kate scanned it and smiled. "Nice. We're lucky to have someone with your expertise onboard."

Chase stared at Jenny, his creased brow shadowing his dark eyes. He turned back to cutting the remaining steak on his plate with clean, sharp strokes. Then he put his knife down and looked up. "Joel, there's something else you should know."

Joel blew out a big breath. "Uh-oh. Something tells me I'm not going to like this."

Jenny shook her head, pleading with Chase not to tell him.

"It's about the fugitive," Chase continued, ignoring her plea. "You knew him as Russ Webb."

Joel's jaw dropped. He stared at Chase as if he didn't recognize him. "You mean, all this time, you've known Webb was in the area, and you didn't bother to tell me?"

Lori tried to intercede. "Joel . . ."

Jenny sighed. "He didn't tell you because he knew you'd react like this."

Joel's eyes narrowed as he shifted to her. "And how long have you known?"

She cleared her throat. "Since last Tuesday."

"And you still want to go on this manhunt?"

"Yes."

Her brother rolled his eyes and focused back on Chase. "What's your plan, Matthews?"

The marshal in Chase took over. "The thefts in the backcountry are mostly near the Cascade Pass area of the park. That's also where my SUV was discovered by Dylan. If Webb is the one doing all this, he's probably hiding out somewhere in that region. What we need to do is scout out the area."

Jenny nodded in agreement. "The nearest place is up on Sahale Mountain. Clint lent me the key to the lookout tower."

A flicker of doubt crossed Joel's face. "That's a long, strenuous climb in the backcountry." He turned to Chase. "Are you up for that kind of punishment?"

Chase shifted to Kate to confirm her readiness.

She responded with a firm nod.

Satisfied, he turned back to Joel. "We're not exactly couch potatoes, you know. We spend a lot of time chasing down felons."

Joel addressed Kate. "I didn't mean to imply that you weren't physically fit. But it takes a certain kind of stamina to hike continuously in higher altitudes. The only way to get there is by foot. There are places too steep and wooded for a chopper to reach. If you get into trouble, help could take hours or days to arrive. You'll be stuck."

She shrugged. "Whatever it takes."

"That's why we're bringing radios and firearms with us," Chase said. "We've all been certified in CPR and first aid too."

"You're not the only one putting yourself at risk, Chase. You'll have my sister with you, and as much of a pain as she can be, Lori and I would still like her back in one piece."

Jenny started to argue. "Joel—"

Chase lifted his hand. "It's okay, Jen." He faced her brother. "You have my solemn word that I'll have Jenny back home safe and sound within a week, if my life depends on it."

The sobriety in his voice made Jenny's blood run cold. She wished he hadn't made the promise. Whatever happened to her was in God's hands, not his.

After dinner, Jenny quickly excused herself to go home. They would all be leaving before dawn, and she still had to pack.

Joel and Lori walked her to the door. Lori gave her a big hug, bordering on tears. "I'll be praying for you. In fact, I'll call the pastor and get the entire church praying for you."

Jenny smiled, touched by Lori's support. "Thank you, Lori. That's why I can go with confidence. Kiss Adam for me and tell him to take good care of the cubs and Sage and Lucy until I get back."

"What about Fred and Ginger?" Lori asked.

"I'm taking them with me."

Chase was standing nearby. "Uh, I don't think that's such a good idea. They aren't trained for manhunts. They could give us away."

"But they're excellent trackers. You saw that with the cougar."

Joel chimed in. "I'd feel better if she brought the dogs with her. They're loyal to her and could provide a degree of protection." He turned to Jenny. "But pets aren't allowed on those trails."

"I know, but Clint got special permission from the park management because the dogs can help us track Russ and Billy. I'll keep an eye on them so they don't harm any animals or terrain."

Chase finally relented, but his frown made it clear he wasn't thrilled.

When Jenny turned to say goodbye to Joel, he gave her a huge bear hug, lifting her off the ground like their father used to. When he set her back down, she wiped a tear from her eye, laughing at herself for being such an emotional mess.

Joel, misty-eyed too, laughed with her.

She took a key from her pocket and handed it to him. "Here's the key to my trailer. I'll leave instructions on the kitchen table for how to feed my animals." She took a deep breath. "Well, looks like everything's settled now."

"You're sure about this?"

"Absolutely." She punched Joel lightly on his arm. "Don't worry about me, big brother. Just take good care of my pets."

Chase and Kate were behind her when Jenny turned to leave. "I'll see you both in the morning, bright and early." With a final wave, Jenny went outside to her pickup.

As she opened the driver side door, Chase appeared at her side. "Jen . . ." The crease on his brow had deepened.

"What is it?"

He met her questioning gaze with stark directness. "I don't think you should come with us."

"Well, that's too bad, because you don't have a choice. You can't go into those mountains without a guide."

"But if Russ knows you're with us, he'll try to use you to get to me."

"Then we'll have to take that chance, won't we?" His troubled expression convicted her to go easier on him. "Look, I'm not afraid of Russ. There's nothing more he can do to me. Don't you see? This is the only way I can be free of him for good." She tried to reassure him with a smile. "Besides, I know you won't let him get anywhere near me."

CHAPTER SEVENTEEN

By FOUR THE NEXT MORNING, JENNY and her dogs had already arrived at the Cascade Pass trailhead. She grabbed her flashlight before jumping out of her pickup and clicked it on as she came around to the truck bed. Lowering the tailgate, she set her restless dogs free, then hauled out her backcountry pack, nearly as tall and heavy as herself.

The beam of her flashlight illuminated Billy's pickup still parked in the lot. Jenny walked over to the passenger side to take one more look. She pulled on the handle. Unlocked. She opened it and shined the light inside. Seeing Billy's worn-out sneakers strewn on the floor of the passenger side gave her an idea. She grabbed one of them and took it with her.

She'd barely finished stuffing the shoe in her backpack when Chase and Kate drove up.

Chase hopped out of the Mustang and strode over.

The Kevlar vest covering his chest reminded Jenny of the danger that lurked on this search. The first rays of dawn revealed his bloodshot eyes under the bill of his marshal cap. He obviously hadn't slept much either. Intensity hardened his handsome features.

Was he ready to face the man who murdered his friend in cold blood?

Was she?

When Chase's gaze met hers, his expression softened. He glanced at the sky, colored with faint streaks of sunrise. "Whose idea was it to come at this crazy hour?"

"Yours."

"Oh. Right." A slight grin melted the remaining frost from his face, and he winked at her.

"The good thing about being this far north is that the sun rises early and sets late. We'll have plenty of daylight to search the area." Jenny switched off her flashlight and shifted to Kate, who had joined them. "Good morning. Are you ready for the hike?"

Kate shrugged. "Yeah, but with all the stuff I brought, my pack weighs more than I do."

A black SUV pulled in and parked. Two men jumped out.

Fred and Ginger barked at the strangers.

Jenny hushed her dogs as she went to meet them.

Like Chase and Kate, the two marshals were dressed in black pants and T-shirts with bulletproof vests worn under sleeveless outer vests with the words 'U.S. Marshal' printed in large, white letters. They eyed the dogs cautiously.

The younger of the two pointed to her pets. "Are those wolves?"

Jenny gave him a reassuring grin. "Huskies, and they won't hurt you. They're coming with us to help track the fugitive."

The men exchanged doubtful glances.

Kate strode up to them. "I'm Kate. We spoke on the phone."

After Kate shook hands with the two men, they relaxed their stance and refocused on Jenny's uniform.

Jenny glanced down at her muted olive-colored shirt and darker shorts, which stood out among the marshals' black clothing. "I'm Jenny. Your guide."

Kate introduced the two men to Jenny and Chase as Buck Taylor and John Crawford.

Buck, the young one with brown hair in a buzz cut similar to the Marines, shook Jenny's hand, grinning with a cocky expression. "Have you ever captured a fugitive before? It's a bit more demanding than a stroll in the park."

Placing her hands on her hips, Jenny returned a confident smile. "I think I'm up to the challenge."

John pushed Buck out of the way and sent him a hard stare. "Ignore him," he said to Jenny. "Buck doesn't get out much."

Jenny had a feeling Buck might need someone to keep him in line now and then. Having a more experienced marshal like John along was a good thing.

Chase addressed John. "I assume you're the one in charge of the search."

"Negative. We've been told it's you."

Chase shot Kate a confused look. "I thought I was only to help to organize it."

She swiveled toward him, grinning. "Congratulations, Chase. Your vacation is officially over."

The dogs wandered around the parking lot sniffing, while John and Buck unloaded their gear from their SUV and Chase and Kate hauled their packs from Chase's Mustang.

Jenny joined the others, her pack in tow. "Looks like you all came prepared with good backcountry gear."

"Kate emailed us a list of things to bring before we left," John said. "We already had most of the stuff at home. The rest I borrowed."

"Good." She pulled out a slip of paper from her back pocket. "I brought a checklist to make sure we have everything."

Chase moved behind her and peered over her shoulder at the list. While the others were busy checking out their new GPS devices, he whispered in her ear. "Are you sure you still want to do this?"

She glanced at him from the corner of her eye. "I'm not backing out. You're not the only one who wants to see Russ brought to justice. I know what he's capable of, and I couldn't live with myself if I didn't do everything in my power to keep him from hurting someone else."

He nodded, appearing satisfied with her answer. Then he addressed the group. "Listen up. Give a shout if you have the items as Jenny reads off the list."

After everything was accounted for, Jenny removed four electronic devices from her pack. "Here. Each of you take one of these, and I'll show you how to strap it on."

Kate studied it. "We already have GPS devices."

"It's not only a GPS. It's an avalanche beacon. I borrowed them from the search and rescue team."

John eyed her with skepticism. "Are avalanches really a threat this time of year?"

"We're going to be climbing in the upper elevations where there is still quite a bit of snow. I checked the forecast this morning, and it's calling for unusually warm weather starting today for the entire week."

Confusion appeared on Buck's face. "A heat wave? Up here?"

Chase frowned. "That will make the avalanche risk go up, won't it?"

Pleased that he remembered, she grinned. "That's right. That's why when we get to the heavy snowpack areas, we'll need to have the beacons on us, just in case."

After she had briefed them all on how to strap the beacons on, she called Fred and Ginger over while the group prepared to leave.

Chase seemed as antsy as her dogs.

The adrenaline rush had sparked a sense of excitement and anticipation in her too. She loved adventure and any excuse to go camping and hiking, but it seemed wrong to be so psyched about a manhunt. Perhaps, a part of her wanted to catch Russ and see justice done as much as Chase.

After helping Kate hoist her pack over her shoulders, Chase came to help Jenny with hers.

She glanced his way. "I hope your team is ready for this. It's not for fair-weather campers, you know."

"They'll be fine. They can pull their weight in gold. By the way, where's your body armor?"

"In my pack. I didn't think I'd need it so soon."

He set the pack on the ground. "Tell you what, I'll put on the beacon if you wear your vest."

She spun around and noted the serious glint in his eye. As much as she wanted to delay wearing the vest on such a warm day, she knew he wouldn't back down. "I guess I can't argue with that." She retrieved it from her pack and put it on.

He lifted her pack behind her so she could slip her arms through the straps and ease it over her shoulders. She turned and faced him. For a brief moment, they stared at each other in mutual understanding and shared conviction—to find Russ at all costs.

He gave her a nod of approval. "Take the lead, Ranger. We'll fall in behind you."

She smiled and about-faced, then started up the trail to Cascade Pass. Despite the adrenaline rush, she hiked at a moderate clip with her dogs at her heels and the marshals close behind. They could be gone for days so they needed to pace themselves.

With the trail closed, they had it all to themselves. But it felt strange absent the usual tourists and hikers. In the secluded forest, ominous noises seemed amplified. Trees swayed in the breeze, whispering secrets, while crows and jays mocked the group in harsh tones as they climbed through the woods on endless switchbacks.

By mid-morning they'd reached the historic pass once traveled by Native Americans and then miners. The snow-laden, craggy ridges of Mt. Johannesburg dominated the landscape as they traversed the rugged trail to an elevation of 5,400 feet.

The periodic crack and thunder of distant avalanches served as constant reminders of the danger lurking in the breathtakingly beautiful wilderness, surrounded by majestic mountains over 7,000 feet high.

From Cascade Pass, Jenny led them to Doubtful Lake on the way to Sahale Arm, a long ridge below Sahale Peak. She hoped Billy might have taken the popular trail. When they reached the blue body of water in a crater-like bowl, they stopped to look around.

Jenny retrieved Billy's shoe from her pack and called Fred and Ginger over to get his scent. "Go find him."

Her dogs sniffed the ground for a few minutes but found nothing.

Jenny and the others circled the area, calling Billy's name.

Growing worried and frustrated after searching the entire place without success, Jenny finally rejoined the others at the trail.

Chase strode up. "Find anything?"

"No. You?"

He shook his head. "We've covered every inch without a trace. If Billy was here, he's not now."

She glanced around one last time. Without the usual number of hikers and backpackers, the place looked beautiful yet forbidden. An uneasy feeling hovered over her.

Before she returned Billy's shoe to her backpack, she noticed its size and shape, smaller and wider than the second set of footprints under her bedroom window that matched the mysterious ones in the woods.

As she led the group up the strenuous climb to Sahale Arm, they made good time. Considering none of the marshals were seasoned hikers, they proved to be in good physical condition, able to acclimate to the high elevation and sure-footed enough to navigate the treacherous parts of the trail covered in snow and ice.

By noon, Chase jogged up to her. "Hold up. I think we should stop for lunch somewhere." He gestured back in Kate's direction, and Jenny saw that she had fallen behind.

"There's a meadow ahead. It'll be a good place to take a break and rest."

She and Chase resumed climbing together.

"How many times have you been here?" he asked.

"A few. There's an old lookout tower where we can camp for the night. We should make it easily before dark."

When they finally reached the stopping point for lunch, Chase looked around in awe. "This is amazing," he said as he gazed at the giant, snow-covered crest of Sahale Peak above and

Doubtful Lake below.

Jenny had led them to a small alpine meadow. Even in full sun, patches of snow remained amid the splendor of avalanche lilies, dainty bluebells, Indian paintbrush, and columbine. An alpine stream formed by glacial melt snaked through the lush, green grass that swayed in the mountain breeze like tiny dancers in a choreographed ballet.

The group followed Jenny to an even better vantage of the neighboring snow-covered pinnacles of Magic Mountain, Mix-Up Peak, and Cascade Peak, which appeared so close you could reach out and touch them. The group quickly stripped off their heavy packs, giving their tired muscles a break.

Placing her hands on her hips, Jenny arched and stretched her back as she stared at the splendid scenery. Her legs ached a little, and her clothes were damp with perspiration, but she had never felt more alive.

She looked at Chase as he set his pack on the ground beside hers. The hair on the back of his neck was damp, and his skin flushed from the vigorous hike. Her gaze wandered over his athletic arms and legs. She sensed the understated strength in them. Not once had he asked her to stop for him. Not once had he complained.

"Spectacular," he exclaimed as they gazed at the mountains and valleys in silence. He turned in her direction. "What are you thinking?"

She smiled. "You'll laugh if I tell you."

"Moi?" He pointed to himself, pretending he was deeply wounded. "Try me."

She considered his challenge. A stray lock of hair blew in her face, and he swept it back behind her ear. It was a simple gesture, but his closeness generated feelings that were anything but simple.

"I'm waiting," he said softly.

"I was thinking that it's hard to imagine a place more peaceful or beautiful than this."

"Not even heaven?"

"Goes to show the limits of my imagination. I'm sure heaven will be even more magnificent." She smiled at him for a moment then turned more serious. "Assuming Russ is still around, how do you plan to catch him?"

"I'm working on that. By the way, what arrangements did you make with Clint when you told him you were coming with us?"

"I told him I'd check in regularly and let him know if we needed assistance. He said he'd tell the other rangers and search and rescue teams to watch for anything suspicious too."

He nodded. "I think you should check in with Clint now."

"Okay. I'll use the short-wave radio. There's no cell service up here."

A loud crack echoed in the distance.

Chase and Jenny joined the others near the ridge.

More strange noises thundered in the mountains.

Chase frowned. "It sounds like avalanches are all around us."

Jenny understood his concern. "All that snow from last winter with the wild weather we've had lately is a deadly combination."

Kate, who was standing close by, overheard them. "Are we in danger?"

"No. Not here. But there are places we should avoid. If we stick to the main trails, we'll be fine."

"I'm so glad you came with us," Kate said, her expression wan. "This isn't exactly my turf."

Jenny gave the young marshal an encouraging smile and patted her shoulder. "You're doing great."

While the others caught their breath and re-hydrated, Jenny spotted a boulder and took a seat, keeping a watchful eye on Fred and Ginger, who roamed around sniffing.

Still no trace of Billy. When she radioed Clint, he had no news on Wendy or Billy. He gave her a weather report and told her the status of the rivers and bridges in the area. She quickly updated him on their progress and signed off.

Her stomach growled from burning so many calories on the hike. She opened her pack and found a bag of trail mix and her water bottle.

Kate staggered over and sat beside her with a weary sigh. "I hope the rest of this trail is downhill from here."

"I'm afraid we still have more climbing to do, but today is the worst of it."

Pulling off her hiking boots, Kate groaned. "Maybe I should have worn my running shoes instead of these."

Jenny's gaze wandered to Chase who was talking to John in the distance. Kate's voice interrupted her thoughts.

"You know, Chase has been through a lot. Jim's death really hit him hard."

Jenny turned to her. "You too, I imagine."

The young woman nodded as she massaged her sore feet. "Yeah. Jim was like a father to me."

"Do you think it was a good idea coming here?" Jenny asked. "It seems a little risky."

"When you're a marshal, there's not much about our work that isn't risky, but the key to catching an escaped felon is the element of surprise. It's hard to have everything planned to the last detail, especially when you never know where they are. You have to be creative, trust your instincts, and expect the unexpected."

Jenny couldn't help but grin at the irony. "Sounds a lot like being a ranger."

Kate laughed, but her smile soon faded. "Chase is one of the smartest marshals there is. He thinks things through before taking action."

"You two must have grown close after Jim's death."

Kate eyed her with the shrewdness of a woman twice her age. "We're friends. That's all. There's nothing romantic between us, Jenny. He's like a brother to me."

"I didn't mean to imply that . . ."

"It's okay. I can sense the love in the air."

Jenny shook her head, despite the blood-rush to her face. "That's ridiculous."

"Why? Isn't Chase good enough?"

"I didn't say he wasn't—"

"Then why deny it? It's obvious you're both crazy about each other. The problem is you're both too stubborn and married to your careers to make room for anyone else."

Jenny was speechless. Who knew this young street-wise woman could be so perceptive when it came to people and matters of the heart?

By five that evening, Jenny, flanked by Fred and Ginger, made it to their destination, the lookout tower. At over 7,000 feet, the old, one-room cabin seated high atop a granite boulder pile, provided a stunning view of the entire range.

Chase had kept pace with her but lagged back as they scaled the last challenging rise of the mountain to stay with the others who fell behind.

After climbing the rocky steps to the tower, Jenny freed herself of the backpack and dropped it by the door. Her dogs roamed the granite pile while she unlocked the padlock to the cabin door with the key Clint had given her.

Inside, the place looked like an old wooden box furnished with two twin-size beds, a small table and a couple of chairs. An antique wood stove filled the center of the room, and large windows on all four sides provided spectacular, panoramic views. The rusted telescope bolted near the western window harkened back to the days when the cabin was used to spot wildfires.

Not bothering to close the door, Jenny dragged her pack to one of the chairs and sat. She unzipped a pocket and felt for the familiar rectangular shape of her small, leather-bound Bible. When she took it out, it fell open to Psalm 87:1.

He has set His foundation on the holy mountain.

A sound at the door caused her to look up.

Chase stood at the open door. His brown eyes were bright with excitement. "Look at that view!" When he entered the room, he saw the open Bible in her hands and paused. "Oh, sorry for interrupting."

"It's okay."

He gravitated to the window for a closer look at the enormous Cascade Mountains.

Jenny laid the Bible on the table and joined him there. She pointed out all the points of interest, including the lofty, snowy crests of Forbidden Peak, Glacier Peak, and even Eldorado Peak, in the distance.

"Amazing," he said in a reverent whisper.

She smiled, pleased he shared her appreciation of the awesome beauty of this special place.

He stared a moment longer and then turned to her. "Does anyone use this tower to watch for fires anymore?"

"No. There are better ways to track forest fires now through modern surveillance devices like satellites and helicopters. The cabin is a relic of the past."

"Have you stayed here before?" The light from the window reflected in his curious eyes.

"No, but I've always wanted to."

"It was good of Clint to give you the key."

"Yes. I wish I had told him about Russ earlier. Yesterday, when I told him, he wasn't happy. I dumped a lot on him before I left. Billy's disappearance. This search. And he's worried about Wendy too. He and Gus are old friends."

"I didn't know." Compassion resonated in his voice.

"At least he sounded a little better on the radio when I spoke to him today."

Chase gave her an earnest look. "We couldn't do this without you, Jen. I know it's put you in a bad position with Clint and your brother."

"They'll get over it," she said with a dismissive wave. "Besides, I want to find Billy."

He gently brushed her face with his fingers, softly tracing the outline of her cheek. "Jen, I . . ."

Buck burst into the cabin. "Awesome!" He fell into one of the twin beds and bounced on it, oblivious that he'd intruded on a private moment. "This bed is mine."

Chase eyed him harshly. "The men are sleeping outside in our tents, Buck. The women are staying here tonight."

Jenny turned from the window. "That's not fair, Chase."

"I agree," Buck seconded. "John and I will stay here, and the rest of you can camp in your tents." He fell back against the mattress with his hands behind his head, until Chase's unrelenting stare finally registered. "After that brutal hike we had today, you're going to make me sleep on the cold, hard ground?"

"Yep," Chase replied.

Jenny glanced down, hiding a grin.

"Heartless." Buck pushed himself up from the bed. "I guess I know when I'm not wanted."

After he left, Chase shook his head and chuckled. "Don't worry about Buck. He still has some growing up to do." Chase faced her again. "Now, where were we?"

His brilliant smile made her forget Buck's antics.

Kate appeared at the door, toting her pack. "I hear we're going to be roomies—oh, am I interrupting something?"

Chase sighed and slumped his shoulders, drawing a laugh from Jenny. He gestured to Kate. "Come on in. I need to go down and help set up camp anyway."

Jenny smiled as she watched him leave.

"Which bed is yours?"

Jenny turned around. "Take whichever one you'd like."

Kate shrugged. "I'm not that picky." She pointed to the one closest. "I'll take this one." She lugged her pack to it and sat on the mattress. "Man, it feels so good to sit on something soft. You know, I don't think Buck is too happy with Chase. I think he might be jealous."

"Of what?"

"In case you haven't noticed, Chase isn't the only one who has his eye on you."

Jenny laughed. "Right."

"Buck's too young for you anyway."

Jenny faked an indignant look. "So you want him all to yourself, huh?"

"Well, he is pretty cute."

"And a little immature."

Kate giggled.

Jenny saw the young woman hidden behind her tough, street-wise facade. Her youthful laughter reminded Jenny of Wendy, and a pang of sadness plucked her heart. The thought of her friend with that scoundrel, Reggie, made her sick to her stomach.

Kate unzipped a pocket in her pack and pulled out her water bottle. "You're right about Buck, but he has good qualities too."

"Like what?"

"Well, he doesn't look down on me because I'm a girl. He treats me like one of the guys. That's more than I can say for most of the men I've known, except, of course, Chase and Jim…" She reached for the book on the nearby table. "Nice Bible. Do you mind?"

"No. Help yourself."

Kate gently thumbed through the pages. "This reminds me of the one Jim gave me."

A wistful smile came to Jenny's lips. "My father gave that one to me."

"Jim used to read the Bible all the time, but I didn't want any part of it at first."

"Why not?"

Kate drew in a deep breath. "Because before I met Jim and Rose, I lived on the streets and did some pretty bad things to survive. I did what I had to do under the circumstances, but I didn't think God could ever forgive me. It was Jim who helped me understand that God's mercy and grace can restore anyone, no matter what they've done."

A deep sense of compassion and concern for Kate flooded Jenny's heart at the toll it must have taken when her foster father, Jim, was murdered. After all, he'd taken her in and raised her as his own daughter.

Then along came Russ to ruin everyone's life once again. How many other lives had he ruined? She still had trouble trying to reconcile the cruel, evil person they were looking for with the charming, handsome man she'd fallen so deeply for as a young woman.

Buck burst into the room again. "Hey, are you two coming or what? We're waiting for you so we can eat." The aroma of stew simmering below wafted to the tower and triggered hunger pangs in Jenny's belly.

Chase was busy stirring a simmering pot on a portable stove when the women joined them. He eyed the small canister Jenny carried with her. "What's that?"

She set it on the ground. "A bear-proof trash can."

He stared at the cylindrical object. "It's not very big."

"I brought an extra one too."

"Guess we should ration the food, and the trash."

Buck interrupted them. "Are we gonna talk or are we gonna eat?"

"Cool your jets, Buck, or you won't get anything." Chase whisked the stew one last time and filled a bowl for Jenny. He did the same for Kate. After everyone else had theirs, he served himself and joined Jenny, who was seated cross-legged on the ground with the rest of the group.

Buck and John didn't waste any time devouring their meal, while Jenny bowed her head with Kate and said a silent prayer before eating. After they'd finished, Jenny looked up and caught Buck and John watching them. The two marshals swapped awkward looks, shrugged to themselves, and resumed eating.

Chase, on the other hand, stared at the ground, waiting patiently until Jenny and Kate were ready to eat.

Despite being freeze-dried, the stew was hearty enough to squelch their appetites, and for the next few minutes, the group ate in silence, relishing the hot meal.

After dinner, Jenny moved to get up.

Chase touched her arm. "Where are you going?"

"It's cold. I'm going to get my sweatshirt."

"Wait. I'll save you the trip." He jumped up and disappeared into his small tent, returning with a bright orange University of Tennessee sweatshirt and his black marshal jacket.

He handed her the sweatshirt. "Here, put this on. It's warmer than the jacket."

"Thanks," she said. After pulling it over her head and tugging at the waist and sleeves, it hung on her like a gunny sack. The bright orange color made her chuckle. "Are you sure I won't give away our position, wearing this? We might as well shoot a flare in the sky."

The group relaxed in a camp circle but skipped the roaring fire that could give them away. The stars and moon, however, illuminated the camp in silvery twilight.

Fred and Ginger rested contentedly beside Jenny and Chase as the marshals shared exaggerated stories of their adventures and misadventures. The oversized sweatshirt kept Jenny warm as she listened to their tall tales. John had more stories than the rest since he'd been a marshal longer. A natural storyteller, he embellished each story with descriptive details and exciting suspense.

After a while, he turned to Jenny. "I bet you've got a few ranger stories. Why don't you share them with us?"

"Oh, I don't know."

"Come on, Jen. I'd like to hear your exploits too." The daring glint in Chase's eye made it impossible for her to refuse.

"Well, okay, I do have one story. It was a couple of years ago when the forest fires ravaged the park. The fires drove the animals out of their natural habitat, and they were desperate for food.

"I got an emergency call about a bear invading a campsite. The smell of bacon cooking that morning had drawn him out, and he was starving. By the time I arrived, he was attacking a tent with a family inside. They were yelling and screaming for help.

"My partner and I shouted at the bear, hoping to distract it and scare him off. We finally got his attention, but instead of running away, he came after us."

She scanned the group's riveted faces. "No matter what you think, you can't outrun a bear. We had to decide real fast whether to shoot him or use bear spray and hope it would scare him away. Hank, my partner, tried the spray but missed and that made the bear even angrier. It swung at me with his paw and knocked me to the ground. My gun went flying, but I was still conscious. I rolled up in a ball and played dead, hoping he'd lose interest in me. Otherwise, I was as good as dead.

"Then he went after Hank, who wasn't a very good aim." The memory brought a rueful smile to her lips. "Hank shot him once in the shoulder. That riled the bear even more, and he reared back to attack. I don't know how, but somehow I managed to crawl to my gun and shoot the bear right before it charged Hank."

Kate's eyes widened in amazement. "Did you kill him?"

Jenny sighed with a pained expression. "Yeah."

Fred raised his head for a moment and whimpered.

Buck eyed her with skepticism. "You made that story up, right?"

"No, it's all true." She removed Chase's sweatshirt and tugged her collar away from her neck enough for them to see the faint, talon-like scars on the back of her shoulder.

The group stared in stunned horror. Except for Chase, who gazed at her with admiration. "You actually killed a bear."

"I had no choice. He would have killed my partner." She pulled the sweatshirt back on.

"Like the cougar."

The meaning of his words sunk in. She peered back at him with a reluctant nod. "Yeah, like the cougar."

Jenny noticed the other three were now staring at her and Chase. "Bears are not man killers by nature. That one was starving, and he smelled food. His instincts took over. Under different circumstances, he wouldn't have been so aggressive. We don't kill people for being hungry."

Buck raised a finger. "We kill 'em for murdering somebody, though."

"Well, since bears don't know any better, and people do, we shouldn't tempt them." She pointed to the small metal can she'd brought with her. "That's why we'll store our trash in the canister so the bears won't smell it and come into camp."

Buck pulled out a small spray vile from his pocket. "I brought this along. It's supposed to work on bears."

"Give me that." Chase snatched it from him. "If anyone's going to use mace on a bear, it should be Jenny." He handed it over to her.

"Hey, that's mine!" Buck protested. "Guess I'll have to use my gun instead."

"I doubt we'll need either one, but if we do, I have real bear spray in my backpack." Jenny inspected the small bottle and shook her head. "I'm afraid you got scammed, Buck. This stuff might put you or me out of commission for a little while, but it's not strong enough for a full-grown bear."

Chase and John erupted in laughter at Buck, while Buck shrugged it off with a sheepish grin.

Jenny held the bottle up. "Do you want this back, Buck?"

"Nah, you keep it. You may have to use it on Chase, if he gets too aggressive."

Chase chuckled. "Very funny. But she'd need the bear-sized bottle to stop me."

"Whoo-hoo! You two sound like a couple of roosters sparring," John hollered.

Jenny slipped Buck's mace in the pocket of her shorts.

Kate ignored the men and turned to her. "Are there many bears around here?"

"They're all over the park, but if we leave them alone, they'll leave us alone."

Buck grinned at Kate. "Don't worry, I'll protect you."

Kate's tough, street-kid facade took over. "How about I use that mace on you?"

Jenny sensed Chase's stare and glanced at him.

He smiled with his brow arched. "You and Kate are a lot alike."

Despite his joking, the truth in his observation made Jenny laugh. "I'll take that as a compliment." Though she couldn't explain it, she felt a certain connection with Kate. Maybe it was their independent spirit, or maybe it was because they'd both lost their fathers recently. Chase had obviously noticed it too.

Jenny yawned. The long day had finally caught up with her. "Chase, what is your plan for tomorrow?"

"Good question." He promptly came to his feet and headed for his tent. When he returned, he unfurled a large map of the park and laid it out on the ground. John brought a flashlight over so they could read it.

Chase drew an imaginary ring on the map. "Because of the thefts, I think Webb has got to be somewhere in this vicinity."

Jenny looked at him. "If Russ is hiding out and moving on foot, he won't summit the mountains because of the snow. It's too steep and treacherous to cross without special gear. That leaves the Horseshoe Basin toward Stehekin, but that's too much territory for us to cover alone."

"I've been thinking about that, but I don't want to call in more troops until we have evidence that he's here. Any chance your dogs could track him?"

"Maybe, but it would be better if they had his scent. Too bad we don't have anything of his we could use."

He acknowledged her comment with a nod and glanced at the group. "First thing tomorrow morning, we'll head down the pass to the Stehekin River. We better head for bed. We have another long day ahead of us."

Jenny illuminated her watch with her flashlight. She groaned at the time. Four a.m. already. After the long day of strenuous hiking, she should be fast asleep right now, but a nightmare woke her early.

The strange dream haunted her still as she recalled the part where she was hiking in the woods and came to a fork in the trail. Chase stood on the right and Russ on the left, each of them urging her to go with him. The sight of Russ sent her flying into Chase's outstretched arms.

Then Chase vanished.

Jenny found herself alone, looking down the precipice of a giant waterfall where the trail dead-ended. Trapped against the rushing water, she heard footsteps from behind. She spun around and saw Russ's scornful face.

In an evil, mocking tone, he taunted her. "You'll never be rid of me, Jenny-girl. Not even in your dreams."

She drew her gun as he edged closer. "Stay away!"

Like a hungry grizzly, he cornered her against the rushing waters near the falls, taking pleasure in her torment. "It's only you and me. No one can save you now." His dark predator eyes burned with malice as he moved in for the kill. "It's time to finish what we started."

With trembling hands, she closed her eyes and squeezed the trigger . . .

A cold chill shook Jenny back to reality. She clutched her sleeping bag and pulled it to her chin. The feel of Chase's warm, soft sweatshirt with his lingering scent calmed her as she listened to the sound of Kate's steady breathing and the occasional stirring of Fred and Ginger sleeping on the floor nearby.

It was only a dream, she told herself, touching the cross her father had given her. Light from the stars and moon flickered through the large window by Jenny's bed. She thought of home and Lori, Joel and Adam, and asked God to bless and watch over them. She stared into the starlit sky and uttered a prayer for Chase too.

When she'd finished, an inner voice prompted. *What about your enemy, Jenny? Don't you have a prayer for him?*

She knew that voice. Deep down, a part of her couldn't forgive Russ for how he'd used her and broken her heart at such a young age. She'd become like Chase, letting past hurts become an obsession and an obstacle to happiness. A deep sadness and remorse plagued her soul at how miserably she'd failed to practice what she professed.

"God, I can't do this without you." Straining against her pride, she managed a prayer for Russ.

Tears flowed from pain and release, like removing a bullet from a festering wound.

CHAPTER EIGHTEEN

"Jenny, wake up!" Kate's voice echoed in the haze of sleep.

Jenny turned over in bed, trying to ignore it, but Kate tugged her arm until she finally gave in and opened her eyes.

"Come on, Jenny. It's five-thirty. The men are already packed and ready to go."

Jenny sat up and rubbed her eyes as the grogginess cleared. "Why didn't you wake me sooner?"

"I tried, but you were dead to the world."

Jenny did a quick scan of the cabin, then unzipped her sleeping bag and jumped out of bed. "Where are Fred and Ginger?"

"Relax. I let them out and fed them already." Kate gave her the once-over. "Still wearing his shirt, huh?"

Jenny glanced down at the orange sweatshirt that hung over her fleece pants. She softened her tone. "Sorry, I snapped at you. Thanks for taking care of my dogs."

"It's okay." Kate headed to the door. "I'll meet you outside."

Jenny changed into her ranger uniform and re-packed in record time. After locking up, she scrambled down the boulders with her backpack, relieved to see the coffee pot still on the small camp stove. She filled her cup and started to drink it, letting out a squeal as it burned her tongue.

"Take it easy. We're not in that much of a hurry."

At the sound of Chase's voice, Jenny turned her head. "Sorry I'm late." Her tongue still throbbed, but she put on a pleasant face.

Chase stared at her, suppressing a grin.

She ran a hand through her hair and realized, in her haste,

she'd forgotten to brush it. "That bad, huh?"

"No, but then you always look good to me."

She blushed at his compliment. In his marshal's jacket with a faint shadow of a beard on his face, he didn't look half-bad either. Her gaze traveled to his eyes, noticing they were hooded and red. "Looks like I'm not the only one running on empty."

Buck came over to refill his cup. He did a double-take at Jenny. "Whoa. What happened to you? A bird could nest in that hair."

"Okay, that's it." She set her coffee mug on a nearby rock and planted her hands on her hips. "The next person who says anything about how I look this morning is going to get punched in the nose."

Buck and Chase swapped shrugs. Buck was the only one crazy enough to speak. "You know, come to think of it, your hair looks good that way." He glanced back at Chase. "What do you think, Chase?"

"It's . . . different."

She shook her head and walked away to finish the rest of her coffee in peace. The glorious sunrise over the mountains quickly took her mind off her appearance. She wished this peaceful moment could last forever, but she knew they needed to get going.

After she'd drained her cup, she headed back to the camp and dug out her hairbrush and an elastic band from her pack. With a few quick strokes, she smoothed her hair and pulled it into a pony tail.

When she rejoined the rest of the party, they were inspecting their weapons with soldier-like discipline.

Chase's friendly demeanor a few minutes earlier had turned deadly serious.

She tried to lighten his mood. "With all this combat readiness, I feel like we're preparing to go to war. Where's the heavy artillery?"

He stared at her as if she'd landed from another planet. "This is a manhunt, not a nature hike. The man we're searching for is armed and dangerous, not to mention a killer. This *is* war."

She bristled at the militant tone in his voice. He turned away and grabbed his gear, setting off on the trail without another word.

John and Buck strapped on their heavy packs. They glanced uneasily at Jenny as they passed by like soldiers following their commander into battle.

Kate came over and touched her shoulder. "I don't think Chase meant to snap at you. He's only thinking about this search." Kate helped her on with her pack. "We'd better get going. They'd be lost without us women, you know."

Kate's words prompted a reluctant smile from Jenny. She secured her shoulder straps and followed the others. Despite her insistence in coming along, she now wanted more than anything for this manhunt to be over. She missed Lori and Adam. She even missed Joel.

By mid-morning, they had descended halfway down the mountain, but last winter's heavy snowpack still covered the trail. Jenny tramped through the slush, her shoulders and back straining against the load she carried. An overwhelming weariness settled over her, not from the physical toll, but the emotional one.

Her earlier motivation for finding Russ and bringing him to justice was gone. The thought of seeing him now made her anxious. He was a cold-blooded killer. What would he do if he was cornered?

The vision of him stalking her like that bear still haunted her. Shaking it off, she pushed herself to catch up with the others.

They descended the trail toward Horseshoe Basin at a steady pace until eleven a.m. Still at an elevation of over 5,000 feet, the slick patches of ice and snow on the steep, rocky trail added to the frustrations of the tired, impatient hikers.

Jenny found a large meadow in full sunlight and decided they should break for lunch. Kate's limp had worsened. Jenny knew her feet must be covered in painful blisters.

The unspoken tension weighed heavily on the group, and everyone seemed to want to eat alone, staking out their own vacant rock or tree trunk to rest upon.

Jenny found a large, smooth boulder with a great view and stripped off her pack. After unzipping a pocket, she retrieved a granola bar and her water bottle. Resting contentedly on the rock, she stretched her back and inhaled the crisp, clean mountain air while she ate.

Buck appeared beside her, uninvited, munching on his chips. "This is a great spot." He proceeded to dig out an assortment of junk food from his pack and set it on the rock.

Jenny stopped eating and stared at the motley collection of food. "You're going to eat all of that?"

"You betcha," he replied. "I've worked up a huge appetite. Help yourself to anything you want."

Jenny eyed the candy bars, donuts, and potato chips with disgust. "No, thank you."

She looked around and spotted Chase, who had been surveying the area with a pair of binoculars. He glanced her way from his distant perch.

The harshness of his earlier rebuke still stung. How dare he lecture her on the seriousness of this mission! She knew better than anyone how dangerous Russ could be.

"Sure is warm today," Buck commented. "Of course, it's nothing compared to Afghanistan."

She gazed in his direction. "You served over there?"

He nodded soberly. "They have a lot of mountains too."

Unexpected compassion moved her heart. In an odd way, Buck reminded her a little of Billy, and a deep sense of sadness and disappointment swept over her from not finding him yet.

So far, her dogs hadn't detected his scent.

Buck swatted at a mosquito. "Gotcha!" He looked at Jenny. "How on earth did mosquitoes get way up here?"

"The snowmelt leaves a lot of standing water where they breed." She opened a small pouch on her pack and retrieved a bottle of insect repellent. "Here. Use this."

He shook his hand. "Nah. I'm good. I can handle a few mosquitoes."

She shrugged at his macho response, knowing he'd regret not using it later.

A gentle breeze blew past her, bringing welcome cool relief from the sun. This kind of heat wave in July was unusual for the Cascades. She twisted off the cap to her water bottle. The sweet, refreshing water quenched her parched mouth and throat as she guzzled it.

Chase wandered over and offered his bag of cookies. "Lori made them."

"Thanks." She took one and munched on the chocolate chip treat. "Did you see any sign of Russ?"

"No."

An awkward pause followed.

Chase glared at Buck sitting nearby. "Buck, why don't you find someplace else to park?"

"Hey, it's a free country, and I was here first."

"Well, there are plenty of other places for you to exercise your freedom. I want to talk to Jenny. Alone."

She sighed. Rather than ushering in World War III, she stood. "Stay put, Buck. I'll go with Chase."

She walked with Chase to the stream and crouched beside it to immerse her hands in its cold, glacial waters. "So?"

"I want to apologize for the way I spoke to you this morning."

She ran her dripping hands over the back of her neck and her face to cool off. "It's okay. I probably had it coming. I didn't get much sleep last night, so I wasn't in the best of moods."

"Are you afraid of seeing Russ again?"

She looked at him, surprised by his question. "No." She read the skepticism in his expression. "Well, maybe a little. Mostly I'm concerned about you."

He raised a brow. "Me? Why?"

"I don't know, but I have a bad feeling. What if we do find Russ, then what? We both know he's capable of anything. He's always scheming."

"Don't worry. I can handle him."

"Can you? Can you really, Chase? I mean, what will you do when you find him?"

"We'll lock him up. I'm trained for this, remember?"

"You're trained for finding felons and fugitives, but are you trained for coming face-to-face with the man who killed your partner in cold blood?"

"Trust me. I know what I'm doing. Now let's get moving. The sooner we find Russ the better for all of us."

Impatience simmered inside Chase as the group hiked for the next two hours. They were all tired and sore from the long journey, not to mention the risk he'd subjected them to coming so far into the wilderness. What if his theory about Russ hiding in the mountains was wrong? He might still have a job, but what good was it if he lost his credibility after this?

And Jenny. The way things were going, she probably wouldn't want anything to do with him once this was over.

The trail finally leveled off and they came to a flooded river with a wild stream of glacial water from the mountain peaks above.

Chase turned to Jenny. "This isn't good. There isn't a bridge. How do we get across?"

"On foot. We need to find enough big rocks close together and cross over. Follow me." She walked a little way down the river where boulders jutted out of the wild, surging water.

The swift and powerful current set Chase's nerves on edge.

One wrong step could send a person downstream in the turbulent rapids. His heart pounded like the raging river as Jenny leapt from rock to rock with her dogs close at her heels.

Not until she finally reached the other side with Fred and Ginger did he allow himself to breathe again. He followed her lead. When he landed on a large boulder in the center of the stream, he decided to wait there to assist the others.

Fred and Ginger barked and growled from the opposite bank.

"Jenny!" Kate's scream pierced the air.

Chase spun around in time to see Jenny waving her arms over her head. She was shouting something he couldn't hear over the rushing water. Then he spotted the bear in front of her.

He skimmed the rocks like a frog. When he reached the other side, he drew his gun. But Jenny's exaggerated motions and barking dogs seemed to be working. The bear backed away and lumbered off with a low growl.

After the animal had disappeared, Jenny shouted, "All clear!"

Chase put his gun away, his head reeling and his stomach lurching. He stripped off his pack and bent over, supporting his hands on his thighs. With a few deep breaths, he re-oxygenated his depleted lungs, and the sickness subsided.

Must be the altitude, he told himself, but he knew it wasn't. His reaction had nothing to do with the altitude, and everything to do with Jenny.

Her voice brought him back to his senses.

Jenny now stood at the waters' edge, encouraging Kate to cross over. "Come on, Kate. You can do it."

Kate was fine. He was the one overreacting. An overwhelming sense of gratitude rose inside. "Thank you, God." The words sounded foreign coming from his parched lips, but he couldn't think of anyone else big enough to thank. The high-pitched cry of an eagle caused him to look up. It soared above them.

When he turned back to the raging stream, John and Buck were crossing with Kate between them, encouraging her.

Babying her sore feet, Kate took careful steps over the boulders until she was one leap away from the last big rock.

After the scare with the bear, the danger of this manhunt weighed on Chase like a backpack stuffed with rocks. He glanced at Jenny. Primal instinct kicked in and compelled him to keep her close. If anything happened to her—

"Kate!" Jenny cried.

Chase spun around as Kate screamed and fell into the whitewater.

Her face appeared above the chop, gasping for air as she fought against the powerful current. "Help!"

"Hang on!" Chase ran along the river's edge to keep up with her. "We'll get you out."

Kate reached for a rock and hugged it, halting her treacherous ride.

Chase prepared to jump in.

"Wait, Chase!"

He glanced at Jenny, who rushed toward him with Buck and John.

Buck shed his backpack. "Let me do it. I used to be a life guard."

"Hold on!" Jenny halted. She dropped her pack and ripped it open, pulling out a rope. "The current's too strong. Try this first." She tossed the rope to Buck.

He caught it and ran to Chase.

Chase unwound it and cast it toward Kate.

With one hand reaching and the other clinging to the rock, she missed.

Chase hurriedly retrieved the rope to try again.

Using both hands to catch it, Kate missed again, and the current dragged her downstream. She disappeared under the water.

"Kate!" A lump lodged in Chase's throat. His heartbeat intensified with each beat. *She can't die, not on my watch.* He glanced at the others. "I'm going in."

Kate came up choking.

Chase took a deep breath, noticing a tree leaning across the water. "Grab a branch, Kate!"

As the current buffeted her, she snagged a low-hanging limb and gripped it with both hands.

Chase ran further down the bank with the rope. "Hang on. I'm coming to get you." He started to tie the rope around his waist.

Buck caught up to him. "Let me. I can do this."

The earnest look in the young marshal's eyes and his training as a lifeguard convinced Chase to give him a shot.

While Buck quickly secured one end of the rope across his mid-section, Chase ran the other end to a nearby tree and tethered Buck to the trunk. Then, standing in front of the tree, Chase held the rope, prepared to pull it in, if necessary.

Jenny and John joined him, taking their places in line, John closest to the water and Jenny between the two men.

Buck gave them a thumbs-up, then turned and jogged into the torrent of water.

"Hurry!" Kate cried. "I'm losing my grip."

With the speed and power of an Olympic swimmer, Buck swam into the chop to where Kate clung to the branch.

Her hands slipped and the current took her.

Chase's throat tightened.

Buck swam downstream and caught her. They floated downriver together until the rope snagged him and held them stationary. He shouted to Kate over the river's roar, "Get your footing and we'll hoof it across the water to the bank."

"Ow!" she cried, attempting to walk over the river rocks. "I hurt my foot."

Rushing water pounded them as Buck removed her pack and slipped it over his shoulders. "Hang on to me."

She clung to his arm as he headed toward the bank.

Chase, Jenny, and John jumped and cheered from their places in line.

A crest of whitewater swept over the pair and they disappeared.

"Where are they?" Chase cried.

Jenny glanced over her shoulder at him. "It's a hydraulic hole. We'll have to pull them out."

"I should have gone in there."

"Chase, focus," Jenny told him as she and John gripped the rope, ready for him to give the command.

He forced himself to concentrate and took a deep breath. "One, two, three, pull!"

The three of them heaved back in unison.

They repeated this two more times.

Like a life-and-death game of tug-a-war, the rope burned Chase's palms as he strained against it.

Finally, Buck and Kate emerged from the water, coughing and gasping, but close enough to reach the bank on their own.

The sudden shift in weight knocked Chase off balance, and he fell on his backside.

Jenny landed on top of him. "Oops. Sorry." She rolled over to her knees and rose to standing. "I hope I didn't break anything."

"Nah. I'm unbreakable."

"Hey, Chase," Buck called to him. "Get over here. Something's wrong with Kate."

Chase jumped up and helped Jenny to her feet. They joined John and Buck where Kate was resting on the ground.

"I hurt my foot," Kate said through chattering teeth from the cold, glacial water. She tried to remove her boot and winced in pain. "I hit it on a rock in the water."

Chase nudged Jenny's arm. "I'll get the first aid kit while you examine her." He quickly returned and set the kit beside her. Kate's shivering made him uneasy.

Kneeling on the ground, Jenny carefully extracted Kate's hiking boot from her foot. "Buck, fetch a blanket out of my pack and put it around her."

Buck returned with the blanket a moment later and draped it

over Kate.

Chase looked at Buck, who was shivering too. "Go put on dry clothes, Buck. We're okay here."

He nodded and disappeared.

Jenny examined Kate's foot and gently touched her toes. Kate cried in pain.

"Your big toe is broken. You may have other broken bones too. Your foot is swelling pretty badly." She looked at Chase. "She can't go on any further."

"I'll be fine," Kate insisted. "Give me a hand."

Chase and John helped her to her feet. When she put weight on her injured foot, she cried in pain.

John and Chase gently lowered her back to the ground.

Chase gave her a brotherly look of concern. "Jenny's right. You can't hike anymore today, and you're freezing cold. We've got to get you warmed up."

Kate pouted. "Then y'all go on ahead without me. I don't want you to stop because of my broken foot."

"I'm not going to leave you behind. We'll have to change plans." Chase rubbed his head, thinking through options.

Jenny looked at the sun in the western sky. "It's getting late. There's a nice place to camp by the river. Why don't we make that our base camp for tonight, and we'll figure out a plan for tomorrow?"

Jenny's suggestion would buy Chase time to think things through. He nodded. "Let's go."

The sound of Fred and Ginger barking in the distance drew their attention.

Chase turned to Jenny. "What is it?"

"I think they have Billy's scent. I'm going after them." She stuffed the first aid kit into a small shoulder bag from her backpack and started jogging toward the noise coming from downriver.

"Wait, Jenny!" When she didn't look back, Chase turned to Buck. "You help Kate to the campground and set up camp for tonight. John and I will go with Jenny."

Once Chase and John caught up to Jenny, they found the dogs a half mile further, circling and pacing around a pile of sticks, rocks, and leaves.

Jenny pointed to a spot at the bottom of the heap. "Look! A hand."

Chase saw it too, his earlier sickness returning from the ominous sight. He gently nudged her. "Stand back. John and I will check it out."

She stepped away while the two men removed the debris. Chase glanced back and saw Jenny kneel beside her dogs, clinging to them for support.

They continued clearing the area until a face emerged. Chase averted his eyes, sickened by the sight.

Jenny came to her feet and inched closer. "I-It's Billy, isn't it?" Her hollow voice echoed the grim reality.

He dropped his head as the truth sunk in.

The rustle of leaves that John swept away roused Chase from his black thoughts, and he helped John clear the rest of the debris from the body.

A red stain marked the center of Billy's shirt. The bloody sight revived the horror of Jim's death. Chase's head reeled as his vision faded.

"Hey, buddy," John said, "are you okay?"

Chase pried his eyes away from the gruesome scene. "Somebody shot him. Check to see if he has a wallet and ID. Also, see if he has any cash or credit cards left."

John took a pair of black leather gloves from his back pocket and searched Billy's clothes. "Nothing. He's been picked clean."

Chase pushed himself up from the ground and saw Jenny's horrified expression. When he stepped toward her, she collapsed in his arms.

"Why? Why did this have to happen?" she sobbed.

"I'm so sorry," he said, cradling her in his arms. "If I'd caught Webb, Billy would still be alive."

She looked up, her eyes wet with tears. "You're not responsible for this. This is Russ's doing. Everything he touches, he destroys."

Chase took her face in his hands and tenderly kissed her forehead. "Not everything."

He wrapped his arms around her. "We'll get him, Jen. I promise you, if it's the last thing I do, we'll get him."

Jenny wished she could have stayed in Chase's arms forever, but Fred and Ginger's barking brought her momentary solace to an end. She looked around.

Chase released her from his embrace. "What is it?"

"My dogs. Where are they?" She called to them. "Fred! Ginger!"

Chase shouted their names too.

A moment later, Jenny heard barking in the distance.

Chase frowned. "Now what?"

"We better go check it out."

He glanced back at John. "Meet you back at camp."

By the time Jenny and Chase caught up with the dogs, they had traveled further down the trail, a couple of miles from camp. They stood outside an old, abandoned mine.

"Someone's been living here." Chase drew his gun. "U.S. Marshal. Come out with your hands up."

No response.

After repeating it once more, he proceeded to go inside.

"What are you doing?" Jenny cried.

"I'm going in. Cover me." He disappeared into the mine before she could refuse.

Jenny drew her SIG and followed him inside.

Using their cellphone flashlight apps, they wandered through the dark, damp cavern that smelled of mold, garbage, and campfire smoke. They came to what appeared to be a fire pit, and a nest of sleeping bags and blankets.

"Not exactly the Ritz," Chase said. He shined his light around and stopped when it illuminated a heap of newspaper, cardboard, and empty cans.

Chase put away his gun and phone, then pulled a pair of gloves from his pocket and tugged them on to sort through the rubble.

Jenny holstered her pistol while keeping her light on the area where Chase worked. She pointed to an item he uncovered. "Hey, that's my shovel!"

Chase found a wallet and opened it. He took out a small card. "It's Billy's library card."

A gasp escaped Jenny's throat.

Chase continued to search the wallet. "The driver's license and cash are gone."

Jenny took out a clean paper bag from her satchel and opened it for him.

He carefully placed the wallet inside. As he went through the rest of the debris, he located something small and wooden.

"My cash box!" Jenny cried.

Chase lifted the lid and showed her the contents. "Looks like the only things left are your fool's gold coins."

She smiled. "They're worth more to me than the money. I never thought I'd see them again."

"At least you'll get them back after the crime scene investigators are finished." He laid the box in Jenny's bag.

"It's hard to believe Russ has been living in this mine all this time."

"Don't ever underestimate the resourcefulness of a desperate man. If this is Russ's hideout, he's been in possession of Billy Norton's wallet, and that makes him a suspect for his murder."

When Chase had finished sifting through the pile, Jenny pointed to an odd-shaped object a few feet away. "What's that over there?"

Chase strode to it and lifted it high so she could see.

It was a bear mask, like the one used at the Trail Break

convenience store robbery.

CHAPTER NINETEEN

Back at camp, Jenny poured Kate a cup of hot tea while the shivering female marshal huddled over the camp stove to warm up. Despite changing into dry, warm clothes, Kate remained freezing cold.

Buck, on the other hand, had come through the river ordeal amazingly well. Because he wasn't injured, he had been doing vigorous exercises to increase his core body temperature.

But Jenny was concerned about Kate. Helping her recover from her fall in the glacial waters was Jenny's first priority.

Even as she focused on Kate, Jenny couldn't get Billy out of her mind. It was hard to believe he was gone. If she'd stopped him from leaving the restaurant that night, maybe he'd still be alive. Nothing could bring him back now.

She looked up when John finally returned to camp. He clutched the radio he'd used to make the patched-in call. "Okay, everyone, listen up. A task force is being organized with members from the local marshal's office, the park service, the FBI, and the local sheriff's office. We'll stand a better chance with a bigger force."

"What about the Special Operations Group?" Buck asked, referring to the special U.S. Marshal unit that was usually called in for high-profile arrests.

"They've been called in, but with the difficult terrain, they won't make it here until the day after tomorrow." He looked at Jenny. "Besides, Jenny's already proven the local rangers know these mountains better than anyone."

She acknowledged the compliment with a humble nod.

Chase spoke up. "What's the plan?"

John's eyes flickered. "You tell me."

A puzzled look crossed Chase's face. "You're the senior marshal. Didn't they put you in charge of the task force?"

"I recommended someone else who's more knowledgeable about the case."

Chase shook his head in protest. "No. You should be leading this, John."

"They agreed to my recommendation."

"I don't care."

"Are we going to waste time arguing, or are you going to tell us your plan?"

When it sunk in that he would be leading the task force, Chase rubbed his forehead, reluctant to usurp John's seniority. Then he gave John a sidelong look. "Thanks."

"For what? He's your fugitive. You know him better than anyone." Despite John's tough act, his genuine respect for Chase was clear.

Jenny agreed with John. Chase was the best person to lead them.

Chase stood and addressed the group. "If we get two other units out here, we can surround the area where we found Billy and the mine, and we can corner the suspect between the river and the mountains." He looked to Jenny. "Do you know who could guide the other two units?"

She thought it over. "There's Clint, and . . . Joel."

Chase looked at her as if she was crazy. "Joel. I can't involve him in this."

"He's already involved. He's your friend and my brother."

"He's got a wife and kid."

"So does John," she pointed out. "And so do most of the people who are going to show up here tomorrow. Lori wouldn't want to keep him from doing something this important."

"I don't know."

"Let me radio Clint and get him to patch me in to Joel's phone." She caught the reproach in Chase's expression. "Don't look at me like that. He can always say no."

"But we both know he won't."

As Chase predicted, once she'd spoken to him, Joel insisted on joining the search. First, she spoke to Lori to gauge how she felt about her husband getting involved, but Lori was totally supportive.

After Jenny told Chase that both Joel and Clint would guide the other search groups, he informed the others. "With two teams arriving tomorrow, we have a busy day ahead of us. Let's finish setting up camp and get dinner going."

Jenny pulled him aside. "I need to speak to you."

She led him to the river near the camp and met his curious expression with frankness. "Kate can't go with you tomorrow. There's no way she can walk on that foot."

He scratched his face. "I can't leave her behind. What do you suggest?"

"I'll stay here with her, and we'll head back in the morning."

"She'll never make it over that river."

"I know. We'll have to take a different way down."

The muscles in his face tightened. "I don't like leaving you two alone, especially with a killer on the loose."

"In that case, what if you and the others return to camp tomorrow night and all of us head out together the next morning? If Russ still hasn't been found, then Joel can help me get Kate back to town."

"I'll have to think it over." He gazed at her with an earnest look. "If anything were to happen to you or Kate, I'd never forgive myself."

She touched his arm to reassure him. "Don't worry. We'll be fine." She sniffed the air. "I smell smoke."

They rushed back to camp and discovered John and Buck had a fire going in the fire pit. Kate was warming herself beside it.

Chase eyed the flames. "That fire is too big. I thought we agreed to use the camp stove."

John shrugged. "We tried, but it's not hot enough. After that spill in the ice water, I'm afraid Kate will catch pneumonia if we don't get a real fire going."

"He's right, Chase," Jenny said. "We have to get Kate warm."

Chase eased off, but Jenny could tell he wasn't happy about the fire. She noticed Buck cleaning fish nearby. "Who caught those?"

Buck stuck out his chest and pointed at himself. "I did, while John and Kate made camp. I'm sick of camp food."

Jenny grinned. "Wow, Buck, you're more of an outdoorsman than I thought. Maybe you should have gone into the park service."

"Are there any openings?"

"Stop trying to recruit him, Jen." The humor in Chase's eyes betrayed his serious facade.

"Okay. I'll take Kate."

Kate peered up and smiled. "Thanks, but I'm afraid I wouldn't be much good to you with a broken toe."

"John?" Jenny asked with an appealing smile.

"No way. I have an aversion to ticks, mosquitoes, and anything else that bites or stings."

Jenny laughed and turned to Chase. "Speaking of stings, did you ever go to the doctor and get checked out?"

He grimaced and looked away. "I didn't have time. Besides, you brought a first aid kit, didn't you?"

"Yeah."

"Then I'm good. I've got a trained professional with me."

She shook her head, frustrated that he'd ignored her advice and neglected his health.

"And I'm unbreakable, remember?"

After dinner, Jenny quickly pitched her tent. When she rejoined the others by the fire pit, the burning embers cast a warm glow over everyone.

Buck melted marshmallows on a skewer made from a long

stick and sandwiched them with chocolate between graham crackers. After he'd made one for Kate, he handed the next one to Jenny.

Jenny relished the decadent treat after the long day.

It was a perfect night for camping. A clear sky, with stars twinkling above them. And the cool night air made them appreciate a warm fire.

Jenny reached down to pet Fred and Ginger, who rested contentedly beside her.

Despite the nice weather and warm fire, Chase stared at the flames with a somber expression. The discovery of Billy's body had piled even more onto the heavy burden he already carried every day Russ roamed free. But Chase's instincts had been right, and, horrible as it was, Jenny was glad they were the ones who found Billy's body. The best thing they could do for him now was to find his killer and put him away for good.

Kate interrupted her thoughts. "Sing us a campfire song, Jenny."

She shook her head. "No, I'm not a very good singer."

"Come on," Kate persisted.

"But I don't know many camp songs. Mostly all I know are hymns."

"Then let's sing Amazing Grace. That was Jim's favorite."

"Okay. But only if you sing it with me."

The two women began the first verse, Kate's soprano to Jenny's alto.

Amazing grace
How sweet the sound
That saved a wretch like me
I once was lost
But now I'm found
Was blind, but now I see

John joined in on the second verse with a surprisingly good

bass.

After they'd finished, Buck clapped. "Hey, not bad."

Jenny glanced at Chase, who was still brooding across from her. "Chase? Are you okay?"

He peered up, his eyes cloudy and sad. The firelight intensified the shadows on his face. "They played that song at Jim's funeral."

"Oh . . . I'm sorry."

Kate, who was seated next to him, gave his arm a compassionate squeeze.

"It reminds me of why we're doing this—for Jim."

"For Jim," the other marshals echoed in solidarity.

A pensive mood overtook Jenny. "That song was my father's favorite too. You know, being out here brings back memories of all the camping trips I took with him."

Kate glanced at her. "Good memories, I hope."

"The best."

They heard a distant yipping sound.

Fred and Ginger's ears perked up.

Kate looked around nervously. "What's that, a wolf?"

Jenny poked the fire with a stick. "No, a coyote, but there have been wolf sightings not far from here."

"Think one will come around us?"

"No. Wolves don't like people much."

"What about bears?"

Jenny smiled at her new friend. "Don't worry, Kate. Bears and wolves are more afraid of us than we are of them. Besides, we have Super-Marshal here to protect us." Her eyes shifted to Chase, expecting a comeback, but he wasn't really listening. "Chase?" she said, hoping to engage him somehow.

"Yeah?"

"Are you sure you're okay?"

He blinked. "Just tired. It's getting late. I'm gonna turn in. Goodnight, everyone."

A chilly breeze caused the trees to sway and whisper as Jenny watched him go to his tent and crawl inside. With Russ on the prowl, bears and wolves were the least of their troubles.

Chase awoke in a cold sweat, his heart pounding like a jackhammer. He'd had another one of his nightmares. But this time, after the gunshot, it wasn't Jim lying in a pool of blood . . .

It was Jenny.

The song she'd sung by the campfire still played in his head. He knew the tune well, but never paid much attention to the words until last night. For the first time, he saw himself in the lyrics.

Lost, blind wretch.

That's exactly how he felt right now.

After Jenny's bear encounter and Kate's close call in the river, he realized how quickly things could get out of his control.

Jenny and Kate. The two people he cared the most about in the world, and he'd put their lives in danger. For what? To catch Russ Webb? He wasn't worth it.

What was I thinking, coming out here? I've got to end this madness before anyone else gets hurt.

The song played in his mind. *Amazing grace. How sweet the sound . . .*

Grace.

That's what I need right now.

A new beginning.

"Jesus," he cried, "please help me."

CHAPTER TWENTY

The next morning Jenny rose before the others. After changing into her ranger uniform, she let Fred and Ginger out of the tent to roam around camp while she tended the stove by flashlight because it was still dark. When she'd started cooking the second batch of pancakes, Chase emerged from his tent and stumbled over.

"Good morning, sleepyhead." She poured a fresh cup of coffee into a camp mug and handed it to him. "Here, this will fix whatever ails you."

"I doubt it," he said as he took the cup from her. He sniffed the air. "Something smells really good."

"I'm making pancakes."

He narrowed his eyes. "*You're* making them?"

"Don't worry, it's from a mix I brought with me. I only added water."

"Whew, that's a relief."

"Very funny." She took a swat at him with the spatula.

"Hey, watch it with that thing. Don't you know it's illegal to assault a peace officer?"

John and Buck rolled out of their tents. Buck sniffed the air and raced John to the stove. "Pancakes!"

Chase nosed Buck out with his plate. "I was here first."

"Don't worry, there's plenty, Buck." Jenny pointed to the first batch covered in foil on the plate by the fire pit. "The syrup is over there too."

Kate crawled out of her tent and hobbled over to the others. "I'm not dreaming. It really *is* pancakes."

After they'd served themselves and sat down to eat, Buck

looked at Chase. "What's the plan, boss?"

Chase had settled on a nearby log and stopped eating long enough to answer. "I've decided to call off the search."

"What?" everyone exclaimed in unison, staring at him in disbelief.

"It's too dangerous to leave Kate and Jenny behind. We either all go together or not at all."

Jenny nearly choked on her food. "Oh, no you don't. We didn't come all this way to turn around now."

"My mind's made up."

"Well, unmake it then."

Kate set her plate on a rock. "Jenny's right, Chase. We know how to take care of ourselves. We're not helpless damsels in distress, you know."

He chuckled. "No, you certainly aren't that. But . . . what if Webb finds you?"

Jenny's grip tightened on her fork. "Heaven help him if he does. He's no match for Kate and me, or my dogs. Besides, it's only for today. Everyone will be back here tonight."

Chase shook his head. "I don't feel right about it."

"It's too late to stop now," Jenny told him. "An entire task force is on its way. You've got to see it through."

Concern and frustration contorted his features. "Why are you doing this?"

"For Jim and Billy. And for you, because you'll never find peace until Russ is caught."

After everyone had eaten to the point of bursting, Jenny and Kate cleaned up.

Chase spread out a large map on the ground and got on the radio to coordinate their rendezvous point with the mobile command station, situated outside the park.

When he signed off, he addressed everyone in the camp. "Okay, listen up. Here's the plan."

Jenny and the others gathered around him.

He located a place on the map with a black marker. "We're

going to rendezvous with Clint and Joel's groups here. If we leave now, we can search this whole area and join them by four this afternoon, then return to camp by six."

Jenny reached for Chase's pen. "May I?"

He handed it to her, and she drew another line on the map. "Clint told me the bridge five miles east of our camp is washed out, and the water is too high to cross Flat Creek." She pointed out their locations on the map. Then she marked a couple of routes with the pen. "These are alternate paths you can take."

His gaze met hers and lingered. "I still don't feel right about leaving you and Kate."

"We'll be fine."

While the men packed their gear for the day, Jenny put the leftover pancakes in a bag and handed them to Chase. "Here. A snack for the road."

"You've thought of everything." He glanced around at the others who were busy with final preps. "Come with me for a minute." He took her hand and led her away from the camp to the river.

Jenny's turbulent emotions matched the raging waters.

Chase stopped on the bank and faced her, his gaze muted with concern. "If you need anything, don't hesitate to radio me, and remember to carry your weapon with you at all times. Promise me you'll be on your guard."

She rolled her eyes. "You sound like my brother."

"If I do, it's because we both love you . . . *I* love you." His soulful eyes reflected the truth of his words. When he moved to kiss her, she stepped away.

"I'm sorry, Chase."

He recoiled as if she had struck him in the face. "I know you care for me—" His tone was hurt and bitter now.

"Of course, I care about you, but feelings are fickle. They come and go like the wind. I want a relationship that will last. I want a man who will be with me in the good times and the bad. . . who shares my values and my faith."

"I know."

She stared at him, surprised. "You do?"

He answered with a slow nod. "And you're right. There are things I need to change. Things in my head and in my heart." Humility resonated in his raw voice. "I need you to pray for me, Jen. Will you do that for me?" His eyes searched hers, pleading.

Stunned by his confession, her heart swelled. "Yes, of course."

He looked down and humbly nodded. "Well, I better be going." He turned to leave.

"Chase, wait a minute."

He stopped and pivoted her direction.

She reached behind her neck and unclasped the chain. Her fingers cocooned the cross in her palm as she stepped toward him. "Hold out your hand."

With a puzzled expression, he acquiesced.

She placed the cross in his palm. "My father gave this to me when I was sixteen. I want you to hold onto it until you come back."

He studied the cherished token of her father's love. "No. I know how much this means to you, and—"

She hushed him with a tender kiss.

Afterward, he stepped back, his eyes flickering with surprise. "But I thought . . ."

She touched his hand and closed his fingers over the cross. "Promise me you'll come back alive, with or without Russ Webb."

He stared at her in wonder, his face bright with renewed hope. "I promise."

CHAPTER TWENTY-ONE

JENNY HELD UP THE CRUTCHES SHE had constructed from two long sticks and duct tape. "Give these a try."

She helped Kate to her feet and handed her one of the sticks.

Kate positioned it under her arm.

Once she'd gained her balance, Jenny handed her the other one.

Kate hobbled around the camp with the crutches. "Not bad. Thanks."

Jenny gave her a sympathetic smile. "I know it's hard being stuck here at camp."

"I wish you could have gone on with the others. I feel like such a nuisance."

"You aren't a nuisance. Besides, who wants to go with a bunch of eager-beaver soldiers on a manhunt?"

Kate laughed at her remark. "Can you give me a hand? I'd like to sit down."

"Sure." Jenny took the crutches from her and helped her to a nearby log by the fire pit. She scooted the roll of duct tape out of the way and sat next to her.

Something in her pocket brushed against her leg. She reached in and pulled out Buck's small bottle of mace. "I totally forgot I still had this."

"Better hang on to it just in case."

Jenny snorted. "This stuff? If we used it on a bear, it would probably laugh at us." She stuffed it into her pocket and stretched out her legs.

Kate stared at her bandaged foot. "You know, I've never seen Chase want to back out of something this important."

"It's understandable. He's concerned about you."

"Uh-uh. That wouldn't have stopped him before. Don't get me wrong. Chase is like the big brother I never had. He's a great guy, but I can tell he's changed. I mean that in a good way. I think it's because of you."

Jenny gave her a dry look. "Maybe that dip in the stream injured your head too."

Kate persisted. "I'm serious, Jenny. The thing is, I wouldn't want to see him get hurt, you know?"

Jenny nodded. "Neither would I." She spotted something on the ground. "Look."

"What is it?"

"A salamander."

"It looks like a lizard. Is it poisonous?"

"No, it's harmless. See, it doesn't have scales like lizards." Kate smiled.

They watched it for a few minutes until it crawled away.

"Chase told me you knew the fugitive," Kate said.

"A long time ago." Jenny grabbed a stick and poked the smoldering coals in the fire pit.

"Were you close?"

"I thought so, until he set me up, and then disappeared."

Kate's head popped up. "This must be really hard for you."

Fred approached Jenny and put his paw in her lap. She rewarded him with a vigorous rub. "I'm over Russ. But I realized after we started this search that I hadn't completely forgiven him for what he'd done to me."

"Have you forgiven him now?"

Jenny took the stick and stirred the ashes until the faint glow of embers appeared. "I hope so. I mean, I can't do it on my own. God has to give me the grace to do it."

"I know what you mean. I've had my own issues to deal with. But Jim wouldn't want me to hate his killer." Kate looked at Jenny. "That's why I'm worried about Chase. I'm afraid he's still seeking revenge for what happened to Jim."

"I know."

"But the fact that he was willing to cancel the hunt is a good sign, don't you think?"

"Let's hope so," Jenny replied.

"To be honest, I don't know how well he's been coping with Jim's death. He's not like us, you know. He doesn't have faith to get him through the tough times. I wish there was something more we could do to help him."

Jenny remembered his last request before he left. "There is, Kate. Let's pray for him."

When Chase finally arrived at the rendezvous point with Buck and John, Joel and Clint were already there. They'd each brought a group of rangers, marshals, and sheriff's deputies with them.

Joel went to Chase and patted him on the shoulder. "Hey, buddy, we were starting to wonder if you'd show up."

Chase nodded. "Me too. The distance is farther than it looks on the map, and we had to take an alternate route because the bridge is out. Good thing Jenny warned us about that before we left."

"Glad that sister of mine is keeping you straight," Joel said with a wink. "Speaking of Jen, where is she?"

Chase blew out a breath, preparing himself for Joel's reaction. "Kate hurt her foot, and Jenny stayed with her. They're waiting at camp for us."

"You mean you left the two of them back there alone?"

Chase raised his hand. "Don't start with me, Joel. You know how stubborn your sister can be."

Joel sighed and relented. "Yeah, tell me about it."

Jenny's radio went off with popping static.

"What's for dinner?"

The sound of Chase's voice brought a smile to Jenny's face.

She pulled the radio from her belt and spoke into it. "Chase? Any luck?"

"No, but we've met up with Joel, Clint and the rest of the task force members. We took your alternate route, but it was longer than we expected so we're running late. We'll be heading to camp as soon as we're finished here. By the way, Clint got a call from Gus. They caught Reggie right outside of Vegas."

She braced herself for the rest of the news. "Was Wendy with him?"

"No, he was alone. He claims he doesn't know where she is. The last time he saw her was Friday night when she left his place."

Jenny closed her eyes, praying that Reggie was telling the truth and that Wendy was okay.

"Jen?"

"I'm still here."

"I'm sure they'll find her. It's only a matter of time."

"I hope you're right."

Impatient from waiting, Jenny checked her watch again. Six p.m. already. Over an hour since Chase last radioed her. She sighed, wishing he would call again.

Kate coughed as she stirred the pot of reconstituted chili on the camp stove near the fire pit.

Jenny's anxiety shifted from Chase to Kate. "Are you okay?"

"I think I'm getting sick."

She felt Kate's forehead. "You're burning up."

"I'll be okay, but I need my jacket. It's so cold."

No, it was warm. The heat wave had spiked the temperature.

Fred and Ginger began barking and pacing around camp with low growls and bared fangs.

Their frenzied appearance drew a gasp from Kate. "What's wrong with them?"

Jenny tried to remain calm for her friend's sake, but the dogs' odd behavior bothered her as well. "I'm not sure. It's probably the rest of the group coming back."

She called to her dogs. "Fred, Ginger, hush!"

They ignored her.

She studied the animals, remembering them acting strange before. The night Joel's dogs were injured and his sheep killed, and when the intruder rummaged through her garbage can. Did Fred and Ginger sense something out there, beyond their camp?

The wind picked up. "I'll be back in a minute. I'm going to fetch our jackets and grab a blanket too." She got up and headed for their tents. After quickly collecting Kate's jacket, she rushed next door to gather her large can of bear spray, jacket, and blanket. She secured the bear repellent to her belt and withdrew her pistol to confirm it was loaded.

Satisfied she'd taken all the necessary precautions, she holstered her weapon and exited the tent.

On her way to the fire pit, a rustling in the bushes stopped her. "Chase?"

A bear cub darted through the thicket.

Jenny froze, staring into the woods as an unmistakable scent pestered her nostrils . . .

The mother burst from the brush with a terrifying roar.

Jenny lost her balance and fell to the ground.

The bear reared up, towering over her.

Fred and Ginger circled the animal, growling and nipping at her like rabid wolves.

The sow took a couple of swipes at them, but lost interest. Sniffing the air, she headed for the fire pit where the chili simmered.

"Bear!" Jenny shouted as she grabbed the spray from her belt and aimed.

Kate gaped in horror at the large creature coming toward her.

"Get on your knees and crawl away backwards, waving your hands over your head."

Trembling, Kate dropped to her knees and slowly backed

away. The dogs' persistent attacks distracted the bear long enough for Kate to hide behind a tangle of fallen logs.

The bear swung around, growling at the nipping dogs.

Ginger lunged, and the sow swatted her head. The dog fell to the ground, motionless.

"Ginger!" Jenny aimed the can and pulled the trigger at the same time the bear spun around.

Missed.

The sow growled and turned in her direction.

Fred leapt in front of her and attacked. The angry mother swiped at him, but Fred fought back. She struck him hard across his body. With a yelp, he hit the dirt.

Jenny gasped, devastated at the sight of her dogs' bloodied bodies.

Another cub darted from the brush, drawing a cautious growl from the mother. It went back into hiding behind a tree.

The sow turned on Jenny, then charged.

Pressing the nozzle once more, Jenny prayed it would hit its mark this time.

The bear halted less than ten feet away. She roared pitifully from the effects of the irritant, and, with a violent shake of her head, lumbered away.

Two cubs appeared from the brush and scampered behind her.

After the bear and cubs disappeared deep into the woods, Jenny ran to Kate. "Are you okay?"

"Uh-huh," the marshal muttered, still in shock.

"That was a close one."

"Too close for me."

Jenny returned the bear spray to her belt and rushed to Ginger. When she saw her dog still breathing, she sighed with relief.

Ginger weighed close to seventy pounds. How would she get her back to camp?

She ran to Kate and lifted the blanket from her. "Sorry, but I need to borrow this."

Ginger was still unconscious when she returned. Jenny spread the blanket and tucked it under her. Grabbing the two ends, she gently pulled the dog to their camp.

After carefully slipping the blanket from beneath Ginger, Jenny went to Fred. Blood oozed from the claw marks on his side. He looked at her and whimpered when she knelt beside him. "I know it hurts, boy, but hang in there. I'm going to patch you up."

Once she'd safely deposited both dogs beside the fire pit, Jenny went to work treating their wounds as best she could with her first aid supplies. By the time she'd finished, they were bandaged and resting on the blanket.

She ducked inside her tent to grab her sleeping bag then returned to Kate.

Kate looked around with a worried expression. "I wonder what's keeping Chase and the others."

Jenny unzipped the sleeping bag and gently draped it over Kate's shoulders. "I don't know. I would radio them, but it might alert Russ if he's close by."

Jenny knew she needed to stay strong for Kate. "You must be starving. Why don't you go ahead and eat?"

"No, I'm not hungry."

"Then rest for a while. No bear would dare attack us again tonight."

"I'm not leaving you out here alone." Kate peered up, her face alarmingly pale. "Do you think Fred and Ginger will recover?"

"I hope so."

A breeze rustled the trees above. Kate hunkered under the blanket. Jenny hadn't re-built the fire from last night in case Russ was around. But she had to do something. After that dip in the river yesterday, Kate could be coming down with pneumonia.

Jenny patted Kate on the shoulder. "I'm going to gather wood and start a fire before the others return."

Kate gave her an apprehensive look.

"Don't worry. I have my gun and my trusty can of bear spray. I'll be all right." Jenny took her radio from her belt and placed it beside Kate. "Here. You hang on to this in case someone tries to contact us."

Jenny wandered to the outer edge of the camp to find an area with dry branches on the ground. She spotted nice wood a few feet away and headed in that direction. Glancing back, she saw Kate huddled under the blanket.

A hand covered Jenny's mouth and pulled her into the brush. Cold metal pressed against her spine, making her gasp.

"Don't try anything stupid, or I'll kill you and that troop of boy scouts who came here with you." The man's tone was low and harsh.

Russ's voice.

"One peep and you're as dead as that firewood. Do you understand me?"

Jenny closed her eyes and nodded. Despairing thoughts plagued her mind as the stench of his body laced with dirt assaulted her nostrils.

"Now slowly remove your gun and hand it to me."

She hesitated.

The cold metal tip plunged deeper into her spine.

She carefully withdrew her weapon.

He snatched it from her. "Hand me the bear spray too."

Angry with herself for letting her guard down after the bear encounter, she pulled the can from her waist holster and handed it to him. Without her weapons, her odds of escaping plummeted.

"Now I'm going to remove my hand, but I've got a rifle pointed straight at your back, so keep your voice down and don't try anything stupid." He thrust the barrel head against her flesh and whispered in her ear. "I've been waiting a long time for this, Jenny."

Desperate, her eyes scanned the woods. She spotted Kate on her crutches, looking for her. If Russ saw Kate, he'd kill her.

She had to distract him. Maybe she could stall him long enough for Kate to see him and get a good aim. "I hear you've gone from robbing banks to murder now."

He snorted. "Whatever it takes."

"That's how you justify killing Jim Tucker?"

"If I testified at that trial, I was as good as dead."

"So it was self-defense."

"Yeah, that's right."

"What about Billy Norton? Was that also self-defense?"

"Who? You mean that hiker? He stumbled on my hideout. If I hadn't killed him, he would have gone straight to the police. I couldn't let that happen. Besides, what's he to you? He was an idiot. The world is better off without him."

"You mean it's everyone's fault but yours. I suppose you've also found a way to rationalize stealing my money, Chase's SUV, and hurting my brother's dogs so you could take his sheep, not to mention shooting Butch Hopkins when you held up his store."

"I did what I had to. It was them or me. Survival of the fittest, baby. You should know all about that, being a park ranger. I'm no different than those pet wolves you love so much. Only they're not much good to you now, are they? You know, I should give them a treat for flushing that bear out of the woods for me." He ran his dirty fingers along her cheek.

She violently shook her head. "Get your filthy hands off me."

"Keep your voice down." He removed his hand and snorted. "You're too good for me now, is that it? I liked you better when you were young and sweet."

"You mean naïve. If I'm a little jaded, it's because you deceived me, then left me high and dry."

"Well, I'm back," he replied in a rough voice, "so get ready to pick up where we left off, like Bonnie and Clyde."

"Bonnie and Clyde ended up dead."

"Yeah, but you and me, baby, we know how to survive, don't we?"

Jenny glimpsed Kate from the corner of her eye. She had

spotted them and taken cover behind a tree. *Keep stalling until Kate can get a clear shot.* "I'm not going anywhere with you, Russ. Why don't you take what you want and leave?"

"What if what I want is you?"

Jenny's stomach lurched. "I'm not the same person anymore."

"It's because of that marshal."

She flinched at Russ's mention of Chase.

"Oh, I know all about you two and your little posse. You think you've been tracking me, when all along I've been tracking you."

"You left the message on Chase's car."

He smirked. "I warned him to stay away from you, but he didn't listen. So here we are. Besides, why would you want him, when you could have me?"

A stab of pain seized her back from the strain of the gun pressed against her spine. "If you think you're so smart, Russ, why don't you get out of here before the others come and take you into custody? You still have time to escape."

"*Escape*? Where would I go? You think I don't know that I'm trapped. There's a bounty on my head, but if you come with me, I'd stand a better chance, you being a park ranger and all," he whispered in her ear.

His provocative tone made Jenny's skin crawl. She gave him a backward jab with her elbow.

He knocked her to the ground.

Kate fired a shot.

Jenny rolled away as the bullet whizzed over her head. She caught a glimpse of Russ clutching his arm and swearing. He'd been hit. She turned and crawled away as fast as she could.

"Hey, you behind that tree!" he shouted. "Put your hands up and come out, or I'll shoot your friend here."

"Don't do it, Kate!" Jenny cried.

All the air from Jenny's lungs escaped as Kate limped from behind the tree, trying to raise her gun and keep her balance.

Kate gave Jenny a woeful glance, leaning against the tree for support.

Jenny turned and glared at Russ as if he were insane. The once-handsome face had become worn and craggy with a permanent scowl and narrow gray eyes, and his thick hair, peppered with gray, was long and shaggy.

She stared at his tattered Nirvana T-shirt.

Billy's T-shirt.

Her heart burned with rage. "Leave her out of this, Russ. It's me you want, remember?"

He glanced at her. "She's a marshal. That makes her a threat. But since you're so worried about her, you won't do anything dumb like try to escape while I get her gun. Otherwise, your little marshal friend will be hurting more than she already is."

"I won't do anything, if you promise not to hurt her."

"Then get up. You're coming with me."

Jenny slowly rose to her feet while Russ kept his rifle trained on her.

Kate's face was deathly pale when they marched forward. She bit her lip and glanced at Jenny.

"It's okay, Kate. Hand him your gun."

Kate scowled at Russ as she relinquished her weapon.

Russ tucked it in his belt. His repugnant grin revealed yellowed, cracked teeth. A life of crime, prison, and living in the shadows had reduced the cunning young man Jenny once knew to a filthy animal, living in a rat hole.

"Looks like my lucky day," he boasted. "Two wildcat women." He glanced at Kate's crutch. "Where's that duct tape?"

Kate kept silent.

He thrust the butt of his rifle under Jenny's chin. "If you want your friend to live, you'll tell me where it is."

"By the fire pit." Kate dropped her head, seized by a coughing fit.

"Good." Russ eased the rifle away and gestured for Jenny to join Kate. "Now turn around and get moving until I tell you to stop." He plunged the rifle into Jenny's spine.

Kate hobbled and fell.

Jenny stopped to help her up.

"Move away from her," Russ shouted.

Jenny aimed a defiant glare at him. "She can't walk."

Russ grumbled something. "Then get her up and keep moving."

Jenny helped Kate to her feet and assisted her as they marched toward the camp.

When they reached the fire pit, Russ shoved Jenny to the ground with his foot.

Fred, who was resting nearby, whimpered when he saw her. He thrashed around, unable to rise. Ginger didn't move, but her rib cage rose as she breathed, giving Jenny hope.

"Now tape up your friend's hands and feet," Russ barked at Jenny.

She hesitated. What would the man do if she didn't comply?

"It's okay," Kate said, trembling with a toxic combination of fever and fear. "Do what he says."

Jenny pushed aside her own predicament for the moment. She had to do whatever she could to save her friend, so she rolled the tape around Kate's ankles. "I'm sorry to do this to you."

"Don't worry. The men will be back any minute. Keep stalling him."

"Hurry up!" Russ shouted, sneering at Jenny as he slung the rifle over his shoulder while pointing the SIG at her.

She eyed the small pocket knife by the fire.

"Don't even think about it."

Jenny turned and saw Russ staring at the knife as if he'd read her thoughts. She paused and looked back at Kate, gesturing with her eyes to the half-empty bag of marshmallows near the marshal.

Kate gave a nod.

Jenny reached for the knife, blocking Russ's view.

He raised his voice. "What are you doing?"

She stopped in front of Kate, giving her friend the opportunity to snatch the bag of marshmallows and slip them into Jenny's side pocket, out of Russ's view.

"I need to cut the tape around her ankles." Jenny said. "Unless you don't want me to tape her wrists."

Russ's eyes narrowed. "Hurry up then."

Jenny quickly slashed the tape and moved behind Kate to bind her wrists.

He came over with the gun.

Fred growled, unable to get up.

Jenny knew Russ would shoot him if he didn't stop. "Hush, Fred!" The dog whined mournfully.

Russ sneered at the dog. "That wolf's a menace. Good thing he can't move, or I'd do to him what I did to your brother's mutts."

Jenny reached behind Fred's ear and scratched to keep him calm while Russ inspected the restraints on Kate.

He tugged at the tape around Kate's ankles and wrists with one hand while keeping the gun aimed at Jenny with the other. "That's the worst taping job I've ever seen, but it'll have to do."

He held out the palm of his free hand. "The knife."

She sighed as she lifted it.

He snatched it from her. "And I'll take that roll of tape too."

She picked it up and handed it to him.

Before he could stop her, she jumped up and grabbed the sleeping bag Kate had been using and wrapped it over her again.

Russ took Jenny by the arm and jerked her. The shortwave radio beside the fire went off, and he froze.

"Jen, it's Chase."

Hope flooded Jenny's heart at the sound of his voice coming over the radio.

"Jen? Jenny, please answer . . ." Concern reverberated in Chase's urgent tone. "Okay . . . in case you can hear me but the radio is malfunctioning—we got delayed again. Clint sprained his ankle and can barely walk, but we're on our way. We should be there within a couple of hours max.

She dove for the radio, but Russ shoved her and snatched it up. He hurled it into the fire pit and grabbed her by the hair. "Get up. You're coming with me."

Fred let out a growl as Jenny muffled cries of pain. She glanced at Kate.

"Please let her stay with me," Kate begged.

Jenny shook her head. "No. It's okay."

"That's right. I'll take good care of her." Russ shoved Jenny forward with the gun at her back. "Now get moving."

CHAPTER TWENTY-TWO

THE EVENING SUN CAST LONG SHADOWS as Jenny stubbornly endured what could very well be a death march with Russ. Chase had said they'd be back at camp within two hours. She glanced at her watch. It was seven. This time of year, the sun didn't set until nine. At the rate Russ was moving, Chase would be an hour or more behind them.

At least Kate had been spared. She thanked God for that.

Her thoughts returned to Chase. As long as he was alive, she still had a chance. That kept her going.

Russ knew it too. Paranoia contorted his face as he eyed her like the mad mountain man he'd become.

The marshmallows in her pocket might be her only life line. It would be risky, but she had to try. She slid her hand in her pocket, pinched off a piece, and rolled the gummy substance between her fingers. Like a secret agent dispatching clandestine messages, she dropped the marshmallow bits to the ground whenever Russ wasn't looking.

As she slipped her hand back in her pocket, her fingers brushed against the forgotten vile of mace Buck had brought. Her hopes surged at the discovery, but she'd have to wait until the right opportunity, or it could backfire. If she could stall Russ long enough for Chase and the others to catch up to them, maybe she wouldn't have to use it.

She stopped and turned around. "I'm not going any further. Not until you explain things."

He waved the gun at her. "Turn your uppity self around and keep moving."

Crossing her arms, she didn't budge. "I'm waiting."

"You're joking, right?" He raised his gun. "Fine. I'll finish you off right here, right now."

"What happened to you? You could have done anything. Become someone great. Instead, you're living in a cave, robbing stores wearing a bear mask, stealing petty cash from my nightstand, and killing innocent people like some kind of wild beast."

His steely eyes grew colder, but his Adam's apple bobbed at her last remark. "You better shut that mouth of yours before I blow it away."

She persisted. "No. I want an answer. After everything you've put me through, you owe me the truth."

He laughed. "And I'm the one they think is crazy. All right, you want an answer, I'll give you one. The truth is, I never had a chance. Sure, I had brains, and I can turn on the charm when I need to, but when your old man is serving a life sentence for killing your mother, it doesn't give you a whole lot to work with, now does it?"

A gasp escaped her lips.

Russ continued. "He would have killed me too, if I hadn't run away . . ."

"How old were you?"

He snorted. "Fifteen." A strange faraway look clouded his eyes.

A twinge of compassion surfaced from deep within her, but even if what he'd said was true, it didn't justify the crimes he'd committed.

Her gaze shifted to his bloody arm. "You should let me treat that wound."

"Nice try, but you're not going to stall me any longer." He thrust the gun closer.

She shook her head and turned around. "Have it your way, but when it gets infected and they have to amputate, don't blame me."

He grabbed her arm and forced her to look at his face. "What you really want to know is if I ever really loved you. I can see it in your eyes." He reached out to touch her cheek, but she recoiled. "Well, I guess I loved you as much as anyone, but not enough for me to change. The best thing that ever happened to you is when that brother of yours found us and broke us up. That's all you need to know."

He jerked her arm and pulled her forward. "We're wasting time."

They'd traveled an hour through the forest, heading east. Russ was following an old mining route along the river. Jenny guessed they were three miles from camp. Her fingers secretly released the last of the marshmallows to the ground.

Russ stopped abruptly.

She noticed the small pup tent ahead. Billy's tent.

"Jenny!" a girl's voice cried.

Her eyes followed the sound until she spotted Wendy seated on a log with her hands and feet bound with ropes. Before she could respond, Russ moved behind her and poked the pistol in her back. "I believe you two know each other."

Jenny tried to turn, but he pressed the gun deeper in her spine. She yelled at him over her shoulder. "Why on earth did you bring Wendy all the way out here?"

"When that marshal man came after me at the Avalanche Grill, I knew I needed insurance in case he found me again. She was easy pickings, like a deer in the headlights."

"If you've hurt her . . ."

"Relax. She's fine." He looked at Wendy. "Tell her you're okay."

"I'm okay." Despite her words, Wendy's voice sounded weak and frightened, but other than her anxious eyes, she appeared unharmed.

Russ laid a hand on Jenny's shoulder and gripped it to the point of pain. "And she'll stay that way as long as you don't do anything stupid or heroic." He shoved her toward Wendy. "Now get over there and park yourself next to her."

Jenny stumbled to her friend and hugged her. "Don't worry," she whispered. "We'll get out of this soon."

Wendy nodded in return.

"Quit talking and move away from her!" Russ shouted.

Jenny shifted and sat a foot away from Wendy. "You told me to sit next to her."

A frown darkened his haggard face. "I changed my mind."

Hope sparked in Jenny. He was losing focus. "Why are you dragging us along? We'll only slow you down. You could escape right now."

"I wouldn't need to escape if you hadn't brought your friends out here to find me. So now you're going to help me get away."

"How's that?"

"You're the ranger. You're going to get me out of these mountains."

"Only after you release Wendy."

His eyes shifted to the gun he aimed at them. "In case you haven't noticed, you're not exactly in a position to negotiate."

"But why do you need her when you have me?"

"Quiet!"

Keeping the gun trained on them, he squatted on a large rock and stifled a yawn. His heavy-lidded eyes gave away his exhausted state.

Jenny knew he must be hungry and thirsty as well as tired. She glanced through the trees at the setting sun. "You only have an hour of daylight left, Russ. The others are probably closing in. If you let her go, we could get a good lead on them. The more time you waste, the less chance you have of getting away."

"Say I do let her go, what guarantee do I have that you won't double cross me?"

"You're the one carrying the gun."

"True." He said with a smug grin. Then he chuckled. "I remember when you couldn't kill a snake if it crawled in your lap and bit you. But you've toughened up since I left. I wonder if you've finally wised up and realized there is no God. There's only us, and it's every man for himself."

An inner strength emboldened her. "I still believe, Russ. Nothing you say or do will ever change that. For once in your life, why don't you stop running and face the truth?"

"The truth?" Russ spat. "Now you sound like that marshal I shot. He told me I could change. I could start over."

At his callous mention of Jim, she fumed, but the inner voice urged her to continue. "You should have listened to him. It's not too late."

He responded with a scornful laugh. "Don't try to save me, Jenny-girl. You of all people should know I'm beyond redemption. But I've decided to take you up on your offer. I'll let Wendy go." He rose and gave Jenny a wary look. "Untie her."

Jenny didn't waste any time undoing the knots around Wendy's ankles. She blocked his view as she untied her hands. "Go northwest," she whispered. "Follow the marshmallow bits."

Wendy nodded.

"Hurry up!" Russ shouted.

After Jenny finished untying her, Wendy slowly came to her feet. Her knees quaked as she nervously rubbed her sore wrists. She glanced at Jenny who sat back on the log.

He motioned with his gun for Wendy to leave. "Go. Get out of here before I shoot you both."

Wendy shot Jenny a woeful look before fleeing through the woods.

Jenny watched her disappear, thankful that she'd been spared.

Russ's mocking voice shattered the triumph of her momentary victory. "Looks like it's you and me, sugar. Now let's get going."

Chase's lungs felt like they would burst when he finally reached the camp ahead of the others on the task force. They'd taken a different route back that gained them some time, and he raced all the way back.

When he saw Kate wrapped in duct tape beside Jenny's half-dead dogs, he broke out in a cold sweat. He rushed to his colleague's side, alarmed by her deep cough and shivering.

A huge smile of relief colored her pale cheeks. "Jenny knew you'd come back. Russ took her with him."

His pulse pounded in his head. "When?"

"Over an hour ago."

"Are you okay?"

"Yes," she replied. "Go find her."

He pointed at Buck who had joined the collection of officers and volunteers surrounding Kate. "Buck, stay here with Kate. Webb has Jenny. I'm going after her."

Clint limped over to them. "Since I've got a bum ankle, I'll stay back and keep an eye on things here too."

"Thanks." Chase turned to Joel and John and the others on the task force. "We need to move fast and stay silent. Let's go."

"Chase," Kate said. "Look for a trail of marshmallows on the ground. I slipped her the rest of them before Russ took her away."

He smiled and nodded. "Thanks." He glanced over at Buck. "You take good care of her."

"Yes, sir."

Chase led the task force along Jenny's marshmallow trail for two long miles. Dark shadows stretched across the trail. He had to find Jenny before all light disappeared.

The sound of footsteps on the trail coming toward them put him on guard. He halted the group behind him then drew his weapon.

"Chase!" Wendy ran to him and collapsed in his arms.

Stunned and confused, he assisted her to her feet. "Wendy, what are you doing here?"

She clung to him, her expression frantic. "Russ kidnapped me."

He paused, trying to make sense of what she had told him. "Are you okay?"

She nodded breathlessly. "Now he's got Jenny. She talked him into letting me go if she helped him escape."

"Where were they headed?"

"I don't know. He let me go before they left his camp."

Chase turned to John. "Take her to the camp. I don't want her traveling alone."

John nodded and moved to escort her in the opposite direction.

After the two of them left, Chase blamed himself. "I shouldn't have left her and Kate alone."

Joel was standing next to him. "Sounds like my sister didn't leave you much choice. Besides, she can outwit and outshoot most men I know. Don't count her out."

"I'm not, but if anything happens to her . . ."

"Turn it over to the Lord, Chase. You're not the one in control. He is."

Chase released a heavy breath, acknowledging the truth in what Joel had said. Then he glanced at the fading sun. "There's not much daylight left. They can't be too far ahead of us."

"Let's make a run for it."

A few minutes later, they found what looked to be Russ's camp, but he and Jenny were gone.

Joel searched the ground. "That's the end of the trail of marshmallows."

Chase remembered the map. "With the rivers flooded and the bridge washed out, there's only one way out of here. We have to make sure Russ doesn't get there before we do."

Jenny stopped at the fork in the trail as déjà vu set in. It was the scene from her nightmare. The vision of Russ cornering her against the raging falls filled her with trepidation.

He gripped her arm. "What's the holdup?"

"There are two paths."

He rolled his eyes. "I can see that. Which one is faster?"

She remembered the bridge up ahead to the left was washed out. But Russ didn't know it. That could buy her time.

Or get her killed.

Either way, it was worth the chance.

"Take the trail on the right," she replied.

He eyed her with suspicion. "No, we'll take the one on the left." Then he jerked her toward the trail.

She dug her heels in, stalling.

"What's your problem now?" he yelled.

Tempted to pull out the mace and spray his face, she reconsidered. With her own pistol aimed at her, she couldn't take any chances. She reached in her back pocket and pulled out a tissue. "Cool your jets, Russ. My nose is running."

"Hurry up."

She defied him as she blew into the tissue.

"You're more trouble than you're worth, woman." He yanked her arm and dragged her down the trail, while she discreetly discarded the tissue on the ground behind her.

Chase and Joel reached the place where the trail split, ahead of the rest of the group.

"Look!" Chase said, "I see something." He rushed to the tissue a few feet down the path on the left. "They went this way."

Joel gave him a confused look. "But the bridge is washed out over the falls."

"We know that, but maybe Russ doesn't."

Joel smiled. "He'll be trapped against the river."

"I hope you know another way around the falls."

"Yeah."

"Good. I have an idea how we can make sure Russ can't get

away this time."

Jenny glanced at the sky. Only a few minutes of daylight left. She could sense the desperation in Russ growing with every step.

He shadowed her like a pesky flea. Her arm ached from his vice-like grip as he jerked her forward.

A desperate fugitive is a dangerous one, she reminded herself. Where was Chase? It would be so much harder to find them after dark.

An off-key bird song caught her attention. She listened carefully. Definitely the worst American Dipper call she'd ever heard.

Then she smiled.

She and Russ reached the waterfall ten minutes later at dusk.

He dragged her toward the rushing, glacial waters that ran over the falls, pulling her to the edge. "Where's the bridge?"

The sound of the falls roared in her ears. She stared at the treacherous current rushing past, only inches from her feet. If he let go of her arm, she would plummet to her death.

He shook her. "I said, where's the bridge?"

She swallowed hard. "It's washed out—but I can still get us out of here."

He snorted like a bull ready to charge. "This is a trap! You set me up. I've had enough of you and your marshals. Now you're gonna pay."

"Like you made Jim and Billy pay?"

"No, I'm giving you a choice: you can either jump or I'll push. It's up to you."

She struggled against him as panic closed in. "Don't do this, Russ. It's not too late, but if you kill me, you'll never get away."

He scoffed. "It doesn't matter, I'm already dead." Then he released her arm.

She teetered for a moment, struggling to regain her balance—

praying she wouldn't fall in.

"Looks like I'll have to push." He shoved her over the edge.

The roar of the falls drowned her scream as she descended. She clawed the air, fighting for her life.

Russ snatched the back of her shirt, halting her fall. He laughed as he dangled her over the water like a bear with a fish in his paws.

Her cries and attempts to reach back and grab hold of him were all in vain. The rapids rushed below like a wild freight train of death.

"What's the matter, Jenny-girl? Are you afraid?" he said in a mocking voice.

Tempted to despair, she reminded herself that death had been conquered. It brought her peace and gave her courage. "I'm not afraid of dying, but I am afraid for you."

He scoffed. "That's funny, when you're the one about to drown. Well, let's see how brave you are on the count of three."

"Russ, please don't!"

"One.

"Two . . ."

"Stop right there, Webb! It's over."

Hearing Chase's command, Jenny's heart surged with hope. Maybe she could still be rescued.

Russ clutched her shirt tighter. "Yeah? What are you going to do about it?"

"Let go of my sister, Russ. You're outnumbered."

At the sound of her brother's voice across the water, Jenny's head popped up.

Joel stood on the other side of the falls, accompanied by a small army of law enforcement officers with their weapons trained on Russ.

Russ yanked her up.

As soon as her feet touched the ground, Jenny lunged to get away.

He caught her by the arm, and pressed the SIG to her temple.

"Not so fast, Jenny-girl." He shouted to the others. "If you try anything, she's dead."

A chopper appeared overhead and circled above them.

Russ glanced up, his face twisted in a scowl.

Jenny struck his arm and stomped his foot. Before he could react, she snatched the mace from her pocket and sprayed his face.

He let out a wild scream, dropping Jenny's gun as his hands flew to his eyes.

She scooped up her pistol and aimed it at Russ, then turned and backed away in Chase's direction. "I've been wanting to do that all day."

Blinded by the irritant, Russ groped for Kate's gun stashed in his pants.

Joel and the others across the river kept their weapons fixed on him.

"If you want to live, Webb, you better drop it," Chase called. "And that rifle over your shoulder too."

Russ spat as he turned around. "So you finally got your revenge." He tossed the weapons to the ground, coughing and squinting his red, swollen eyes.

"Now raise your hands over your head and slowly walk toward me," Chase shouted.

Russ lifted his arms in surrender, grimacing in Chase's direction as he stepped forward.

When Chase ordered him to stop, two other officers moved to cuff him.

Chase guarded Russ, his gun steady, while other members of the task force searched him for weapons and secured him in a waist chain.

For the first time since Jim's death, Chase felt a small measure of satisfaction. Russ's capture wouldn't bring Jim back, but at least when he was finally behind bars, he couldn't hurt anyone else.

This is for you, Jim. Rest in peace, buddy.

After the officers had finished securing him, Russ sneered at Chase. "Hey, Marshal, whatever happened to that friend of yours? You know, the one I shot. He died, didn't he? Died like a dog. That's why you came all the way out here, isn't it? To get your revenge. In the end, there's really no difference between you and me."

More than anything, Chase wanted to rid the planet of Russ Webb. "Shut your trap, Webb, or we'll put ankle chains on you and drag you back to prison."

Russ shook his shackled hands and rattled his chains. "Go ahead. Settle the score. I know you want to."

Chase's finger tightened on the trigger. He suddenly found himself in his nightmare, pressing his hands over Jim's bloody thigh.

The pastor's words echoed in his mind. *So what's keeping you from God? Will you trust Him with whatever it is?*

"No, Chase. Don't."

The sound of Jenny's voice cleared the crimson fog. He snapped back to the present and removed his finger from the trigger, then clicked on the safety. After holstering his gun, he sent Jenny a reassuring wink.

Her anxious expression relaxed into a smile of relief.

Chase looked Russ in the eye. "You're wrong, Webb. There's a big difference between you and me."

With a criminal like Webb in their custody, no one got any sleep at camp that night. Most of the men stayed awake playing cards, keeping a watchful eye on him. They were killing time until first light when they would head back to civilization.

Chase stoked the blazing fire, glancing at Russ.

Russ glared back, sneering.

Chase focused on the fire. While the flickering flames

engaged his eyes, his mind was preoccupied with thoughts of Jenny, and his future. When he returned to Tennessee with the fugitive, how could he go back to his former life without Jenny? But he couldn't ask her to give up everything here to follow him. Besides, she deserved someone with an unshakeable faith like her own. He was only beginning to discover God personally, and still had a long way to go.

Jenny lay awake in her sleeping bag, bundled in the warmth of Chase's sweatshirt, with Wendy on the other side of Fred and Ginger in the crowded tent.

Wendy finally spoke from the shadows. "Are you awake, Jenny?"

"Yeah. I can't sleep."

"Me neither."

Jenny propped her head on her elbow. "You gave us quite a scare, you know. We all thought you ran off with Reggie."

Wendy looked down. "I know. Dad told me over the radio earlier."

"I drove past Reggie's cabin last Friday on my way home and saw you two arguing outside."

Wendy glanced up. "Yeah, it got pretty ugly. After our lunch at the lake, I decided I wasn't ready to get serious with anyone yet, much less someone I barely know. I stopped by his cabin to break it off. He was packing like he was moving out. When I asked him where he was going, he got all weird and said he wanted me to come with him to Vegas. Now I know he just wanted to keep me quiet. He probably would have dumped me like a hot potato once we hit Nevada. What a creep. If you hadn't warned me, Jenny, I could have made the biggest mistake of my life."

"You've had a pretty crazy summer so far, haven't you? I bet you can't wait to get back to college now."

"Actually, I've been thinking about that. I've decided to

transfer to Washington State."

Jenny stared at her, surprised. "Really? Why?"

"I think my dad is lonely with me gone so much. Besides, I kind of miss it here. Who knows? Maybe I'll become a park ranger, like you."

Jenny liked the sound of that. "Hey, I almost forgot." She grabbed her backpack and retrieved Wendy's cell and wallet. "They found these on Russ. Chase asked me to give them back to you."

"Thanks." Wendy punched the power button. "The battery's dead. Guess I won't be texting anyone tonight." She opened her wallet and pulled out the fake ID. "Please take this and burn it in the coals tomorrow morning before we leave."

Jenny took it from her and smiled. She put the card away and rolled over to go to sleep. With Russ in camp, she doubted she'd get very much.

CHAPTER TWENTY-THREE

Jenny woke early and quickly changed into her ranger uniform. While Wendy and her dogs snoozed, she opened the door flap of the tent and crawled out.

The first streaks of daylight greeted her in hues of pink, purple, and orange. She inhaled the fresh, clean air. They were finally going home.

"Well, look who's up." Chase strode over and offered her his fresh cup of hot coffee. "Did you sleep?"

She rose to her feet and rubbed her palms together to remove the dirt before taking the cup. "Not much. How about you?"

"I spent most of the night thinking."

She took a sip of the drink. It wasn't Cascade Java, but it tasted good on the cool morning. "Thinking about what?"

He shrugged. "Just stuff . . . How are Fred and Ginger?"

"I think they're going to pull through."

"Can they make it back down?"

"Joel offered to make a litter for them. He'll go with Clint and Kate, so I can guide the group."

Chase nodded. "By the way, Kate's looking much better this morning, but it will be tough for her to hike with that foot."

"I wish there was another way back, but I'm afraid she and Clint will both have to tough it out until we get to an area where a chopper can land. Speaking of Clint, have you seen him this morning?"

"Yeah. He's still limping from that sprained ankle. He's been going around to everyone on the task force, making sure we're all wearing these." Chase opened his marshal jacket, revealing the avalanche beacon strapped on. "He even put one on Webb."

"Good. Because of the flooding and washed-out bridges, we'll take a quicker, but more rugged route that passes through an area with heavy snowpack, so it's best to take precautions."

He examined her ranger shirt under her jacket. "Where's yours?"

"Still in my pack. I haven't had a chance to put it on."

Gazing at the sunrise, a wistful smile appeared on his face. "I'll miss these mountains."

"When we get home, you can go hiking anytime you want."

"It'll be harder to do that from Tennessee."

She shivered as a chill set in. Sadness at the thought of Chase's departure tempered her relief at having Russ in custody. "When will you leave?"

"I have to fly Webb to Tennessee tonight."

"That soon?"

He gently lifted her chin with his finger. "Don't look so sad. We knew this day would come."

"I know. I've gotten used to wearing your sweatshirt. That's all."

"Keep it until I come back."

"I like the sound of that."

"What?"

"You coming back."

He smiled. "Me too. Hey, that reminds me." He reached in his pocket and held out the silver cross. "Thanks for loaning this to me."

She touched his fingers and folded them over it again. "Hold on to it until you return. Then we'll do an exchange."

He returned it to his pocket. "Deal."

After her conversation with Chase, Jenny found Clint who was searching through his bag. "What are you looking for, Clint?"

When he saw her, his brow wrinkled. "Avalanche beacons. I looked for you and Wendy earlier to give you one, but now I'm out. Did you bring any with you?"

She'd given all of hers to the search party three days ago. Seeing his disturbed expression, she smiled to set his mind at ease. "Don't worry. I've got it covered."

Jenny doused the coals after she and Wendy burned the fake ID in the fire pit. When they came to her tent, Jenny found her backpack and pulled out her beacon to give to Wendy. "I want you to put this on."

Wendy gave her a curious look. "An avalanche beacon?"

Jenny tossed her an easy smile, not wishing to alarm her. "It's a transmitter so we won't lose you again. Come on, I'll show you how to strap it on before we break down the tent." Jenny zipped her jacket over her bulletproof vest. She'd be hot, but no one would notice her missing beacon. It was only a precaution anyway.

After Wendy had been rigged with the beacon, Joel joined them at their site. "Need a hand with your tent?"

"Sure." Jenny turned to Wendy. "Since Joel is here, why don't you see if Clint needs help with the dogs?"

After Wendy left, Jenny tried to appear casual. "Did you know Chase plans to fly to Tennessee tonight?"

Joel pulled the tent spikes from the ground. "I figured as much. It won't be the same without him around. He's become like one of the family." He stopped and looked at her. "Something tells me you don't want him to leave either."

She shrugged. "I kind of got used to him hanging around."

"It's more than that, and you know it."

"Maybe, but what if he goes home and forgets all about us?"

"Don't give up on him, Jen. He needs us now more than ever, whether he knows it or not."

She nodded. "You know, sometimes you're not such a bad guy to have for a big brother."

"Only sometimes, huh?"

She laughed. "We better get moving, or they'll leave without us." She glanced at Chase, who was mustering the marshals and the other members of the task force for the return trip. A chill shot up her spine at the thought of him guarding Russ on the journey home. "I wish they could get a chopper up here to take Russ away."

"Me too, but it can't land with all the trees and rugged terrain."

"Between you and me, I really dread this trip. I wish there was another way home."

"Unfortunately, the route we're taking through the mountains is our only option." Joel gave her a reassuring grin. "It'll be okay. You know the way, and Chase and his team are professionals."

"Under normal conditions, I would agree," she replied with a serious look, "but you and I both know there's nothing normal or predictable in the mountains."

The rising sun in the clear blue sky promised another beautiful, warmer-than-usual day, but clouds still hovered over Jenny's thoughts. This might very well be the last chapter of her life with Chase Matthews. A chapter she didn't want to end.

Jenny and Wendy waited at the front of the group while the task force officers, covered in body armor and weapons, formed a line in front and behind Russ.

Chase watched as John checked that Russ's hands were secured in the cuffs and waist chain. In order for Russ to hike the rugged terrain, his feet had to be free.

The thought of Chase guarding Russ on the journey bothered Jenny. She turned to Wendy and masked her concern with an upbeat smile. "I bet you're ready to go home, huh?"

Wendy nodded emphatically. "I can't wait to see Dad. I know he's been worried sick about me."

When the group was ready to start the hike, Jenny took the lead. She positioned Wendy next to her so she could keep a close eye on her.

They traveled a couple of miles along the winding path through thick forests. Snowmelt had degraded the trail into a muddy bog.

Jenny called out to the others behind her to watch their step in the slippery ooze.

Tiny birds flew up and bugs scattered as they plowed through a dense thicket.

"Ouch," Wendy cried. "I think something stung me."

Jenny looked over her shoulder. "Are you okay?"

"Yeah—oh, no!"

Jenny halted and spun around. "What is it, Wendy?"

"My phone. It must have fallen out of my pocket. I've got to find it." Wendy did a one-eighty and began dodging around the task force officers before anyone could stop her.

"Wendy, wait!" Jenny cried.

Wendy wove around the officers through the mud and maze of thick foliage without stopping.

Jenny called to the officers nearby. "Somebody stop her!"

Chase noticed an impediment in the route and halted. The dense brush and slippery path would add a new challenge. "Hey, Buck, tell the group to hold up."

The young marshal stopped and ordered the officers further ahead to wait.

Chase frowned as he surveyed the sticky situation. The bushes squeezed the trail, and the mud was slick. Despite Russ being confined to the waist chain, Chase couldn't take anything for granted. There was only room for one person at a time to clear the narrow opening in the thicket. With John guarding Russ's rear, Chase moved in between Russ and Buck. Once he'd taken his new position, he gave the order to proceed.

He peered over his shoulder and caught the smirk on Russ's face.

Facing forward again, Chase felt something sting his neck.

Jenny shed her pack to go after Wendy.

Clint blocked her path. "Where do you think you're going?"

"It's Wendy. She went back to get her phone—" Jenny slipped past Clint and the other task force members who had halted because of Chase's order.

Through the foliage in the distance, she spotted Chase stumble to the ground.

An officer moved in front of her.

She struggled to get around him.

"We have a situation. I can't let you through."

Realizing it was a losing battle to get past the big man, Jenny turned back and detoured off the trail through the brush until she reached a spot with a view of Chase. Trapped behind a briar patch, Jenny watched in horror as Wendy emerged from the thicket near Chase and slipped in the mud, landing at Russ's feet.

Peering up at her former captor, Wendy froze.

As John reached to assist her, Russ landed him a sharp kick in the groin.

John cried out and doubled over in pain.

Chase and Buck both drew their weapons and fired at Russ as he dove in the mud, dodging their bullets. In a split second, he flipped over, swiveled his legs, and kicked the gun out of Chase's hand while evading Buck's second shot. Sliding toward the pistol, Russ maneuvered it into his cuffed hands before Buck and John could get a good aim. Then thrusting his foot out, he took the two marshals down in the mud with him and Chase.

Jenny bushwhacked through the bramble, branches and thorns tearing her flesh.

But it was too late. Russ's legs were wrapped around Wendy's neck in a choke hold as he swiveled Chase's pistol toward the back of her head.

Jenny froze, assessing the situation. Russ now had the upper hand. For Wendy and Chase's sake, she couldn't risk making any sudden moves.

A couple of officers emerged through the narrow clearing and halted, assessing the situation.

Clint stopped behind her. He had hauled her pack with him from the front. They exchanged alarmed glances.

Then she turned toward Chase, mystified by his affliction. Why was he laying in the mud, unable to get up? His condition alarmed her. If Russ realized how incapacitated Chase was, he might exploit it to get back at her. If only she could go to him.

Sprawled on the ground, Chase met her gaze with a painful grimace. "Bee . . ."

"Take one more step and your little friend here dies."

Jenny halted at Russ's harsh voice.

With amazing agility, he released his legs from Wendy's throat and rose to his knees, keeping his weapon fixed on her. Restricted by the chain around his waist and attached to his cuffs, he prodded Wendy with the gun. "Now get up slowly, sweetheart."

He poked her with the butt of the Glock as he came to his feet, and she gasped. "Move toward me," he ordered as he pressed his back against the thicket.

Trembling, Wendy obeyed.

Torn between saving Chase or Wendy, Jenny knew she had to do something fast. "Chase will die if I don't give him an injection, Russ."

"Then tell your friends to hand Wendy the key to the cuffs, drop their weapons, and beat it." He eyed Chase with cool detachment. "Better act quick. Your marshal is fading fast."

Jenny fingered her weapon, hoping for a break. But with Russ using Wendy as a human shield, it was too risky.

Buck and John had frozen in the mud, not wanting to rile Russ.

Chase fought for breath, too weak to push himself up from

the bog.

Jenny had endured enough of Russ's sick little spectacle. Time was running out. She turned to John. "Hand Wendy the key, John. Chase will die if I don't give him an injection."

John hesitated only a second, then removed the key from a pocket. He cautiously crawled to Wendy and handed it to her.

"The rest of you, drop your weapons and go," Russ shouted. "Any sudden moves and the co-ed is dead."

Buck and John left their weapons in the mud, cautiously rising to their feet and backing away. They joined the other two officers who had laid their weapons on the ground. Then they stealthily disappeared in the bushes.

Russ nudged Wendy with the gun. "If you want to live, pretty girl, and you want your friends to live, you'll turn around and unlock my cuffs."

Wendy glanced at Jenny, who gave her a nod. "Do what he says, Wendy."

Slowly, Wendy turned until she faced him. Hands shaking, she took the key and unlocked his handcuffs and chain while he kept the Glock aimed at her.

He smirked at Jenny. "You know, you haven't changed one bit, Jenny-girl. You're still as gullible as the day I met you."

She held her tongue. All that mattered now were Chase and Wendy.

When Russ vanished through the bushes, Jenny rushed to Chase's side.

Clint joined her with a first aid kit.

She grabbed the EpiPen and quickly went to work.

Wendy stood by watching. "He's not going to die, is he?"

"No!" Jenny replied, banishing the prospect of his death from her ears and her thoughts.

The two officers came to retrieve their weapons and quickly left to search for Russ. Then Kate appeared with Joel, who pulled Fred and Ginger on a litter.

After Clint and Joel turned Chase over on his back, Jenny

raised the needle. "I'm sorry, baby, but I have to do this."

He nodded weakly and barely winced when she stabbed his thigh with the injection.

She softly kissed his forehead then held his hand and rubbed it while he slowly recovered. "You're going to be all right."

He blinked a couple of times. Soon his ragged breathing relaxed.

Joel helped him sit up. "You've got nine lives, buddy."

Chase exhaled a long breath. "I don't deserve friends like you." He glanced from Joel to Jenny. "You've saved my life twice now. Once, I could dismiss, but not twice. I'm beginning to believe what you've been saying to me all along, Jen. Maybe there's hope for me yet."

He tried to get up.

Joel laid a hand on his shoulder. "Wait a minute. Where do you think you're going?"

"To get Webb."

"Don't worry about him right now. The others will catch him."

A few minutes later Chase's radio went off. "Chase, it's John. Are you there?"

Chase pulled the radio from his belt. "Roger that."

"Man, it's good to hear your voice. Are you okay?"

"I'm not a hundred percent yet, but I'm getting there. What's going on?"

"We found Webb. He's heading up the mountain."

"I'll be right there."

Jenny glanced at the snowy peak of Mt. Buckner high above them. "He'll never make it."

"Maybe not, but we've got to make sure he doesn't." Chase reached for John and Buck's weapons. He holstered one, and handed the other one to Joel. Then he attempted to stand with Joel's assistance, stumbling as he came to his feet.

Jenny shook her head. "You're in no shape to go."

"I've got no choice." He stared at his hands. They trembled

from the effects of the adrenaline. "Besides, I feel like I've been launched from a rocket after that shot you gave me."

"Then I'm going with you."

"What about Fred and Ginger? You need to see to them."

Clint, who'd stayed behind because of his ankle, spoke up. "Don't you worry. I will see that Wendy, Kate, and your dogs get home. You do what you need to do."

Adrenaline from the EpiPen and the hunt for Russ kicked in and fortified Chase with enough strength to keep pace with Jenny and Joel. When they met up with the others, Buckner Mountain towered over them, white and foreboding. Its glaciers and snow-filled crevasses glistened in the sunlight.

At the beating sound of a helicopter, Jenny looked up. She could see it through the trees, circling above them.

"There he is," Chase said, pointing to the figure climbing the steep slope. "I'm going after him. He's getting away."

Jenny grabbed his arm. "No. He's too far up."

He reached for the gun in his holster.

She touched his hand. "Don't, Chase. It's too dangerous. With all that snow and this warm weather, it's the perfect conditions for—"

A huge wall of snow broke off from above them and tumbled down the mountain like a white tsunami.

"Avalanche!" Joel shouted as the snow hurtled toward them. "Run!"

Chase grabbed Jenny's hand. They raced with the others away from the cascading snow.

Jenny glanced over her shoulder at the huge white wave hurtling toward them, the muscles in her legs burning as she panted for air.

The earth shook with the thunderous noise as the avalanche closed the gap behind them.

She let go of Chase and lifted her hands to thrash the

incoming snow. "Swim, Chase!" She looked his way, catching a fleeting glimpse of him before the white monster descended and separated them. She kept swimming with her hands and feet, breaking up the snow as much as possible before it buried her completely. A moment later all went silent.

And dark.

She tried to move but couldn't budge. The avalanche had entombed her in snowy cement.

Buried alive.

Don't panic. You've got time.

One hand was stuck near her face. She wiggled her fingers a little, making a tiny air pocket so she could breathe.

She shouted at the top of her lungs and waited for a reply.

Dead silence.

She yelled again, but the snow muffled her cries.

Icy cold stung her skin. Her lungs ached for oxygen.

Her heartbeat, amplified and desperate, screamed through the tomb-like silence. *You're going to die. They'll never find you in time.*

"No!" She pushed the morbid thoughts away.

The faint sensation of warmth teased her other hand. She tunneled her freezing fingertips through the white cement until she touched the source.

Chase's fingers.

They held hers and squeezed them, assuring her that he was there. Alive.

She closed her eyes and thanked God.

Faint sounds of voices calling from above buoyed her hopes. A search party. She yelled again as loud as she could, struggling to free herself from the snowy straight jacket.

She heard the muffled sound of Chase's voice shouting too.

Joel called from somewhere above. "Chase! Jenny!"

Warmth filled her heart and a tear escaped her eye. Joel was all right. She shouted his name as loud as she could. The feat left her gasping for air.

The weight of the snow crushed her chest. Her pounding heart echoed in the silent white tomb while she fought against panic and her collapsing lungs.

Chase squeezed her hand every second, encouraging her to hang on.

Her thoughts wandered to the top of the mountain where she floated, looking down at its splendor. She must be dreaming or dying, for she felt light and free now. Panic had been replaced with peace unlike any she'd known before.

She didn't know how much time passed, but somehow she didn't care. Then, suddenly, a bright light appeared in the distance. She could no longer see the mountain below or anything but the brilliant light. She heard familiar voices from inside the light calling her name.

"Come back to us, Jenny. Jenny, honey, wake up!"

She gasped and coughed as her eyes fluttered open, squinting into the sun's radiance. She saw familiar faces hovering over her, twisted with shock and concern.

"She's okay," Chase yelled to the others.

"Praise God!" Joel shouted with raised hands.

Chase, who was kneeling beside her, took her hand in his and rubbed it, restoring warmth to it. "Jenny, sweetheart," he said in a soothing, loving tone, "we were buried alive in the avalanche, but Joel and the others found us and dug us out, thanks to those beacons. Joel administered CPR and saved your life."

His wet clothes were caked with mud from his battle with Russ. Her gaze traveled to his face, so full of concern for her.

His exuberant smile.

The intensity of his gaze.

He really loved her.

Joel knelt beside her and took her other hand. "Hey, sis."

Warmth flooded her heart at seeing her brother again. "Hey, Joel. Thanks for saving my life."

He shrugged. "That's what big brothers are for."

She smiled back. "What about the others?"

"Six people were buried, including you. Now everyone on the task force is accounted for. We found you just in the nick of time too. Everyone had a beacon except you."

Wendy knelt beside Joel.

"Wendy, what are you doing here? I thought you were with Clint."

"We heard about the avalanche over the radio so we all came to help with the search." She displayed the beacon Jenny had given her earlier. "This one is yours, isn't it?"

Jenny smiled, happy to see her young friend. "Guess it worked, huh?" She turned back to Chase. "What about Russ?"

His smile abated as he shook his head. "We'll keep looking until we find him, but I don't think there's any way he could have survived under all that snow."

She pushed herself to her elbows, moaning from her stiff limbs.

"Hey now, take it easy." He helped her sit up. "You've been through a lot."

"I'm fine. Give me a hand, and I'll be ready to go." Chase took her arm and helped her to her feet. She fell against him. "Whoa," she said, touching her forehead. "I guess I need a few more minutes to catch my breath before we hike back."

"We're not hiking. A chopper is picking us up. The avalanche cleared a place for the chopper to land. Some of the rangers went to fetch Clint, Kate, and your dogs, so they can go back with us."

She exhaled a deep breath. "That's a relief. I wasn't exactly looking forward to a long hike after this."

Buck ran toward them, breathless and excited. "Russ is dead. He must have forgotten about the beacon when Wendy took off his cuffs. It led us right to him."

CHAPTER TWENTY-FOUR

A BEAUTIFUL SUNSET PAINTED THE SUMMER sky with brilliant pinks, yellows, and reds. Jenny took a moment to enjoy the scene framed by distant mountain peaks before heading to Lucy's cage.

"When are Fred and Ginger coming home?" Chase stepped into view on the edge of her yard.

His arrival brought a happy smile to her lips. She turned as he strolled into her backyard. "They'll be at the animal hospital in Watkinsville a few more days, but they're getting better. You came in time for Lucy's sendoff into the wild."

"Here, let me." He strode to the maimed fox's cage near the pet carrier and bent to peer inside at the baby cougars. "You know, these cubs need a bigger home."

"Actually, I'm taking them to the wildlife refuge tomorrow. Want to come with me?"

"I wouldn't miss it."

"Adam is coming too."

Chase lifted the fox's cage and set it on the ground beside Jenny. "Lucy's finally getting her freedom . . . Strangely enough, I can relate."

Jenny laughed. "Me too. When I think about being buried under all that snow, it still makes me shiver."

"Actually, I was referring to something else."

She gave him a curious look as she crouched by the cage to say goodbye to Lucy.

"Jenny, there's something I want to tell you."

"This sounds serious."

He knelt beside her. "It's all so new to me, I'm not sure I can explain. When the avalanche buried us under the snow, I thought it was over. A million things crossed my mind at that moment, but one thought stayed with me. If I survived, I promised God I would change. I don't know what took me so long to trust Him. I guess I was afraid to let go." Chase scoffed at himself. "It's not like I had any control over anything anyway. Now I know my life is in much better hands than it ever was with me in the driver's seat."

Joy overwhelmed Jenny as she came to her knees and reached to take his hand. "You've finally found your burning bush."

Chase looked down and chuckled. "I was a hard case, wasn't I?" His gaze met hers. "I'll need you to keep me honest."

Her fingers threaded his. "I'll be with you every step of the way." With a teasing glint, she added, "and in case you do stray off course, I'll carry a spare EpiPen with me."

He grinned, his eyes reflecting the sunset. "You'd do that, wouldn't you?"

She stared him down until he laughed. Then the reality of him leaving filled her with sadness "You know, it won't be easy keeping tabs on you with me in Washington and you in Tennessee."

He glanced at their entwined fingers. "I've been thinking about that, and I've decided I don't want to go back to my old life in Tennessee."

She gazed at him, her hopes rising. "What do you mean?"

"I want to be here, with you. This is where I belong. I realize that now. It's funny. My life has been completely turned upside down, but I've never been happier." He smiled, his eyes sparkling with vitality and warmth.

Excitement bubbled inside her like a mountain spring. "Now I have something to confess."

"Uh-oh. Look, if you're a fugitive from the law, I don't want to hear it."

Jenny shook her head, laughing. "Don't worry. It's nothing like that. It's about us."

He sat on the ground. "Us? This I wanna hear."

She joined him, sitting cross-legged. "You know, while we were buried under the snow, the only thing that kept me focused was your hand squeezing mine. When I lost consciousness, I thought I'd died, but your voice drew me back, and I realized how much you mean to me."

He took both of her hands in his and kissed them. "Jenny, I know I have a long way to go, but I do want to be a better man." Lowering his gaze, his voice resonated with sincerity and love. "And one day, I hope to marry you, if you'll have me."

A rush of happiness flooded her heart. "Is next summer too soon?"

His face lit in a brilliant smile. "You mean it?"

She nodded, grinning.

Leaning closer, he pressed his lips to hers in a fervent kiss. Then he smiled, regarding her with love and anticipation. "When can we send the wedding invitations?"

She giggled. "It's still a year away."

"I don't care. I want to tell the world." He jumped up and reached for her hand. "Come on, let's start with Joel and Lori."

"Wait. First things first." Jenny opened the door to the cage.

The fox paced around nervously, not sure what to do.

"Go on, Lucy. The world's waiting for you."

The little creature stared at her for a moment before taking off toward the trees.

Chase helped Jenny to her feet and wrapped his arm around her as they watched the fox vanish into the woods.

The sun had slipped below the horizon, leaving the sky streaked with color. A deer and two fawns grazed in the nearby meadow.

He pointed upward. "Look, an eagle." It soared above them like an unfettered kite.

Jenny's gaze drifted to Chase. "You don't think you'll get bored living out here, away from all the big city action?"

He drew her close, kissing her again. "Not a chance. Besides,

I can't imagine anywhere more exciting than right here with you."

Author Note

The seed for the story of *Avalanche* was planted when I learned about a fox injured in a trap. She chewed off her leg to escape, yet survived to live a remarkably normal life. It made me think about those of us, who, like that fox, have been hurt, sometimes outwardly, but more often, inwardly. So we go through life with hearts and souls trapped, not knowing how to break free. *Avalanche* is about freedom and healing of the heart and the soul.

I chose the North Cascades National Park for the setting because it is the perfect place for a wilderness adventure. Its spectacular mountain scenery and rugged backcountry are a hiker's dream, but there are a few hazards too. One summer, while hiking in the Cascade Mountains, I noticed the trails closed due to the avalanche danger. At that time, I didn't know avalanches could occur in summer months, and the idea intrigued me. Thankfully, I've never been caught in one!

I hope as you read *Avalanche* you experience the joy and wonder of God's creation, and the peace and freedom of His love.

Learn more about Gayla on her website at:
www.gaylakhiss.com
Join her on Facebook at:
https://www.facebook.com/profile.php?id=623160321192569

Book Club Questions

1. Jenny has withdrawn from God after her father's death. When have you been tempted to withdraw from God? What was the result?
2. Jenny treasures the cross her father gave her for her 16th birthday. What does the cross mean to you?
3. Chase doesn't want to forgive because then he would have to give up his desire for revenge. Which aspects of forgiving others do you find most difficult? What blessings have you received when you have forgiven someone?
4. After the cougar is killed, Jenny is angry with Chase, though he saved her life. What helps you see the big picture when you are hurting?
5. Chase has trouble fully committing to God and trusting Him with his life. In which areas of your life do you find it difficult to trust God? What are some easy areas to trust Him with?
6. Jenny wants to marry someone who shares her faith. What challenges are there to marrying someone who doesn't share your faith? What benefits are there in marrying someone who does?
7. Jenny has to face several crises like being threatened at the falls by Russ and being caught in the avalanche. What helps you through the crises in your life?
8. As Chase draws closer to God, he wants to be a better man. How has your faith transformed you into a better person?

Now, A Sneak Peek at Book Two

Dangerous Ground

CHAPTER ONE

THE SOUND OF RAIN DRUMMING on metal roused Kate Phillips to her senses. Slowly, she opened her eyes. Battered and sore from the airbag and seatbelt, she gingerly touched her face, tracing the stray tear on her cheek—or was it blood?

Images and sounds replayed in her mind . . . the stormy night . . . a hooded man crossing the road . . . his bandaged face and wild eyes before she swerved to avoid him . . . the large tree in her way . . . the crash of metal and glass . . . the silence of darkness. The impact from the collision had scrambled her brain. Where was she?

A bright beam illuminated her car. Shielding her eyes, Kate squinted as a man came into view, holding a flashlight.

He shouted through the glass. "Are you okay?"

She nodded and touched the button next to her. The window wouldn't open. She tried the door. Jammed.

The man panned his light to her passenger seat.

Kate gasped at the massive tree trunk that had crushed the front right side of her car.

"I'll be right back," he said, then disappeared.

Alone in her confusion, Kate relied on her instincts. Shifting toward the door, she attempted to shove it open, but the pain forced her to stop.

The light returned. When she saw the man carrying a crowbar, she exhaled with relief.

"I'll pry it open," he shouted.

She pushed from inside while he inserted the crowbar into the crack and pressed against it, using his body for leverage.

The door gave way and Kate lurched, her seatbelt preventing her from falling out. She spotted the man searching the autumn leaves on the ground in the rain. "Are you all right?" she called.

"I lost my flashlight." He found it and scooped it up. After wiping his muddy palm on his soaked jeans, he clicked it on as he came toward her.

"Where are we?" she asked.

His brows pinched together with concern as he stared at her. "Great Smoky Mountains National Park."

"Now I remember. I was on my way to the campground."

"Camping tonight, in this rain?" He glanced at the downpour. "You'd be better off staying at the motel in Tyler's Glen. It's only five miles away."

He touched her wrist and she jumped.

"It's all right," he said in a calm, reassuring voice. "I'm only checking your pulse."

Watching him with a wary eye, she didn't know if she should thank him or draw her gun.

"Good. It's strong and steady." When he released her hand, his gaze traveled past her to the passenger side of her Miata. "I wish I could say the same for your car. You're lucky to be alive."

He shined the flashlight toward her eyes. "Now look at me."

She squinted into the light.

"Your eyes aren't dilated. That's a good sign."

"But now I'm blind," she replied in a dry tone.

The corner of his mouth ticked up. "Only temporarily."

As the fog in her brain lifted, a sea of emotions rolled in, bringing tears to her eyes. *Lord, if this is a nightmare, please wake me up.*

She released her seatbelt and moved to get out.

"Whoa," the man said, gently touching her shoulder. "Sit still for a minute. You're still in shock."

She ignored him and pulled her backpack from what was left of the passenger seat to get her phone.

"What are you doing?"

"Calling 911."

"I'm the closest thing you'll find to a paramedic around here tonight. I'm a member of the volunteer fire department."

She sighed and reluctantly put the phone away. "So what now?"

"Let me give you a ride into town."

"Look, I really appreciate you rescuing me, but I think I'll take my chances on my own. After all, I don't even know your name."

He bent on one knee to look her in the eye. "I'm David Jennings. Nice to meet you." Raindrops dribbled down his forehead into his eyes, making him grimace. "We've got to get out of this storm."

Lightning streaked the sky, followed by a loud boom.

Startled, Kate clutched David's jacket and clung to him.

"It's okay," he said in a soft, consoling voice. "It's only thunder."

She gazed into his riveting blue eyes. For a moment, she almost forgot about the accident and the storm.

He gently coaxed her. "Come on, let's go."

Slowly, she released him. "Sorry. I don't usually react like this. The accident must have affected me more than I realized."

"It's okay. You know, they say lightning never strikes the same place twice."

"Then this should be the safest place on earth."

A lightning bolt struck a tree nearby, sending sparks flying in the air.

Kate grabbed David again as the deafening roar of thunder pounded her ears.

"Then again, I never believed that old saying." He swept her into his arms as rain mixed with small chunks of ice pummeled the ground.

She yelled over the wind and torrential downpour, "What are you doing? Put me down."

"In case you haven't noticed, it's hailing." Carrying her, he quickly ascended the embankment to the highway.

Despite her protests, she clung to him. The warmth and strength of his arms calmed her and made her feel safe.

When they reached his dark gray pickup, he opened the passenger door, stepped on the running board, and gently set her inside. "I'll go get your things."

His departure gave her time to think. She scanned the dark forest by the road, realizing she didn't have many options. Her hands trembled from the shock of the accident. Vigorously, she rubbed them, hoping to steady herself.

Her gun! It was still in her backpack. She had to get it.

David returned with his hands full.

When he opened the driver side door, she pounced before he had time to get out of the rain. "Where's my backpack?"

Stepping away, he stared at her. "Take it easy. It's right here."

When he lifted it so she could see, she snatched it from his hands.

"You're welcome," he said in a dry tone.

While he stowed her tent, sleeping bag and two small pieces of luggage in the back seat of the cab, Kate searched her backpack. She breathed a sigh of relief when she found her Glock and her wallet with the mysterious business card that had led her to Tyler's Glen.

David hopped in and started the engine.

The tapping of the rain and a country song softly playing on the radio filled the awkward silence as they waited for the windows to defrost.

Kate studied the man from the corner of her eye. He appeared about her age, in his late twenties, but his dripping black hair curling around his handsome face reminded her of a boy who had been playing too long in the sprinklers. His rain-soaked T-shirt and jeans, however, revealed strong muscles and a lean physique.

He sneezed.

She hoped he wasn't catching a cold. Guilt needled her for being so harsh. "I'm sorry. I didn't mean to sound like I was ordering you around, especially after everything you've done for me."

He gave her a slight nod. "It's understandable considering what you've been through tonight." Reaching for the handle of his door, he glanced her way. "I'll be back in a sec."

"Wait. Where are you going?" she cried when he jumped out. Still shaken from the accident, she didn't want to be alone.

"Here," David said when he returned. He handed her a wool blanket and a bottle of water as he got back in. "You're shivering."

A sigh escaped her lips as she took the items from him. "Thanks." She tugged the blanket around her shoulders and drew it close. "What about you? You must be freezing in those wet clothes."

He shrugged it off. "I'm okay."

"Where did you get the water and the blanket?"

"I carry an emergency kit in the back of my truck."

She smiled, impressed. "You must have been a boy scout."

"Eagle."

"Really?"

"Scouts' honor." He gave her the three-finger scout salute.

"When are you going to tell me how your Miata ended up wrapped around an oak tree in the Smoky Mountains?"

She rubbed her forehead. "It was dark and rainy. A hooded man crossed the road right in front of me. I swerved to avoid him, and that's the last thing I remember."

He frowned. "Not the best night for a walk in the park. At least you didn't hit him."

"No, I'm thankful for that, but it was so strange . . ."

"What?"

"How he came out of nowhere, and he had a bandage on the right side of his face. His hand was wrapped too."

David's eyes flickered with interest. "Sounds like a zombie. What else do you remember about him?"

"That's it, really, except for his terrified expression when he saw my car headed toward him." She touched her forehead. "What was I thinking coming here? I could be warm and dry at home right now, and my car would still be operable."

After checking his mirrors, David put the truck in gear and drove onto the highway. "What is a girl from Nashville, driving a red Miata convertible, doing way out here in the Smoky Mountains on a night like this?"

She eyed him indignantly. "You have something against red Miatas?"

His heart-stopping smile revealed straight, white teeth. An amused gleam twinkled in his eyes. "No, but I do wonder how you packed so much into such a tiny car."

"It wasn't easy," she replied with a slight grin. "How did you know I'm from Nashville?"

"I saw your license plate when I went to get your luggage. It said Davidson County."

"Oh."

"You're here on vacation?"

"Sort of." She watched the lightning show in the clouds overhead. "Actually, I'm here on business, but decided to take some time off work."

"Business, here in the park?"

"In Tyler's Glen, but since it's so close to the park, I thought I'd do a little camping."

He laughed.

She gave him a curious glance. "What's so funny?"

"Tyler's Glen isn't exactly Wall Street. These days, the main businesses in our booming metropolis are farming and funerals. Oh, and the new chemical plant."

His humorous reply relaxed her and made her laugh. "Well, I'm not a chemist, and definitely not a farmer or an undertaker."

"So the lady can smile."

"My teeth are the only part of me that doesn't hurt."

His expression switched to concern. "Are you in a lot of pain?"

"I'm sore all over."

He reached across her to open the glove compartment and took out a small bottle. "Here."

She read the label on the over-the-counter painkillers. "You are an Eagle Scout, aren't you?"

"You didn't believe me?"

She swallowed a couple of pills and chased them with a sip of water, then set the bottle and pills in the console between them. "I do now. Seriously, I appreciate you stopping to help me. I don't know what I would have done if you hadn't arrived when you did."

He shrugged modestly. "I never could pass up a red Miata convertible in distress. What kind of business do you have in Tyler's Glen, if you don't mind me asking?"

She shrugged. "I'm looking for Lester Crane. Do you know him?"

"The lawyer?"

"Yes."

"He has an office on Main Street. I'll show you where it is on the way to the motel."

"Thanks. You didn't know a man named Dwight Bentley by

chance, did you?"

He gave her a double-take. "Dwight? He lived down the road from me. Why?"

Before she replied, she paused and considered how much she should share with someone she barely knew. "I read the local paper online and saw an article about his death. It said he died in a fire."

David released a long sigh. "The whole town is in an uproar over it."

"What happened?"

"It looks like a freak accident. There was a propane tank explosion. His house burned up with him in it."

They passed a reduced speed limit sign. The next sign read 'Tyler's Glen, population 552'.

"Which motel are you taking me to?"

"The only one in town, Tyler's Glen Motor Inn."

He turned on Main Street and pointed out the lawyer's office. Then he slowed as they approached the large neon sign for the motel.

"Here we are," he said, driving into the parking lot. He passed the long, one-story building with a string of efficiency units and stopped in front of the office before turning off the ignition.

"You think they still have vacancies?" Kate asked, looking at the number of cars in the lot. "It is tourist season in the park."

David glanced around. "This isn't exactly the Opryland Hotel, and it's a Sunday night. You should be able to find a room. If not, Gina, at the front desk will refer you to the bed and breakfast in town. It's only a block away. I can wait and take you there, if you'd like."

She smiled, touched by his offer. "You've done more than enough for me tonight. I can take it from here."

When David got out, Kate removed the blanket and grabbed her backpack to exit the truck.

From the back of the cab, he peered at her over the console.

"By the way, the local sheriff's department has a website with a number you can call to report the accident."

"Thanks." She peered at the dark sky and falling rain, then opened the door to make a run for the motel.

"Hold on," he said. "Don't forget the water and pain pills. You're going to need them in the morning."

"You've thought of everything." She put the items in her backpack and hopped down from the truck.

He joined her under the awning outside the motel office, hauling her bags and camping gear. "You should stop by Doc Granger's first thing tomorrow and get checked out—"

"Let me guess. He's on Main Street too."

"No. He needed a bigger office and moved to a new building on First."

She laughed. "It's good to hear at least one other business is growing here besides farming, funerals, and chemicals."

He chuckled. "I'm not sure a growing medical business is anything to brag about. You know, I'd feel better if you let me take you to the doctor's house tonight to be on the safe side."

"I really appreciate your concern, but I'm fine. All I need is a nice hot shower and a good night's sleep."

"At least let me pay for your room. I know you were planning to camp tonight and the motel is more expensive."

"I can't let you do that."

A flicker of disappointment crossed his face.

"Hey, if not for you, I'd probably be wandering around in the pouring rain like that guy I almost hit." She extended her hand to shake his. "Goodnight, David."

He received her handshake with an amiable smile. "Take care of yourself, and stay out of trouble, okay?"

After the young woman entered the office, David waited outside long enough to make sure Gina had room for her at the motel. He didn't want her to walk to the bed and breakfast in the rain.

Glancing through the large window of the motel office, he saw the pretty young blonde with shoulder-length hair checking in. He'd been so consumed with helping her, he hadn't thought to ask for her name and number. Now he wished he had.

She saw him and waved, giving him a grin and a nod to confirm she had a room.

Satisfied, David returned to his truck. The temperature had dropped after the storm, making it colder than normal for October, especially since he was completely soaked. After starting the engine, he chuckled at the irony of her coming here on business when most people came to the Smokies to get away from business. And what sort of business would a woman like that have with Lester Crane? With the election next month, Lester was more focused on his bid to become mayor than practicing law these days. Maybe she worked for his campaign.

By the time David pulled out of the motel parking lot, the rain had let up. When he came a stop sign, his thoughts returned to the woman's description of the man she almost hit. He sounded more phantom than human, except for the bandages. Somewhere out there was an injured man, who was lucky to be alive.

After a long, hot shower, Kate emerged from the small bathroom dressed in her pajamas. The airbag and seatbelt had bruised her face, shoulder, and chest. Fighting exhaustion and pain, she sat on the bed and carefully reclined until her back rested against the sheets.

It was good she had called the sheriff's office and her insurance company to report the accident immediately after she'd checked in, before it got any later. The sheriff's deputy she'd spoken to had given her the number of a local car mechanic in town. She'd called him next and asked him to tow her car to his shop. Her Miata was probably totaled, but she'd see what the mechanic had to say in the morning.

It had been one of the longest nights of her life, and yet she was thankful to be alive—and grateful that David had stopped to help her.

She lay on the bed resting and relishing the comfort of being warm and dry again. Hopefully, David was faring as well right now. Her Good Samaritan had been a Godsend, getting her out of that jam. But when she first saw the blinding beam of his flashlight, she wondered if she had died and gone to heaven. With his wet, curling locks and clear, blue eyes glittering in the darkness, the striking man appeared almost angelic.

She smiled, recalling him standing outside the motel office. He might have an angelic side, but the warmth in his lingering gaze as he said goodbye was more like flesh and blood.

Reaching for her wallet on the nightstand, her aching muscles induced a groan. Her wallet fell open to a photo of a smiling, middle-aged couple. She gingerly removed the picture and caressed it with her finger. The picture of Jim and Rose Tucker brought back happy memories of the times they'd shared together, as well as a painful sense of loss.

Jim, her father figure and a deputy marshal like herself, had been killed four years earlier by the felon he was guarding as a witness for a high-profile case, and Jim's wife, Rose, had recently died from a stroke. Though she was a young teenager when they took her in fourteen years ago, Kate thought of them as her parents.

With Rose and Jim gone, Chase and Jenny Matthews were her closest family now, though they weren't related by blood. Once her mentor with the Marshal Service, Chase had always been like a big brother to her. Now he lived with his wife, Jenny, in Washington State, where he worked for the sheriff's department. Kate couldn't have made it this far without Chase and Jenny's love and support. They encouraged her to come stay with them after Rose's funeral, but with Jenny now expecting her first baby, Kate didn't want to intrude, though she missed them terribly.

She hadn't felt this lonely since she was a teen, living on the streets. She set the picture of her foster parents against the lamp beside her bed. The pain from her grief and sorrow hurt more than her bruises. *Lord, if I have any family left, help me to find them.* She kept her head bowed for another moment until a sense of peace washed over her.

Releasing a deep sigh, she moved to close her wallet. Her gaze fell on the business card that had mysteriously arrived in the mail last week and led her to Tyler's Glen. She took it out and re-read Lester Crane's name and law office address on the front, then turned it over to see the anonymous handwritten note on the back.

Contact Lester Crane in Tyler's Glen, TN. Tell him your mother is Dwight Bentley's sister.

Releasing October 1, 2017